She owed it to her children…and to this baby not yet born

Wendy had finally made her decision. No matter how hard it would be to put up with a stranger, a man who wasn't Matt, she owed it to her children and their future to get the best possible price for the resort.

No one would pay top dollar for a run-down operation. If Josh Walker could help get things in shape around here, it would be a way of honoring her husband's memory. She couldn't let Moon Lake Inn deteriorate; Matt had given too much of his life to this place. Even if financial circumstances had forced her to put the resort on the market, she had to preserve what she could of their hopes and dreams.

And only one man could help her do that.…

Without further ado, she pulled out the phone book and looked up the number for Josh Walker's hotel.

"Hello?" came his distinctive voice on the third ring.

"Hello, Mr. Walker. It's Wendy Sloan. I have an offer for you.…"

ABOUT THE AUTHOR

Rebecca Winters is a writer, teacher and mother of four. She's currently teaching French and Spanish to junior high school students—but despite her busy schedule, she always finds time to write. She's won a number of awards, including the National Readers' Choice Award; in 1995 she was named the Utah Writer of the Year. Rebecca, who also writes for Harlequin Romance, has become known for her dramatic, highly emotional and always imaginative stories.

Books by Rebecca Winters

HARLEQUIN SUPERROMANCE

THE FAMILY WAY
Rebecca Winters

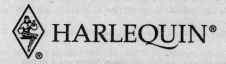

HARLEQUIN®

TORONTO • NEW YORK • LONDON
AMSTERDAM • PARIS • SYDNEY • HAMBURG
STOCKHOLM • ATHENS • TOKYO • MILAN • MADRID
PRAGUE • WARSAW • BUDAPEST • AUCKLAND

ISBN 0-373-70875-0

THE FAMILY WAY

Visit us at www.romance.net

Printed in U.S.A.

THE FAMILY WAY

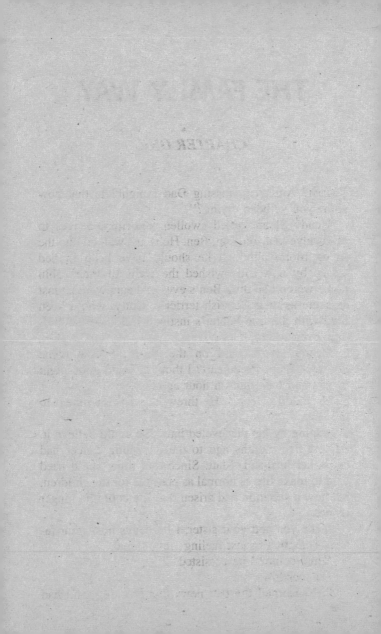

CHAPTER ONE

"MOM? ARE YOU missing Dad tonight? Is that how come you've been crying?"

Wendy Sloan turned swollen, red-rimmed eyes to her twelve-year-old son, Ben. He'd just walked into the living room, although he should have been in bed asleep by now. She wished the walls of their cabin home weren't so thin. Ben's eyes and ears were almost as acute as their Scottish terrier's; Cutty, who'd been bred with the true hunter's instinct, followed the children everywhere.

Wendy sat forward on the couch. "How come you're still up, sweetheart? I thought I said good-night to you and Kim half an hour ago."

"I couldn't sleep." He threw himself down next to her.

Judging by his disheveled hair, she could believe it. Almost five months ago to the day, lung cancer had taken her husband, Matt. Since that time, she'd tried hard to make life as normal as possible for the children, but now a situation had arisen that she could no longer ignore.

"Like you and your sister, I'll always miss your father. Tonight I'm just feeling...emotional."

"How come?" he persisted.

How come?

She'd learned the bad news this morning, and had

been struggling all day for the right way to tell the children. Up until her talk with the banker, everything had seemed to be part of some strange dream she'd been living. But no longer. She was awake now, staring reality in the face.

At the moment, she didn't think she could handle Ben's reaction as well as her own pain, but it didn't look as if she had a choice. She had to tell him the truth. Her son wanted answers, and he obviously wasn't going back to his room without them. Maybe it would be better just to get it over with.

"Mom? I know you went to the doctor today. Is something wrong with the baby?"

She shook her head. "Oh, sweetheart, no. The doctor said my pregnancy is coming along fine."

"Do you know if it's a boy or a girl?"

"No. I'm not even sure we want to know. I think it'll be fun to be surprised."

There was the slightest hesitation. "Did Dad know you were going to have a baby before he died?" Ben had never asked this before, but he must have wondered.

She paused for a moment, trying to get her emotions under control. "No. I didn't realize I was pregnant until...afterward. I've decided it was a blessing. Otherwise he would have agonized about the baby when he was already so worried about leaving you and Kim without a father."

Ben's light-blue eyes grew suspiciously bright. "Do you think he knows now?"

Eyes brimming with tears, she pulled him into her arms and gave him a huge hug. "I'm sure he does."

After several sniffs, Ben let go of her. "I hope it's a boy."

"Kim told me she wants a sister."

"What do *you* want?" he inquired, always concerned about her feelings.

She loved him for it. "I'll take whatever we're sent."

Six months before his death, Matt had been diagnosed with terminal cancer. He'd never even smoked, and for a while Wendy had found it difficult to suppress her bitterness at the unfairness of life. For his sake, and for the children, she'd managed, somehow, to accept the fact that this had happened—that her husband was dying. An operation could have been performed to extend his life by as long as three months. After considering everything, Matt decided not to put off the inevitable. He'd had some pain, but it was manageable. Five weeks before he died, they'd made love for the last time. After that, his condition worsened and he was finally hospitalized.

"Are you happy about the baby?"

"Of course!" she answered honestly. "Thrilled! A baby is a miracle. Your father gave me three very special gifts. Every night when I go to bed, every morning when I wake up, I'm thankful for my children, including the one who isn't born yet. You fill my life with joy and purpose."

He pondered her comments before he said, "Then why were you crying? I'm not a little kid, Mom. You can tell me the truth."

"I know I can." Ben was as straightforward as his hardworking father. In fact, he'd inherited many of Matt's endearing qualities. "You're the most wonderful son a mother could have." *But my news is going to topple your world.*

"Are you scared to have the baby alone or something?"

Or something.

She took a deep breath. "No. Besides, I'm not alone. I have all of you." She tousled his hair. "No. This doesn't have anything to do with the baby.

"The truth is, now that your father's gone, I won't be able to open up the cabins. This is the year he'd planned to do a lot of repair work to get them in shape. That's very expensive... I can't do that kind of work myself, and there's no extra money in reserve, so they'll have to stay closed. Without them, we can't make this place a paying proposition. We've already lost the ski crowd, and it's only going to get worse for us financially. S-so we'll have to sell Moon Lake Resort and move."

Like the calm before the storm, there was a tense silence while the announcement settled in. "Sell—" Suddenly he jumped to his feet. "No way!"

Ben's horrified cry of protest didn't come as any surprise. She'd been imagining and dreading this moment for a long time; the banker had only confirmed what she'd already suspected. Since her marriage to Matt thirteen years before, they'd struggled to build a business from the small property Matt's father had left them on the Nevada side of Tahoe.

But without her husband and no capital backing them, the banker advised her to sell while the resort was in its best shape. She'd probably make enough money to pay off their bank loan and still have some left to buy a small home in the city and tide her over for a while.

"I know exactly how you feel, Ben, but there's no other solution."

He bowed his head, gazing intently at his hands; it reminded her of Matt who used to do the same thing when he was upset about something. "Before Dad died, he told me to be the man of the family and take care of you, Mom. That's what I'm going to do. I don't have to go to school. I can stay around here and do all the stuff he did."

"I love you for saying that, but no! Your job is to go to school. My job is to worry about how this family is going to fare."

The last thing she wanted was for Ben to grow old overnight trying to be the head of the Sloan family. It was a burden no child should have to carry.

"I've thought it all out. We'll move to Sacramento near Grandma and your Aunt Jane and Uncle Bob. You'll be able to play with your cousins every day, and I'll have family around to help us after the baby comes. In time I'll get a job. Things will work out, and we'll be happy. You'll see."

Tears spilled down his splotched cheeks. "We're not leaving Moon Lake, Mom! This is our home. Dad said it would be ours forever!"

"I know he did," she said in a choked voice. "But life sometimes has a way of going in a direction that's different from what you've planned. Dad's gone now. We have to do what makes the most sense. I'm six months along. The baby's due at the end of June. That's not very far away. I'll need to be in the city near a hospital. Your grandma and aunt will be there to help take care of you children."

She could see her news had torn him apart. This was worse than any nightmare, worse even than she'd expected it to be.

"Ben—please listen. From the sale of the property,

we can buy a nice little house. You'll make lots of new friends, and life won't be as hard for us." She gave him what she hoped was a cajoling smile. "Every time we go to California to visit Grandma, you always tell me how much you like it there."

"For a visit, yeah. But not to *live!* We can't leave Moon Lake!" He sobbed openly, ignoring her comments. "What'll happen to Magpie and Rusty?"

She swallowed hard. "Mr. Lott in Carson City is taking good care of all the horses, including yours and Kim's. He said he'd buy them if the new owner doesn't want them."

"No." He shook his head violently. "You can't do it, Mom. I told you. I'll work hard. So will Kim."

"Ben..." She moaned in exasperation, her heart aching with new grief. "You already do work hard. Too hard! You've both been a tremendous help to me. The best! But in order for us to stay here, I'd need to hire a man like your father—someone who's a building contractor and a handyman and a manager.

"Unfortunately, no man with those credentials would work for us because I could only offer room and board. There's no money to pay him a salary. As it is, we'd have to give up one of the cabins for him to live in, which would cut down on our revenue even more. Finally, I'd need him to be with us for several years, at least. If you were older you'd underst—"

"But—"

"There's no 'but,'" Wendy interjected in a firmer tone. "No such man exists!" She eased herself off the low couch and put a hand on his shoulder. "What I need from you is your support. You can help me most by convincing Kim that this decision is for the best. I don't think you realize how much influence you have over her. If she believes you're happy about the move, she'll go along with it much more willingly.''

He refused to look at her. ''Have you already put our place up for sale?'' His voice was barely a whisper.

She bit the underside of her lip. ''Yes. I signed with a Realtor today.''

His flushed, pained face was the last thing she saw before he left the living room on a run. Cutty darted after him. At least her son had a loving dog who would lie next to him during the night and give him comfort. And I have my baby, she reminded herself, turning out the lights and making her way to bed.

It would take Ben a long time to come to grips with the situation. But at least the truth was out in the open. She could only hope they'd find a buyer before another school year started in the fall. The sooner they moved to Sacramento and got settled, the sooner they could start to create new memories and separate themselves from the worst of the pain.

Tomorrow would be here before she knew it. Thursday was the cook's day off. Wendy would have to prepare all the meals at the coffee shop and try to fix a plumbing problem under one of the kitchen sinks.

Matt had taught her and Ben how to do small plumbing and carpentry repairs. But electrical wiring problems, construction problems and snowmobiles were beyond her scope of expertise. Since Matt's death in early November, she'd closed up the guest cabins and locked the snowmobiles in the garage. She couldn't cope with everything and a heavy winter snowfall, as well.

Being pregnant had complicated her life in ways she would never have imagined. This third baby had brought low back pain, something she hadn't suffered when she was pregnant with Ben and Kim. Lately she'd had to stop and rest while she was making the beds in their own cabin. Scouring the bathroom, especially the floor of the shower, had become an almost impossible chore.

A couple of local teens still helped at the coffee shop after school and on weekends. But she didn't know how much longer she could pay their salaries, not when she had to pay Ada Morse, their cook, who worked days while her husband drove the school bus.

Kim helped with the laundry, and Ben assisted Ada in the kitchen when he got home from school. Unfortunately, no matter how hard they all worked, neither the coffee shop nor the gas pump brought in enough revenue to pay all the bills.

She was getting further and further behind. Vital items needing repair or replacement were mounting without the money from the guest cabins to pay for them. It had been a relief to speak to the Realtor today. She simply couldn't go on like this much longer.

But Wendy was well aware that this move would be as traumatic for her as the children. Moon Lake Inn had been their dream, hers and Matt's. Tears crept from beneath her lashes before she settled under the covers, exhausted.

"I'M GOING TO REITERATE what I told you kids in class yesterday. The President of the U.S. wants to bring all public schools into compliance with the latest technology standards by the twenty-first century." Mr. Finch, the computer lab teacher, gestured expansively as he spoke.

"You're lucky to live in this school district because we've received a special grant that will fund your web sites for one week on the district's server. This is an

exciting project, and I want to see some great ideas—
okay, class? You've already had half an hour to get
started, so let's not waste any more time.''

Ben's palms rested on the edge of the table while he
proofread his work.

Picture yourself in paradise. In other words, the
rugged Sierra Nevada Mountains near Lake Tahoe, Nevada. It's the perfect getaway where you
can ski, snowmobile, horseback ride, climb, hunt,
fish, canoe, kayak, hike and swim in virtual iso-
lation.

Moon Lake Inn, which is a small but fabulous,
family-owned resort for up to twenty-four guests,
needs a general handyman who will live year-
round in his own modern cabin. All meals, laundry, plus full use of the facilities and a truck are
included. Possibility of a salary at a later date.

If interested, please contact Mr. Benjamin Sloan
for further details by writing to him care of Moon
Lake Inn, PO Box 2750, Stateline, Nevada, 06172.
Or phone Mr. Benjamin Sloan at 1-775-555-6000
after 4:00 p.m., Monday through Sunday.

Ben read it several more times, decided he couldn't
improve it, then got up from the chair. He stood by his
teacher, who was helping one of the other kids set up
a password.

''Mr. Finch?''

''Yes, Ben?'' The teacher glanced at him.

''I've finished creating my web page.''

''Already? Good for you! That's what I like to hear.

A lot of the students haven't even come up with an idea yet."

"Yeah, well, I like playing around on the Internet. It was easy."

"All right, then. Let's see what you've got."

Mr. Finch followed him back to his spot in the computer room and looked at the screen to inspect his project. He frowned. "This is an ad for a Help Wanted column. I explained that I wanted you to create an informational site about the Tahoe area, like your favorite fishing spot, interesting facts about the local geography, history of the area—like the mines, for example."

"I know," Ben muttered. "But my ad *is* informational." No matter how hard he tried, he couldn't get rid of the lump lodged in his throat. It had been there since last night when his mother had told him they'd have to sell everything and move.

He and Kim hadn't slept all night, trying to figure out what to do. Toward morning they'd thought up a plan and sworn each other to secrecy. He'd hardly been able to wait until school started so he could get to his computer class.

His teacher studied him for a moment. "That's true. This is a very well-thought-out, appealing ad. But you can't put it on the net because people will respond."

"Isn't that the whole idea? To create a web site that will produce inquiries?"

"Of course. But since it's a bogus ad, I couldn't allow it to go out over the net."

"Bogus?" Ben hadn't heard that word before.

"It means, there *is* no job opening. You'd be generating interest under false pretenses. In other words, it would be a lie."

"No, it wouldn't!" Ben argued. "My dad died a while back," he began in a tremulous voice.

"I know," Mr. Finch murmured. "I'm sorry about that. It must be tough going."

"Yeah. It is. Especially for my mom. She's looking for a man to help us do the chores around the resort. We've already started advertising by putting up a Help Wanted sign in the coffee shop."

Ben had told only a partial lie. Mr. Finch didn't need to know that the Help Wanted sign had been in the coffee shop window ever since he could remember. His dad had placed it there to attract local teens.

"But if I send this ad out over the Internet for a week, I know I could find us some help a lot faster. My mom's going to have a baby in three months. It's getting harder and harder for her to manage the heavy stuff."

Compassion entered his teacher's eyes. "I can see why you're in such a big hurry. Under the circumstances, I commend you for your plan to help your mother. If your father were alive, he'd be proud of you."

The teacher patted his shoulder. "I think your ad just might work. It's worth a try, anyway. But you'll have to make a few changes."

"What changes?"

"Well, if you're going to advertise over the Net, hundreds of thousands of people will see it. You never want to put out your name, the name of the resort or your phone number."

Ben shook his head. "Why not? I don't get it. How will anyone be able to answer the ad, then?"

"Not everyone's trustworthy. You can't afford to invite some undesirable to come nosing around your place. Unfortunately there are a lot of weirdos out there these days, so you have to protect yourself. You're also going to have to ask any applicants for references.''

"What are those?''

"The names and phone numbers of places where they've worked before so you can check to see if they were good employees.''

"Oh, yeah. I get it.''

"And remember—don't give away any information that someone can trace directly to you. I'll come back before the bell rings to look over your work again.''

"All right. Thanks, Mr. Finch.''

Euphoric, Ben sat down and began revising his rough draft. He left the first paragraph alone. In the second, he took out the words *Moon Lake Inn* and replaced them with *this small, but fabulous family-owned resort.*

In the third paragraph he deleted some more words and put

If interested, please write ASAP to Cutty, PO Box 2750, Stateline, Nevada, 06172. Please send references. If everything checks out satisfactorily, employment will start immediately.

Pleased with the wording, Ben ran the computer spellcheck, then hurried to find Mr. Finch. As soon as this went out on the web, he figured that hundreds of unemployed men would respond to the ad, if only for the chance to live and work in the out-of-doors. He and Kim would choose the best one.

No way was Ben going to leave Moon Lake! He'd made his dad a promise to look after the family. His dad had always said their home in the mountains was paradise on earth.

Ben agreed with him.

So did Kim. So did Cutty and Magpie and Rusty. Their new brother or sister would love Moon Lake, too.

Ben liked to think his dad was watching over all of them. Maybe he'd even sent Ben the idea for this ad.

It *had* to work....

"JOSH? HOW ARE YOU this morning? How does that leg feel now?"

Special FBI Agent Joshua Quincy rested his crutches against the wall and sat down on the chair in the doctor's examination room. "Better than I expected."

"Let's have a look."

Josh rolled up his pant leg. To his relief, the gunshot wound that had fractured the weight-bearing bone below his left knee had been healing nicely since the rod had been put in. He hoped to get back to work soon and counted on this visit to give him the needed clean bill of health.

"You're right, Josh. You have good fixation, but according to this X ray, you're not out of the woods yet."

Sighing in frustration, he told the doctor, "I can't handle being laid up like this anymore." He missed flying. The walls of his borrowed condo were closing in on him.

"I understand. But you have to be in top shape to go back to the Bureau. You've made excellent progress; however, you're still not a hundred percent. Right now, if you had to jump or run in the course of duty, you'd undo the healing process and create all kinds of complications. At least, you've improved to the point where I can recommend the use of a cane instead of your crutches.''

A cane? Lord. That was all he needed.

Resigned to the inevitable, he asked, ''How much longer do you estimate it'll take me to recuperate?''

''If you want a leg that's almost as perfect as the one God gave you, it's my medical opinion you should have another three to four months' leave of absence. During that time, you'll need physical therapy at least twice a week.''

Josh groaned. *Another three to four months?*

''Here's a prescription for more painkillers—a smaller dosage, though. When you return the crutches, they'll fit you with the right-size cane. I'll leave it to you to make an appointment with a good therapist. I've written down the names of several in the Cleveland area.''

Taking the notes from him, Josh got out of the chair and reached once more for the crutches. Thank heaven he'd be getting rid of them after he left the doctor's office.

''There's nothing to prevent you from doing light household chores or going on short walks. Good judgment is the key here. The cane will give you more freedom, which should help you regain your full strength.

''Just don't rush it. Nothing can improve on nature's way of healing the body. Don't forget that physical therapy is vital. If you must fly, let someone else be the pilot.''

Though Josh hated to admit it, the doctor made sense. ''I won't forget. I'm obliged to you for all your help.''

The other man grinned. ''You didn't say that to me

three months ago when they wheeled you into the operating room.''

''I apologize,'' he said wryly. ''I'm afraid I wasn't at my best right then.''

Another agent, Barry Shaw, one of Josh's closest friends, had died of a gunshot wound to the head during the same shoot-out. His death had taken an emotional toll on Josh.

Until then, the two of them had spent the previous sixteen months flying surveillance missions to trace drug-traffic movement between motorcycle gangs and corrupt law enforcement officers within the U.S.

After Josh and his partner had supplied the Bureau with the necessary photographic evidence, two hundred FBI agents had closed in at various rendezvous points around the country to make simultaneous arrests.

Josh and Barry, disguised as businessmen, had flown by private plane to a small airport outside Topeka, Kansas, to participate in the final effort. But one of the targeted policemen, disguised as airport security, was waiting for a drug supply from South America and must have sensed a setup. He opened fire on Barry as he left the plane.

Josh had been only two steps behind him, and took a bullet in the lower leg before he shot the other man. Tragically, Barry never regained consciousness. The fact that those arrests broke up one of the largest and best-organized drug operations to date brought him little joy.

''Don't worry about it, Josh. Agents in your kind of work make the worst patients. I guess it goes with the territory. Good luck.''

They shook hands, and then Josh went down to the main floor of the clinic to rid himself of his crutches.

Twenty minutes later, he entered his supervisor's office in downtown Cleveland.

Harve Pearson's expression brightened when he saw him. "Josh! You're a sight for sore eyes." He crossed the room to give him a bear hug. "That cane makes you…interesting. What did the doc say?"

Josh's quick smile vanished. "Three or four more months."

"That soon? I thought it might be longer."

"Very funny, Harve. Please don't tell me I can fill an entry-level position at some resident agency. I need a total change of scene."

His superior nodded in understanding. "You're going to get your wish. As you know, a contract was put out on you after your last case. We're moving you to a new location where the risk to you and the people around you will be negligible. Three or four more months in hiding should put an end to any worries in that department, plus it'll give your leg time to heal completely."

Harve sat back in his swivel chair. "How would you like to spend the rest of your medical leave as a handyman?"

He blinked. *A handy-man?* "Where?"

"In the mountains near Lake Tahoe, Nevada. It's either that or a custodial job at a dental office in Seattle."

"It rains too much in Seattle," Josh muttered. "Besides, I've never been to that part of Nevada."

"Tahoe's an incredible place. Trust me on this. Some kid at a junior high placed an ad on the Internet for a handyman to live in one of the cabins at his family's resort. It's legitimate. Our guys have already done a background check. The resort is called Moon Lake Inn.

"It's a struggling mom-and-pop outfit. They can't pay a salary, just room and board. Apparently the owner died, leaving a family who can't manage things any longer, so it's up for sale. In the meantime, they need the help of a general fix-it man.

"I'd say Moon Lake would be the perfect spot for you to lie low and stay busy at the same time. Even when it changes hands, I'm sure the new ownership would keep you on, but we'll worry about that when we have to.

"The point is, you'd have a total change of scene, you'd be in a safe location and you'd be doing work that won't interfere with the healing process of your leg." He twiddled his thumbs. "So…you interested?"

Josh let out a resigned sigh. "As I see it, I don't have much of a choice."

Though the years he'd spent in the Navy and the FBI had sent him to all parts of the world, Josh had grown up on his grandfather's farm in Ohio. The idea of living and working in the Nevada mountains would never have occurred to him. He had to admit it held a certain appeal.

"At sixty-five hundred feet, you'd see a lot of blue sky and breathe pure, dry mountain air. It would give you a chance to stay physically active until I can put you back on official duty. And it'd give you the anonymity you need."

How many more ways could Harve restate this? He obviously considered it the right solution. Josh grinned. "You've convinced me."

"Good. Then let's discuss the cover I've worked out for you. Go ahead and use Brenda and Henry for references. There's no point in changing them when they've worked well for you in the past. As for getting you hired, you're going to bypass answering the ad through the PO box. There's a Help Wanted sign in the coffee shop window. That will be your entrée.''

For the next hour they got down to business, finalizing plans and details, then Josh headed for the underground carpark where one of the guys was waiting to drive him to his claustrophobic condo. He hated it. He'd hated the long dark winter of his confinement. He despised even more this dismal March weather of eternal gray. You couldn't even distinguish the sky from the horizon.

Josh had always needed movement, an outdoor life, the sun on his face. The agency psychiatrists had told him he'd fallen into a serious depression and he knew it was growing worse because of physical inactivity. He'd declined medication; he believed strongly that for him it wasn't the right approach.

Still, there'd been too many endless nights when he'd been tortured by thoughts of what he could have done differently to prevent his partner from being killed. Since the shooting, Josh had been haunted by Barry's death. It had darkened his world to the point that he didn't feel like socializing. In fact, he hadn't found pleasure in anything lately.

Normally he enjoyed female companionship—time and opportunity permitting. He'd always imagined that one day he'd get married, but so far he hadn't met the right woman. During his convalescence, it hit him that he was thirty-five years old and still a bachelor. If this downward spiral continued, marriage might always elude him.

Since his release from the hospital, he hadn't been

out on a date. He didn't seem to know any women who were capable of holding his interest. That was his fault, not theirs. He began to worry that while he was waiting to return to active duty, his morbid state of mind might turn into a permanent condition.

Perhaps a new environment in another part of the country was exactly what he needed. If that didn't change his state of mind, he'd be forced to seek further professional help. But he wasn't ready to travel down that road quite yet.

Once inside the condo, he fixed himself a TV dinner, then sat down at his computer and looked up Lake Tahoe on the Internet. There were hundreds of web sites extolling its various virtues, particularly the casinos and nightclubs around the lake.

After half an hour, he started to get up to exercise his leg when he caught sight of an ad that grabbed his attention.

Picture yourself in paradise. In other words, the Sierra Nevada mountains near Lake Tahoe, Nevada. Josh read the entire piece with uncommon interest. Maybe this was the ad Harve had referred to in his office.

Josh had never been kayaking, and had never gotten on a horse. For the first time in months, something intrigued him enough to jar him out of his morose spirits. He wondered who Cutty was. It might be interesting to find out.

"WE'LL BE BACK in a minute, Mom."

Carol Irvine, Eric's mother, nodded. Ben and his best friend jumped out of the van and ran into the Stateline post office to get the mail from their boxes. Sometimes she drove them into town; sometimes Ben's mother did.

With trembling hands, Ben inserted the key in the lock and opened the box while Eric did the same thing a little farther down the row. Ben pulled out some bills and junk mail, but there was no envelope addressed to Cutty.

His heart dropped to his feet. Ten whole days and no response. Not one. He couldn't understand it.

There'd been more than a thousand visitors to his web site before the week ended and he'd had to take it off the net. Mr. Finch had praised him in class for obtaining such impressive results.

Ben had received an *A* on his computer project. But with the threat of leaving Moon Lake, he couldn't appreciate anything just now. His mother had been right. It didn't matter how beautiful the scenery was or that they were offering good food and a nice cabin to live in, no man was willing to do a job without being paid for it.

"You didn't get a letter, did you?" Eric said quietly.

"Nope!" Ben fought tears as he shut the box and shoved the key in his pocket.

"Maybe there'll be something tomorrow."

Ben shook his head fiercely. "No, there won't. It was a stupid idea."

"It was a *great* idea! And I'm not giving up yet. Heck, I don't want you to move."

They hurried out of the post office toward the van waiting in the parking lot. "Why don't you sleep at my house tonight? We can think up another plan, just in case."

"Okay," he muttered without enthusiasm. "But I have to go home first and help Ada in the kitchen. Then I'll ride my bike over."

"Okay."

"Don't say anything to your mom about this."

"No way."

Twenty minutes later, Ben waved off the Irvines, then he ran through the back door of the coffee shop. He left the mail on his mom's desk in the office, and washed up in the employee bathroom before reporting to the kitchen.

"Hi, Ada."

"Hi there, Ben. Glad you're here. Cindy couldn't come in to wait on tables, so you're going to have to take over. Your mom wants you to get a fire going in the fireplace. Then you can put the water pitchers on the tables."

"Okay."

Business used to be good year-round. They'd had a number of regular week-long visitors, as well as those who stopped by for a night or two. But since tourists had found out Moon Lake's cabins were closed, only a dozen or so people driving through the area came in to eat dinner on any given night. After their meals, they'd move on to find lodgings elsewhere.

Ben hated losing their business, but there was nothing he could do. His mom was in charge and could no longer extend herself physically. Anger over his dad's death made him work faster.

As he set down the last water pitcher, a tall stranger with medium-length dark-brown hair and a cane entered the coffee shop.

Ben didn't mean to stare, but he couldn't help it. The man, dressed in well-worn jeans and jacket, looked familiar. The more Ben scrutinized his profile and stature, the more he was convinced it was his movie idol, Mel Gibson.

The man nodded. "Hi," he said in a deep voice.

"Hi. My name's Ben. Welcome to Moon Lake Inn, sir. You can sit anywhere you'd like."

"Thank you."

With the help of his cane, the stranger walked over to the table next to the fireplace and sat down, stretching his bad leg in front of the flames with a sigh.

Ben hurried over to him and filled his water glass. Up close, he could see the man wasn't Mel Gibson, after all. "Would you like a cup of coffee or a soft drink for starters?"

"Coffee sounds good."

"I'll be right back with a menu."

"You don't happen to have any pie, do you?"

"Sure. Apple, cherry and pecan. You can have it plain or à la mode."

"I'll have some hot cherry pie with vanilla ice cream."

"Coming right up."

Ada was busy slicing the pot roast, so Ben poured the coffee and got the pie ready. As he went out front and served the stranger—their only customer at the moment—he heard the man say, "I noticed a Help Wanted sign in the window. What kind of help are you looking for?"

Ben thought he must be dreaming. "Are you asking about a job?"

"As a matter of fact, I am. This leg of mine needs to mend, so I can't do the kind of work I normally do. I thought I wouldn't mind sitting around until it got better. But that got boring, so I've been on a long vacation. Now that the fun's worn off, I want to try my hand at something to stay busy."

After receiving no response to his ad, Ben couldn't

believe this was happening. Although it probably *wouldn't* happen once the man heard the truth.

"When my dad died, we had to close the cabins," Ben told him. "My mom would have to hire someone like you so we can keep the place running, but she can't pay a salary. All she could do is offer you room and board. Our place is up for sale," he added, trying to keep his voice from wobbling.

"I noticed the 'For Sale' sign. Where's your mother, Ben?"

"Home, but she'll be here any minute now."

"Do you think she'd be willing to talk to me if I made an appointment through you? My name is Josh Walker."

Ben was incredulous. "You mean you'd be interested in coming to work for us without any money?"

"That depends on a variety of things."

His heart started to hammer. "Don't go anywhere, Mr. Walker! Stay right here. I'll get my mom and be back in a sec!"

CHAPTER TWO

"MOM? WHERE ARE YOU? Mom?"

"Ben?" Her son sounded out of breath. It filled her with alarm. "What's wrong?"

Wendy had just finished dressing to go and wait on tables. She rushed out of the bedroom and felt a twinge of pain in her side. When was she going to remember that at six-plus months, she had to move slowly?

Her son met her in the hallway. "Remember what you said about needing a man who could do the work here—like Dad?"

Oh, no. They weren't back to that, were they?

"Yes?" She tried to keep an impatient note out of her voice. At least this wasn't an emergency. She should be grateful for that much.

"Well, there's a man named Josh Walker who came into the coffee shop a little while ago. He asked me if he could talk to you about a job."

What job?

She forced herself to count to ten before responding. "Why would he do that when we're not looking for anyone and the place is for sale? What have you been up to, sweetheart?"

"Nothing!" he said so defensively she was positive he must be hiding something. "He said he saw the Help Wanted sign in the window."

Wendy moaned. She'd forgotten all about that. Matt

had put up the sign years ago to attract local teen help. It had become a permanent fixture.

"That's why he came in the coffee shop in the first place. He's cool, Mom. I mean really cool. I thought he was Mel Gibson. He even kind of sounds like him."

Oh, Ben. You're so desperate you'd say or do anything to stay here. Trying to remain calm, she finally said, "Did you tell him we're not hiring because there's no money?"

"Yeah. He said he still wants to talk to you."

"Ben!" she cried in exasperation. "If a man who looks like Mel Gibson has shown up in a place like this wanting a job that doesn't pay a salary, there's got to be something wrong with him."

"There is."

His admission took her by surprise. "What do you mean?"

"He has to walk with a cane."

She sighed. "That's terrific. An incapacitated vagrant who knows how to make people feel sorry for him. No doubt he's looking for someone to wait on him, too." Why not prey on a destitute widow?

Wendy stopped short of revealing all her thoughts— like the fact that if the drifter *did* look like Mel Gibson, he probably got a lot of mileage out of it with the female population.

"I'm sorry, Ben, but I'm not falling for it. You'll have to tell him to move on."

"Maybe he's as desperate for work as we are for help," her son said quietly, sounding very much like his father. "Maybe he got hurt in an accident or lost his wife and family in a fire or something. Maybe people are scared off by his cane. Maybe he became a homeless person and it's not his fault.

"It happens all the time to good people. At school, we did a unit on the homeless and the students donated a whole truckload of stuff to the food bank. Remember? How can you just turn your back on him without giving him a chance?"

Despite everything she'd said, Ben was fighting for the home he loved. She couldn't fault him for his compassion, though, another trait he'd learned from Matt. His words tugged at her emotions. Damn. She was still so vulnerable, it frightened her.

"All right. I'll tell you what. I'll talk to Mr. Walker, but don't get your hopes up—and don't forget the resort is for sale."

"I could never forget that, but at least you're willing to see him." His eyes filled. "Thanks, Mom." With some difficulty Wendy hugged him. At times like this she realized how large she'd grown.

When she'd been six months pregnant with Ben, no one had even guessed. Being pregnant with a third baby—and at thirty-two instead of twenty—was quite a different proposition.

"Do you want me there when you interview him?"

Always the protector. She gave him a tremulous smile. "No, sweetheart, but thank you anyway. Please stay here and eat your dinner. It's in the oven. Kim should've been home from the Nymans' before now. I don't want her coming into an empty house to eat alone."

"Okay."

"By the way, Eric phoned. He says you have plans to sleep over at his house tonight."

"I was going to ask you if I could, but I've changed my mind. I'll call him."

Ben helped her on with her parka, which she could

no longer zip up, and walked her to the front door. She could see the pleading in his eyes. With a sigh, she started along the wet path through the pines to the coffee shop.

He was begging her to do what he saw as the right thing. But in her view, the right thing was to send the stranger on his way. One day, when Ben was much older and wiser, he'd understand why she'd had to do this and forgive her.

Her heart heavy, she entered the coffee shop through the back door and walked straight to her office. She noticed the pile of mail—with another bill from the vet in Carson City on top—and grimaced. After removing her parka, she hung it in the closet, then headed for the kitchen.

"Good evening, Ada. How are things going?"

"Just fine, except water keeps backing up in the left sink."

"I'll take care of it."

"The food's ready. You've only got one customer so far. He's working on a second piece of your cherry pie. You know who he kind of reminds me of?"

"Mel Gibson," Wendy muttered irritably.

"Yes. How'd you know?"

"Ben said the same thing."

"Between you and me, the guy out front is better-looking."

Wendy couldn't take much more of this. "It'll be our secret, Ada. Thanks for everything. Have a good night. I'll see you in the morning."

"You bet. Bye."

Right now, before anyone else showed up, would be the best time to get the conversation over with. She moved through the swinging door and looked around for the stranger.

He was seated at the table nearest the fireplace. His cane lay across the chair next to him. One of his legs was stretched out. As she moved toward him, their eyes met over the rim of his coffee mug. Even from several yards away, she could tell that those eyes were as deep and riveting a blue as Lake Tahoe under a summer sky.

Matt had always been so entrenched in her heart, she'd never given any real thought to another man. But the stranger's slow perusal made her distinctly aware of her pregnancy.

It also made her aware of herself as a woman, and that hadn't happened for many, many months. Not since before Matt's death, when he'd made love to her for the last time and left her carrying his child.

Her black leggings and pale-green maternity jumper could hardly be considered alluring. She chastised herself for that reaction. Why should she care how she looked to him?

Certainly the stranger had an arresting presence. Though his dark hair and complexion bore some resemblance to the famous actor, this man's features were more rugged, his demeanor less approachable.

If he was a vagrant, you wouldn't know it by the attractive crew-necked black sweater and well-washed jeans. His boots were obviously expensive, like the lined sheepskin jacket thrown over the other chair.

Whoever he was, he kept himself amazingly fit, despite his bad leg. When she stood next to him, she immediately noticed his immaculate nails. He was also clean-shaven and smelled of soap and some faint, piney aftershave.

"Hello, Mr. Walker. I'm Mrs. Sloan. My son said you wanted to see me."

"How do you do." His voice was low, cultivated, impressing her when she didn't want to be impressed. "Thank you for being willing to talk to me. You have a fine son there."

"Thank you. Now, what can I do for you?"

Wendy hadn't meant to sound so curt, but suddenly she didn't feel like herself at all. She was sharply, intensely conscious of him, a sensation that made her uncomfortable. It had to be because she was pregnant, she decided, and awash in hormones.

Using his cane, he got to his feet, then shook hands with her. Her fingers disappeared in the warmth and strength of his. She certainly couldn't fault his manners. Being five feet four, she had to tilt her head to meet his unwavering gaze.

Matt hadn't been quite six feet. This man stood several inches taller than her husband, though why she'd even made the comparison was beyond her. She wished she could still wear Matt's rings, but her hands had swollen with this pregnancy.

"Please. Sit down," she urged him, not liking to feel at a disadvantage.

"If you'll sit with me."

That made perfect sense, but his suggestion sounded personal. Intimate. Cross with herself for overreacting, she eased onto the chair opposite him.

"I'm sorry if that sign in the window led you to believe I'm looking for help. Over the years we've left it there for local teens who want occasional or part-time work. The fact is, I'm selling the resort. I've already put it on the market, so it's only a matter of time until the place falls under new ownership."

"Ben said as much."

Ben? He already knew her son's name?

Vexed by the knowledge, she said, "Then he's informed you that there's no money to pay a salary for extra help."

"Yes. However, I'm not looking for a salary. Only for a place to live and make myself useful until this leg heals properly."

Maybe she had him all wrong. Maybe he wasn't a drifter but someone running from the law, someone who needed a safe hideout.

"I'm a farmer from Ohio," he supplied, as if he could read her mind. "Three months ago a tractor accident mangled my leg."

Wendy couldn't prevent a compassionate murmur. "I'm sorry," she added.

"As soon as I was released from the hospital, my fiancée left the country on business. We're planning to be married this fall when my leg's completely healed.

"In the meantime, the surgeon took me off crutches and gave me this cane. He told me I can't do any heavy farming for at least three or four months, but I'm now permitted to do light chores.

"With my fiancée gone and time weighing heavily on my hands, I decided to visit some friends on the West coast. They told me I should see Lake Tahoe, so I flew to Reno and rented a car. Now I find I don't want to leave the area yet.

"Tahoe's a beautiful place, especially here, around Moon Lake. With spring coming, I'd like to stay for a while. When I stopped for coffee and saw the Help Wanted sign in your window, it seemed as if this was somehow…meant to be. I felt compelled to come in and find out if you'd consider hiring me.

"I don't need the money. What I want is a change of scene and a constructive way to spend my time. Could you use some help around here until you move? If nothing else, I make a good dishwasher."

Wendy sat back in stunned surprise. Like anything too good to be true, there had to be a catch somewhere. "My husband died five months ago of lung cancer, Mr. Walker. W-without him, we can't make it." Her voice caught. Damn.

"I'm very sorry."

"That's why I'm selling the resort. It could happen any day now. I'm afraid staying here wouldn't be worth your trouble."

He'd been studying her closely the whole time she'd been talking, making her feel more vulnerable than ever.

"Why don't you let me be the judge of that? I crave a new diversion, even if it's short-lived."

The man was practically begging for the job. No matter how good his reasons sounded, she didn't buy them. Especially since she could sense some inner turmoil emanating from him.

What fiancée in her right mind would have left a man like this alone for months if she truly loved him?

Maybe they'd quarreled. Maybe he hadn't wanted her feeling sorry for him and told her to stay away until he was back to his former self. Matt had been a little like that. He'd had a lot of pride and hated the idea of anyone pitying him.

Maybe you're insane to give this stranger another second of your time when you've got problems of your own to solve, Wendy Sloan.

"Look, Mr. Walker. My husband was a licensed building contractor. He knew how to fix anything from a generator to a snowmobile. He kept the accounts and did the taxes.''

''On the farm I have the same responsibilities. I may not be familiar with snowmobiles, but I'm no stranger to machines, believe me.''

I don't know what to believe. But if you're a farmer, I'm an astronaut.

His mouth twitched in amusement. He seemed to know exactly what she was thinking, which made her feel even more out of sorts.

''Naturally I can supply references. I'll jot down a few names and phone numbers for you. Then I'll head back to Stateline for the night. I'm staying at the Silver King Hotel. If I don't hear from you in the next couple of days, I'll know you're not interested.''

Against her better judgment, she said, ''I'll think about it, Mr. Walker.''

''That's good enough for me.''

He pulled out a pen and used the back of a paper napkin to write on. When he'd finished, he glanced up to meet her eyes. ''Thank you for your time. Since you've got customers, I'll get out of your way now.''

Wendy hadn't noticed. She'd been too busy concentrating on this stranger. He used his cane to rise to his feet, and as he shrugged into his jacket, she realized she was staring at him.

Averting her head, she quickly stood up. Too quickly. Another pain in her side made her gasp.

His expression sobered. ''Are you all right?''

''Yes, of course. It was just a muscle twinge.'' Embarrassment flooded her cheeks with hot color.

His concerned blue eyes played over her features. ''If you're sure.''

''I am.''

He nodded. "Good night then, Mrs. Sloan. Please thank your son for me. I've never met a brighter, more polite young man. Obviously, a lot of the credit goes to you."

He left a ten-dollar bill on the table and walked to the door, his limp barely discernible. "By the way," he added over his shoulder, "the cherry pie was the best I've ever tasted. My compliments to the chef." Then he was gone.

In a daze, Wendy pocketed the money and napkin.

Her customers looked at her expectantly.

She blinked.

Menus.

They needed water, coffee and menus. In that order.

"COME ON, CUTTY. That's a good girl." Ben shut the front door behind their terrier, then ran to catch up with his sister.

"Now remember what I said, Kim." She was only nine and sometimes forgot to do what he told her. "While we're cleaning up the coffee shop, pretend you don't know anything about Josh Walker. If we talk about him, it'll just make Mom mad. This is our only chance, so don't blow it!"

"I won't."

"Be super nice to her. Do everything she tells you and don't whine if she doesn't want you to sleep over at Misty's tomorrow night."

"Okay. Do you think she's still talking to him?"

"I don't know."

"Is he really nice?"

"Yeah. Like I told you. He's cool."

"How come he needs a cane?"

"He didn't tell me, and don't you dare ask Mom."

"I won't! Maybe he almost died in an accident."

"Well, whatever happened, he's okay now and he walks really well."

"Ada doesn't like dogs. Do you think he'll like Cutty?"

"Heck, he'll love her!"

"Does he smoke?"

"I don't think so. I couldn't smell it on him."

"Mom hates that, and drinking."

"I know."

"What if she hires him, and then catches him doing stuff?"

"We'll warn him not to do anything around her."

"She always finds out."

"You're right." Their mom had got rid of a summer stable hand who'd been caught drinking on the job. They hurried inside the back office of the coffee shop and took off their parkas. "Okay," he whispered. "Let's go. Don't forget what I told you."

She zipped her lip as they walked into the kitchen. Ben looked quickly around. "Mom's out front. Find the stool and get busy stacking the dishwasher. I've got to fix the sink."

A minute later, their mother came through the swinging door with an armload of dishes. "Hey, you two." She set them down on the counter, then gave Kim a hug. "Hi, lovey."

"Hi, Mom."

"I didn't know there were elves working back here. When did you get home from the Nymans'?"

Ben flashed his sister a warning glance.

"A little while ago. I ate all my dinner. The biscuits were yummy."

"So was the meat loaf," Ben chimed in.

"Well, I'm glad you liked everything. As soon as I clean up the dining room, I'll help you finish the dishes and we can call it a night."

He shook his head. "That's okay, Mom. We'll take care of them. Why don't you go back to the house and put your feet up?"

"Wouldn't I love to do that, but I can't go anywhere until I unplug the drain pipe under the sink."

"I put Drano in. The water's already started to go down."

"You're kidding! Thank you, Ben. What would I do without you guys?"

"You cou—"

"Mom?" Ben broke in before Kim said something she shouldn't. "Did you turn off the gas in the fireplace?"

"No. Not yet," she said, wetting a clean dishcloth to wipe off the tables.

"Then I'll do it."

He threw his sister a warning look, then followed his mother through the swinging door. Before he could reach the large stone hearth, she caught him by the shoulders and turned him to face her.

"Ben—you don't need to do this."

"Do what?"

"The angelic behavior you and your sister have been demonstrating doesn't have anything to do with Mr. Walker, does it?"

"Heck, no! We want to help you." Suddenly resigned to the fact that their family would have to move to California, he said, "I know you sent him away."

His mom had hazel eyes. They turned a really pretty green when she laughed or cried. But when she stared through him like she was doing now, they went kind of dark.

"How do you know that?"

He shrugged his shoulders and stared at the varnished pine floor. "I just do. Even though Mr. Walker wanted the job and said he'd work for nothing, I guess it's too hard for you to think of anyone else doing what Dad did around here."

Breaking free of his mother's hold, he turned off the gas and fled from the dining room. "Come on, Cutty," he called to his dog as he ran through the kitchen. Kim asked him where he was going, but he kept on running.

"YOU'VE REACHED THE Greater Bank of Cleveland. If you know your party's extension, press one for more options. If you want to know today's account balance, press two. If you've lost or wish to purchase an ATM card, press three. If you wish to speak to a customer service representative, press four. If you—"

Wendy pushed four and waited impatiently, still haunted by the bleakness in Ben's eyes when he'd run away from her last night.

After sleeping poorly, she had awakened with a colossal headache. Unfortunately she didn't dare take any painkillers because of her pregnancy and hoped a can of cola might help. Caffeine wasn't good for her, either, but the doctor hadn't yet eliminated it from her low-salt diet, as long as she kept the drinks to two per week.

This morning she'd fed her taciturn children and had seen them off on the school bus without a smile from either of them. Now it was time to get dressed and report to the coffee shop.

But she couldn't forget about that damn napkin with those names and telephone numbers. She felt like the villainess in a melodrama and found she couldn't toss the napkin in the trash as she'd intended. At least not until she'd satisfied her conscience, or possibly her curiosity. Or both...

"This is customer service. How may I help you?"

"May I speak with Brenda Rasmussen?"

"Just a moment, please."

While Wendy waited, she took a long swig of her drink.

"This is Brenda."

"Hello. This is Wendy Sloan calling from Moon Lake, Nevada. A Mr. Josh Walker has applied for temporary employment, and he gave me this number as a reference."

"Yes, Ms. Sloan. I'm the bank manager and I know him very well. Mr. Walker has done business with us for years, as did his grandfather, Ray Walker. We've handled several farm loans for Josh.

"It's a shame about his leg. He could have lost it. I don't know if he mentioned, but one of the hands accidentally ran over him with the tractor," she said in a confiding tone. "I didn't realize he was out of the hospital until he came in to get some traveler's checks. He said he couldn't farm again until his leg healed, so he decided to take a trip. What kind of work has he applied for?"

He really was a farmer. Wendy couldn't believe it.

"I—I own a resort in the mountains and need a general handyman to keep the place in good condition until it sells."

"Well, he runs a prosperous farm outside Cleveland, which means he knows how to work hard and can probably fix anything. All the farmers around here are pretty self-sufficient.

"Of course, I'm no expert in that department, but I can certainly vouch for his character and honesty. I've pulled up his file on the computer. As far as I can see, he's never been late with a payment on his loans, never written a bad check. He has a substantial sum in both his savings and checking accounts. Does that answer your questions?"

I would say so.

"Yes. Thank you very much for your time."

"Not at all. Call again if you need to. Goodbye."

Wendy clicked off and looked at the other number Josh had written down last night. Compelled by a force she didn't understand, she punched in the digits.

"Hello?" The voice sounded gruff.

"Hello? Is this Mr. Henry Kendal?"

"Who's this?" Like many old people over the phone, he was abrupt.

"My name is Wendy Sloan. I'm calling from Nevada."

"Don't know anyone in Nevada. Never want to—"

"No! Wait—don't hang up. I'm phoning about a man named Josh Walker."

"What's he done?"

Wendy blinked. "Nothing. He gave me your name as a reference because he's applied for work at my resort."

"Restless, is he?"

"I'm sorry? I don't understand."

"If you've got Josh there, then you know he has a game leg. Darn fool didn't see that tractor coming. I knew he was champing at the bit 'cause he couldn't get back to work, but I never figured him to head straight for those showgirls."

She didn't know whether to laugh or cry. "Is Josh a friend of yours?"

"That depends."

"On what?" A smile broke out on her face.

"His grandpa and I didn't exactly see eye to eye, but Josh is all right—most of the time. Except when he comes over to my farm and starts trying to help me do my own job. What he needs is to settle down and raise a family, but that fancy fiancée of his took off again."

"He told me."

"She's a damn fool. I bet if that high-strung filly knew he'd landed in sin country and planned to hang out for a while, she'd hightail it back here on the double!"

Sin country?

It took every bit of self-control Wendy could muster not to burst into laughter. But eccentric though Mr. Kendal might be, his explanation verified what Wendy had been thinking. Josh and his fiancée were having problems.

"So, if I were to hire him as a handyman, you think he'd do a good job?"

"Well, let's just put it this way. I'd be right proud to call him my own son."

High praise, indeed.

"Thank you for talking to me, Mr. Kendal. I appreciate it."

"You're welcome. Next time you see Josh, you tell him to be careful."

"Careful?"

"Yup. Mood he's in, he's liable to fall for one o' them showgirls. When his fiancée finds out about that, all hell will break loose."

Her mouth curved in a smile. "I'm afraid there aren't any showgirls around here. Just a lot of repairs that need doing to the cabins and barn."

"Barn? You have horses?"

"We have had." Her voice trailed off.

"Well, now. I guess I better let you in on a secret then."

"What's that?" To her own amazement, she was actually enjoying this conversation.

"Josh has never been on a horse. If he told you different, he was lying."

"Really. How do you know that?"

"Because when he was just a youngster, he watched his grandma get thrown from one at a county fair. Broke her neck and died. His grandpa raised him after that. Josh has been scared of horses ever since. But don't you tell him I told you."

By now her smile had faded. "No. I won't."

There was a lot more she would've liked to ask the old man, but she didn't dare. It was none of her business. In fact, she'd already learned more than she had any right to know.

"Thank you for the information, Mr. Kendal."

"That's all right. You tell Josh to call me some time."

She could hear the affection in his voice and wondered if he wasn't a little lonely for Josh, or just lonely, period. "I'll tell him. You were very kind to talk to me. Goodbye."

She suddenly realized it was almost nine and she hadn't yet opened the coffee shop. She hurriedly threw on her clothes, but the action pulled at her side once again. She groaned at the pain; what she really wanted to do was howl.

She had no legitimate reason not to hire Mr. Walker, particularly when there was so much work to do. She had to keep the place up until she found a buyer.

Her son knew instinctively why she was resisting. The words he'd spoken last night wouldn't stop resounding in her head.

I guess it's too hard to think of anyone else doing what Dad used to do around here.

Ben had an understanding beyond his years.

Guilty as charged, sweetheart, she murmured inwardly as she let herself in the back door of the coffee shop. Ada arrived a few minutes later.

The first thing her cook did was declare that the sink was still backed up, which meant Ben's solution to the problem hadn't worked, after all. Shouldering yet another worry, Wendy waited on customers, then left to do her own housework. But by the time she reached home, the issue of the sink had forced her to make a decision.

No matter how hard it would be to put up with a stranger, a man who wasn't Matt, she owed it to her children and their future to get the best price possible for the resort.

No one would pay top dollar for a run-down operation. If Josh Walker could help get things in shape around here, it would be a way of honoring Matt's memory. She couldn't let Moon Lake Inn deteriorate; Matt had put too much of his life into the place. Even if financial circumstances had forced her to put the resort on the market, she had to preserve what she could of their hopes and dreams. She wanted to feel that he'd be proud of her efforts. She wanted, needed, his blessing...

Without further ado, she pulled out the phone book

and looked up the number for the Silver King. Seconds later, she asked the front desk to put her call through to Mr. Walker.

"Hello?" came the distinctive voice on the third ring.

"Hello, Mr. Walker. It's Mrs. Sloan. I have an offer for you. You work for me for a month, and if we're both happy, you can stay until you're ready to move on, or until the place sells. Is that satisfactory with you?"

CHAPTER THREE

JOSH FELT A SENSE of elation; he recognized that it was out of all proportion to the situation. He loosened his grip on the receiver, unaware until now that he'd been holding his breath. Somehow he hadn't expected Mrs. Sloan's capitulation. Certainly not this soon!

Last night he'd left the resort convinced he'd have to tell Harve he'd take that job in Seattle, after all. By the time he'd reached the hotel, he'd decided it didn't matter where his supervisor sent him.

He'd tried to entertain himself, but the slot machines didn't hold his interest and he could find nothing worth watching on television. His sleep had been fitful. This morning when he'd awakened in a particularly foul mood, he realized it *did* matter. For some unfathomable reason, he'd wanted her to hire him.

Maybe it was because he'd seen how hard she'd fought against the idea. Maybe because she represented a challenge. Maybe it was some latent protective urge. Josh was delighted by the chance to stay at Moon Lake Inn.

"Thank you, Mrs. Sloan. I'll do everything in my power to justify your faith in me. In case you were wondering, I'm available now," he inserted, not wanting to give her time to renege on her decision. Instinct told him this was a fragile moment. One wrong word, and she might change her mind.

There was a slight pause. "Are you still driving a rental car?"

"That's right."

"Why don't you return it, and I'll pick you up in front of the Silver King at two this afternoon? While you're in my employ, you'll be given the use of my husband's truck. Just so you know, I'll be driving a white four-door Corolla."

She was all business. No chitchat.

"I'll be waiting for you. There's still a few hours before you get here. Are there any supplies you need? I'd be happy to pick them up to save you time."

Another long pause ensued. "That's very thoughtful of you, Mr. Walker."

"If I'm coming to work for you, I might as well make myself useful as soon as possible. By the way, the name is Josh, unless you prefer to keep things on a formal basis."

"No," she answered quietly, "of course not. Feel free to call me Wendy. If you have a pen and paper handy, I'll tell you what I need from Bintz Restaurant Supply in South Lake Tahoe. It's not far from Stateline. We have an account there."

"I'll be happy to do that." He took down her order—napkins, coffee, a few other items. "Anything else?"

"Not that I can think of at the moment. Wait—I'm out of nine-volt batteries. You could pick up a couple at Rymer's Hardware, where we also have an account. It's on the east side of South Lake Tahoe."

"No problem. I'll find it."

"Thank you, Josh. I think that's all for now. I'll see you at two."

"I'll be here."

As soon as he hung up the receiver, he checked the telephone directory and jotted down the addresses of the hardware and restaurant supply stores. While he was at it, he added the names and addresses of several physical therapists. As long as he was looking, he might as well scout for a good one. Twice a week, his doctor had said.

Filled with purpose, a sensation he hadn't felt since before he was shot, he picked up a map at the front desk. The therapy clinics were all relatively close to the hotel, so he visited those first.

He was satisfied with the third therapist he saw. He liked the sound of her methods and said he'd be calling to set up semiweekly appointments. With that taken care of, he began his errands.

The clerks at both stores accepted his job status at Moon Lake Resort without question. The older woman at the hardware store made the comment that although she admired the grieving widow, she felt Ben and Kim's mother had always worked too hard for her own good. The minute that husband of hers became ill, someone else should've been hired to take over the heavy load, especially when she discovered she was pregnant.

From the things the loquacious woman *didn't* say, Josh got the distinct impression she found fault with Mr. Sloan. Evidently the clerk wasn't aware of Moon Lake's financial problems. Even so, it was only natural that Wendy Sloan would want to hang on to the resort to honor her husband's memory. No doubt she was trying to carry out his wishes, as well as her own. Clearly the place had meant a lot to both of them. Would she remain in the area if she did sell? he wondered. If he'd been the one facing that decision, he figured he'd want to stay.

Josh had only been in Tahoe for a few days, but already the majesty of the mountains had affected him. It was the right word to describe the spectacular Sierra Nevadas, which were slowly giving up their snow to the glorious sunshine of spring.

Harve hadn't exaggerated. It *was* beautiful here. And at this altitude, the crisp dry air had cleared more than Josh's lungs. For the first time in months, he realized he hadn't been wallowing in the pain of his partner's death, and that felt good. Something else felt good, too, but he couldn't put a name to it.

It was an expectant feeling, like the kind he occasionally experienced in the cockpit doing photographic surveillance when he knew in his gut he was on to something big.

Ten minutes after turning in his rental, he spotted a white Toyota, which had joined a long line of cars waiting to check in to the busy hotel and casino. With a sense of anticipation, he went out to greet his attractive new employer. He asked her to open the trunk so he could store his suitcase and the purchases he'd made.

"You'll have to adjust the seat on your side or you'll never get your legs in," she called out to him.

He did, pleased over her concern for his comfort. Once he'd entered the passenger side of the car, he placed the cane between his legs.

"Don't forget to fasten your seat belt."

He grinned. She had no idea she was talking to a pilot who did that automatically. "I won't."

"I'm sorry," she said in an embarrassed voice. "I'm

so used to being with the children, I forgot. Please forgive me.''

"Think nothing of it.''

She worked the car back onto the street and they merged with the traffic. "Did you encounter any problems doing the errands?'' she asked.

Problems?

Distracted by the sheen of ash-blond curls against the foil of her black turtleneck, he almost lost his concentration. "No. None at all.''

"That's good. Well, unless you need to do anything else, I'll pick up the mail and we'll head straight over to Moon Lake.''

"Thank you for mentioning it, but no. I'm ready to go whenever you are.''

"I'm glad you said that, because I'm running late and I like to be home when the children get off the school bus.''

"How many do you have?''

"Two and about two-thirds.''

He chuckled, enjoying her sense of humor. "Ben must be your oldest. Still, you look too young to be the mother of a boy his age.''

"If you're trying to flatter me, you're doing a splendid job. Ben is twelve, but thinks he's much older.'' Josh had already figured that out. "I also have a nine-year-old daughter, Kim. Then of course there's Cutty.''

Ah, yes. Cutty. Josh had been waiting for all to be revealed. "A dog?''

Her eyes left the road long enough to dart him a surprised glance. "How did you know?''

He fought not to smile. "Just an educated guess. Children, mountain cabins and dogs sort of go together.''

She fastened her attention back on the road. "You're right. Cutty's our Scottish terrier. She'll defend any of us, but she's in love with Ben."

By this point, there was no doubt in Josh's mind that the ad on the Internet had been her son's doing. From their first meeting, Josh had taken a liking to the boy. But the knowledge that he'd gone behind his mother's back to try and find help for her touched Josh deeply. Such devotion spoke volumes about the love abounding in the Sloan family. The death of husband and father must have been devastating.

Thank God Josh's partner hadn't left a wife and children to fend for themselves. Premature death was a risk when you worked for the Bureau. Yet it happened to people in other walks of life, as well, like Mrs. Sloan's husband. There were no guarantees.

Deep in thought, he hadn't realized they'd already arrived at the post office. Fortunately she had even more difficulty than he did making a speedy exit from the car. He was able to get out first and open the door for her.

A becoming blush filled her cheeks. "You didn't need to do that."

"I'm afraid it's a habit my grandmother instilled in me. You may be my employer, but you're a woman first. I hope you don't mind."

He thought she might be offended, and forbid him to do it again. Instead she surprised him. "No. Every woman should be so lucky."

Slender legs swung to the ground. She looked smart in the brown maternity jumper toned with the black sweater. As she stood up, the noticeable mound beneath the soft wool drew his gaze. The growth of an unborn baby was miraculous. A man could only marvel.

"Would you prefer that I not go in with you?"

He sensed her hesitation, but she surprised him a second time. "It's probably a good idea if you do. When I'm too busy at the coffee shop to leave, or it's inconvenient for my neighbor to take Ben on errands with her, I'll probably ask you to drive to town for supplies. It'll be a great help if you could stop here to pick up the mail, too."

"I'll be happy to do that."

Using his cane, he accompanied her inside the building. Strange how he had to control an urge to clasp her elbow.

Under normal circumstances, he would do that for any woman he was escorting. But Wendy Sloan was not his date. She was his employer.

If this situation was going to work, he'd have to continue reminding himself of that fact.

She stopped at one of the mailboxes and took out her key.

Box 2750.

Proof positive of Ben's culpability. Well, if his mother ever found out her son had advertised over the net, she wouldn't have learned it from Josh.

He watched her retrieve the mail and give the half-dozen envelopes a cursory glance. Judging by the lack of expression on her face, he assumed they were bills.

I wish my mom would hire someone like you so we could keep the place running, but she can't pay you a salary.

According to Ben's ad, their resort could accommodate up to twenty-four people at a time. If the place had been closed to guests for the winter, then she'd lost a major part of her income for the year. Tahoe boasted some of the greatest skiing in the country. Because of that attraction alone, she could have filled the cabins every night of the week.

His mind spun with fresh possibilities. The advent of spring meant the ski season was winding down. But there was a host of other activities to draw tourists. Perhaps it wasn't too late to recoup some of her losses. He was sure he could help with that. But he had to check out a few things first.

Fired by new energy, he opened the doors for her and followed her to the car. As soon as he'd helped her into the driver's seat, he went around to the other side and they were off.

"Obviously there's a Moon Lake, but I have yet to see it," he commented as they headed back to the resort.

"Our property takes up seven acres of land, part of which borders on a tiny mountain lake. You don't know it's there until you suddenly come upon it.

"The legend goes that in the 1840s, one of John C. Fremont's men discovered it during the night of a huge harvest moon. Its reflection lit up the water, and from that moment on, he called it Moon Lake. I don't know if it's a true story, but it's fun to tell.

"In the summer, families rent canoes and kayaks from us. There's one fishing boat. We don't allow any motorized craft, no jet skis."

"How is the fishing, by the way?"

"A mountain stream feeds into the lake. A good fly fisherman will have success casting along the bank. But my husband was the only man I ever knew to catch his limit of German browns." Her voice trailed into a private world where Josh couldn't go.

"How about you?" he inquired mildly.

"What do you mean?"

"Are you an expert with the fly rod, too?"

She shook her head. "Heavens, no. When I fish, I want comfort. Let me troll on Lake Tahoe with a spinning rod in one hand and a soda in the other."

Comfort. He'd bet she hadn't had a moment's comfort or relaxation since she'd learned her husband was going to die. Unlike many people—and that included Josh when he'd been on medical leave, suffering over his partner's death—she didn't seem to wallow in self-pity. Considering her pregnancy, he admired that quality in her more than he could say. He admired it in her son.

Instead of rebelling against the tragedy that had robbed their family of its protector and provider, Ben had come up with a pragmatic solution to advertise for help. Incredibly, it had worked. Josh's presence in Wendy Sloan's car was evidence of that.

"Have you done much fishing, Josh?"

He shifted in the seat to flex his leg. "Not in years."

"If your farm's anything like our resort, there's always something that needs doing. If you don't make time to play, you probably won't."

When she put it like that, he figured he hadn't played in years. Not since college. In order to really play, you needed someone to play with. The right kind of someone...

"Speaking of things that need doing, what tops your list?"

She darted him an impish glance. "That depends on how many hours you've got to listen."

He chuckled. "That many."

"I thought it'd be better to give you the bad news

first. Then you can't go anywhere but up." He could tell she was smiling. "And Josh," she added, "in case you were thinking that you don't want to do this as badly as you thought you did, there's still time to turn around."

If this was her way of telling him she'd changed her mind and would just as soon watch him disappear, he had news for her. "You know, Mrs. Sloan, I think I'm going to like working for you."

"That's good, because there's a sink of standing water in the coffee-shop kitchen with your name on it. If the pipe doesn't get fixed, I'm afraid my cook, Ada, is going to quit."

She might make light of it, but Josh knew that if he hadn't come along, she would have tackled the plumbing problem herself. Getting under a sink required a few bodily contortions. Being six months pregnant would only make the task that much more difficult.

"Since my mouth's watering for another piece of her cherry pie, I'll get to work on it the second we arrive."

"I was only teasing, Josh. Naturally you need time to settle in. Tonight I'll make a list of the things that should be taken care of first. Tomorrow will be soon enough to get started."

Though he had his own ideas on that score, he murmured his assent.

"Please don't think I'll forget our bargain. If the job isn't what you had in mind, after all, you can leave at the end of April with no qualms. Likewise, if you should experience any problems with your leg, you're free from any obligation to me."

Josh wondered how much longer she was going to try getting rid of him. The more she spoke, the more he realized she was praying he'd let her off the hook.

No way, Mrs. Sloan. You hired me and by damn, you'll just have to put up with me for the next thirty days.

"Josh?" she prodded.

"I would never have applied for the job if I'd had any concerns about injuring it further."

"Nevertheless, with marriage plans in your future, I'd feel terrible if you suffered a setback while you were working for me."

He lurched in the seat. He'd almost forgotten about that lie. Lord. He had a manufactured fiancée to provide him with the needed excuse when it came time to go back on active duty. It was part of the cover story Harve had invented for him last week, before he'd met Wendy Sloan. Already he'd almost blown it.

"Barring something unforeseeable, I plan to be a hundred percent recovered before long, but I want you to know I appreciate your concern. As long as we're talking about my leg, I meant to tell you that I'm supposed to have physical therapy twice a week.

"I'm mentioning it now because we haven't discussed my work schedule yet. If I could have either two mornings or afternoons off on weekdays, then I'd be around the rest of the time, particularly weekends. I assume you're swamped Saturday and Sunday."

"Be that as it may, I wouldn't expect you to work on Sundays. As for your therapy, arrange it however you can. That's fine with me."

"Thank you."

"I'll open a cabin for you as soon as we reach home. Each has a different view. You can take your pick."

He liked the sound of that. "Which is your favorite?"

"They're all wonderful, but I like the one where you

can see the mountains forming the Tahoe Rim. Matt
and I planned t—''

She stopped herself before she revealed anything
more.

He grimaced. With her husband's death only five
months ago, Josh imagined she'd do quite a bit of that
for a while.

Taking advantage of the lull in the conversation, he
fastened his attention on the magnificent alpine scenery. The mountain road wound through dense forests
of tall, snow-dotted pines and firs.

How had he lived on this earth for thirty-five years
and not known such a heavenly place existed?

Heavenly was the name of the local ski area. He'd
seen the word on his map of South Tahoe. Now he
knew why....

''I guess the one thing we haven't talked about is
your meals,'' she began, speaking again. ''I open the
coffee shop in the morning, cook breakfast and make
the pastry. Ada comes in a little after I do and fixes all
the other meals.

''You can eat in the dining room or the kitchen
whenever it suits you. Treat the coffee shop like your
own home. If you feel like raiding the fridge at two in
the morning, go ahead.''

So she made the pastry. The woman did everything
and still managed to make the best pie he'd ever tasted.

There were a few female agents in the department
whose performance ranked higher than the guys'. Josh
thought of them as superwomen. But after meeting
Wendy Sloan, he decided she'd redefined the term. The
battleground might be different, but the struggle for
survival was no less precarious. In some ways he
thought it might even be more so.

They rounded another bend in the road. As he caught sight of the log-cabin coffee shop with its wide picture window, he felt an inexplicable sense of homecoming.

The faded Help Wanted sign was still in one corner of the glass. Such an insignificant piece of cardboard, it had provided him with an entrée into a totally different world. So far, he liked everything he'd seen. He liked everyone he'd met....

She pulled into a driveway that ran past the gas pump and stopped in front of a large garage around back hidden by trees. A blue Ford V-8 half-ton pickup with a winch and trailer hitch stood parked under one of the biggest pines. The truck was probably ten years old, but seemed in good condition.

"The garage serves as a workshop and storage facility. Later, I'll give you a set of keys to the resort and show you around. Right now I thought you might like to freshen up. Ada will fix you a sandwich while I gather some bedding and towels for your cabin."

He'd already grabbed lunch at the hotel, but decided against saying anything and simply nodded. Perhaps while she was busy, he could take a look at her sink and fix it. He assumed there was a closet with tools and janitorial supplies. Ada, the friendly cook who'd waited on him last night after Ben had run to get his mother, would show him where to find things.

It felt good to be needed again.

This time Wendy got out of the car before he could help her, so he reached for the supplies he'd picked up in town. With the aid of his cane, he followed her along a soggy path to the back of the coffee shop. He'd return later for his suitcase.

Little by little the snow was disappearing. Since he couldn't do any skiing, he didn't mind seeing the last of it. The sun had been out most of the day, and it seemed to be chasing away the dark shadows that had haunted him for months.

Together they entered the coffee shop and walked through to the kitchen, where he set down the sacks on the gleaming, stainless-steel counter. The interior, which was spotless, looked surprisingly modern.

Ada had been slicing potatoes with a food processor, but she turned off the machine when she saw him with Wendy.

"Mrs. Morse? You met Josh, Mr. Walker, last night. He asked for a job and I decided to hire him until the place is sold. You'll be seeing a lot of each other during the next few weeks, so I'll let you get acquainted while I run back to the house. I don't suppose he'd say no to one of your chicken sandwiches, Ada." He smiled in response.

"Josh?" Her hazel eyes flicked to him, but he could tell she was distracted by other matters. For a short time, he'd had her undivided attention. Perhaps he'd be able to capture it again later. "The children are due home any minute now. Once I've seen to them, I'll show you to your cabin and take care of you."

He liked the sound of that. "Fine."

"One more thing," she said as if he hadn't spoken. "The employee bathroom is the door on the left, where we came in. The door beside that is the laundry room."

"I'll find everything."

She clapped her palms together in what he assumed was an unconscious gesture. "Okay, then. I'll see you in a little while."

As soon as she'd left, he turned to the older woman. "Ada? Before I do anything else, I want to fix the sink."

"Hallelujah!"

He liked her already. "Where can I find a bucket, a wrench and some rags?"

"Follow me."

"ARE YOU STILL MAD at Mom?"

"Aren't you?"

"I guess."

The kids on the bus waved to Ben and Kim as they clambered off.

"Don't you get it? Mr. Walker said he'd work for no money."

"That's 'cause he loves it up here, huh?"

"Of course. If Mom had let him, I bet he would've stayed, and we wouldn't have to move."

"I don't want to go to dumb old Sacramento and leave Magpie."

"We're not going if I can help it."

"What can we do?"

"I don't know yet. Eric and I are thinking up another plan." They kept walking. "Are you hungry?"

"Yes."

"Let's get a candy bar out of the pantry before we go home."

"Okay. Just don't tell Mom."

They hurried in the front entrance of the coffee shop and passed through the swinging door to the kitchen.

"Hi, Ada!" they said at the same time, intent on their destination.

"Hi, kids!"

But Ben came to an abrupt halt when he saw the subject of their conversation stretched out on his back, his head half-hidden under the kitchen sink. The cane lay next to his long, jean-clad legs. There were tools and bucket close at hand.

"What the heck?" Ben walked over and crouched down to see. He thought maybe he was dreaming. "It really *is* you!"

Mr. Walker grinned. "I sure hope so."

Ben grinned back. "How come? I mean, what happened?"

"Your mother phoned me this morning. We had a talk, and she hired me for a month."

"A month—" he cried out. Ben had been ready to shout for joy. But Mr. Walker's last words dashed his dreams.

"We decided to wait a month to see how everything works out. If at the end of that time, she's happy with my work, and I'm happy to be here, then I'll stay for a while longer."

Ben jumped to his feet. "Yes!" But his euphoria was short-lived. He leaned over again. "How much longer?"

"I don't know. That all depends."

Mr. Walker had said the same thing last night. *That all depends.* It could mean anything.

"Who's the little golden-haired, blue-eyed princess peeking over your shoulder?"

"That's my sister, Kim."

"Hello, Kim."

"Hi."

"Why don't you two call me Josh?"

"Okay."

Ben felt her crouch down next to him. "If you want to keep your job," she whispered, "don't let my mom see you smoke or drink around here."

"She really hates that," Ben said, supporting his sister.

"I hate smoking myself. As for drinking, I might have one when I go out for an evening with my fiancée or my friends. Ben? How about handing me that smaller wrench."

"Sure."

"What's a fee-awn-say?" Kim piped up.

Ben knew what it meant. Eric's older sister had one. "That means he's getting married."

"Your brother's right, Kim."

"When?" Another lump had formed in Ben's throat. Every time he thought he was home free, Josh said something to destroy his hopes.

"In the fall."

"Does she live around here?"

"No. She's a freelance journalist from Ohio. That's where I live."

Kim had moved in closer. "How come she isn't with you?"

"Because she's covering an earthquake story in South America."

"But you're sick!"

"I was, but I'm almost better now."

"Then how come you have to use a cane?"

"So I won't put too much weight on my bad leg. It's still healing."

"Is it ever going to get well?"

"You bet. Another month and I'll be able to throw the cane away."

"Can I have it?"

Ben heard Josh chuckle. "If you want it, it's yours."

"How did you get hurt?"

"A tractor ran over me."

"Did it hurt a lot?"

"A lot."

"Are you a farmer?"

"I sure am."

"You don't look like one."

"What do farmers look like?"

"They're old and have beards and wear overalls. Yuck."

Ben thought Josh was laughing again. "Some of them are younger."

"My brother thought you were a movie star."

"Me?"

"Yeah," Ben muttered. "You kind of looked like Mel Gibson when I first saw you."

"I thought the same thing," came Ada's comment from the background.

"Well, I'm glad I'm not a movie star."

"How come? Misty's mom says they make lots and lots of money."

"Money isn't everything, Kim," Josh murmured.

"If we had money, we wouldn't have to move to California, huh, Ben?"

"Heck, no!"

Suddenly Ben heard the back door open and close.

"Ada?" his mom called out in an anxious voice. "Have you seen the children? They're not home yet, and I'm worried!"

"We're right here, Mom!" Ben shouted as his dog preceded her into the kitchen and nosed her way under the sink.

"Yeah, Mom," Kim echoed.

"Well, hello there. You must be Cutty. You're a nice dog." Josh's voice floated out from under the sink.

Kim smiled at Ben in secret understanding. "He's ours."

"Come out of there, Cutty. Come on. Leave the poor man alone," their mother urged.

"It's okay, Mrs. Sloan—Wendy. We're all getting acquainted."

"I can see that."

"The sink is fixed, guys."

That ought to make his mother happy. The plumbing had been giving her trouble for weeks.

Ben watched the way Josh smiled up at his mom. But she just looked down at him with this weird expression on her face.

Was she mad or something?

Heck—did she think their dad was the only man who could fix things around here?

CHAPTER FOUR

WENDY FELT AS IF they were all in a play, but she was the only one without a script.

Three happy faces stared at her. Four if she counted Cutty's. Even Ada wore a wider smile than usual.

This scene of domestic bliss was as unexpected as it was troubling. For months she'd been working to recover some semblance of order and normalcy in their family life. She'd made decisions she'd believed were for the best.

Then Josh Walker had come into the coffee shop last night, and suddenly everything was different. He was like a magnet attracting iron to itself in a distinct pattern. She no longer felt in control.

Overnight Ben had changed. And where her brother went, Kim followed.

Starved for Matt's affection and attention, they were vulnerable to any man who showed them the slightest kindness. Now this stranger had come along, seemingly able to solve all their problems.

Though his position was just temporary, Wendy had made a mistake in hiring him. A big one.

She took a deep breath. "You children empty the bucket and put the tools away, then you can help Ada get things ready for the dinner crowd. I'm taking Josh to his cabin. Come on, Cutty. You can't stay in here."

Wendy knew exactly what Ben and Kim were thinking; everyone had been having such a good time, then the wicked queen had come along and ruined it.

Wendy refused to look at her children's crestfallen faces. But she couldn't help glimpsing their terrier's sad eyes as she bade Ben the most soulful farewell Wendy had ever witnessed. Oh, brother. Fortunately Ada seemed to realize what was called for and told the kids to get busy.

Cutty trotting beside her, they moved quickly along the path. Too late she remembered to slow down in deference to Josh's leg. She could sense he was close behind, no doubt endeavoring to keep up. What was wrong with her?

When they reached a fork in the fir-lined path, she turned but didn't look at him.

"I left your bedding and towels in the house. Just a moment and I'll get them."

Forgetting her condition, she dashed off. By the time she'd raced up the steps and entered the cabin, she felt the familiar pain in her side. She sat on the couch for a minute until the worst of it subsided. Cutty had flattened herself on the floor and stared up at Wendy, waiting.

After catching her breath, Wendy gathered up the things she'd come for. "All right, girl. Let's go."

The load felt heavy and cumbersome as she made her way out of the house. As soon as Josh saw her, he started in her direction. Their eyes met briefly. His seemed to ask permission before he relieved her of the burden and placed everything under his free arm.

Part of her resented the ease with which he'd already insinuated himself into her world. Then she chastised herself for such an uncharitable thought.

He'd been hired to help.

And that's what he's doing.

In fact, if it had been any other person with her, she would have *asked* for assistance. But for some reason she couldn't explain, Josh Walker's presence had a disturbing effect on her.

Far more aware of him than she wanted to be, she murmured her thanks, then made a determined effort to pull herself together. Walking slightly ahead of him, she moved along the path that led toward the cluster of log cabins hidden among the pines.

When Wendy had met Matt at college in Reno, he and his father had been in the process of building them. Each cabin had been placed higher up the mountain at a different level and angle for privacy.

She and Josh had to trudge through melting snow to reach the farthest cabin. Her favorite, with the best view... How many times had she shown guests to this cabin?

Yet this time was different. This guest was different. He would be living on the property. They would see each other coming and going at all hours.

Relieved that a late-afternoon sun still made everything visible, even here, deep in the woods, she pulled the key ring from her parka pocket and opened the door. But she'd forgotten about the shuttered windows. They closed out the warm rays.

For that moment, when she and Josh both stepped over the threshold, the darkness seemed to take on a certain intimacy. Until she flipped the light switch, she'd actually felt...

She didn't know what she'd felt.

No doubt her breathless state had everything to do with her pregnancy. Her reactions toward this man were absurd. He'd done nothing she could fault.

Maybe that's what's wrong, she muttered inwardly as she turned on the heating unit against the wall. From there she moved to the utility closet, where she flicked another switch so he'd have hot water.

So far, Josh had been nice, pleasant, polite, helpful. He'd done the shopping for her. Thanks to him, the kitchen sink would no longer give her grief.

Couldn't she just be grateful that he'd asked for work? Why not take advantage of what he had to offer and stop feeling so…threatened? As long as the children realized the resort could be sold any day, why should she worry over Josh's temporary employment?

For all she knew, he and his fiancée might decide to get married earlier.

He might even be gone before Wendy had a buyer. She would drive this point home to the children.

"You should have hot water within twenty minutes. In the meantime, I'll go back to the shop for a hammer to open those shutters."

He'd already started making up one of the double beds. "Thanks, but that won't be necessary. I left my suitcase in your car. When I go back for it, I'll borrow the one I saw hanging in the kitchen closet."

She nodded. He was so self-sufficient, she felt superfluous.

After putting the towels and soap in the bathroom, she checked out the rest of the cabin. The bedside lamp, clock radio and TV appeared to be in good working order.

"You'll notice there's a phone by the bed, but I had the service disconnected when I closed the cabins. There are three phones in the coffee shop. One's a pay phone inside the front door for customers. There's another for our use on the wall behind the front counter.

And there's a third phone in the office at the rear of the restaurant. You're welcome to use any of them, but you probably have a cell phone.''

He shook his head. ''I left it in Ohio. If I need to make a call, I'll use the pay phone.''

Surely there'd be times when he'd want to talk to his fiancée at length. Neither the pay phone nor the resort phones would afford him much privacy, but of course that was his affair.

Clearing her throat, she said, ''We start serving dinner in the next half hour. Come whenever you're ready. I'll give you a key to the truck. I can't remember if I mentioned it earlier, but please feel free to use it in the evenings and during your days off when you have to go to town for therapy. Just fill it up at the pump whenever it needs gas.''

''That's very generous of you.'' He finished slipping the second pillowcase on the pillow.

''You may not feel that way when you have to fix something first so it'll start.''

He flashed her a quick smile. ''Now you're making me feel right at home. My own truck has been known to have the occasional temper tantrum. In any event, I don't plan to drive more than I have to.''

Wendy refrained from comment. He might say that now. But as Mr. Kendal had implied, Josh would grow bored after a week without his fiancée and would want to make the rounds of Lake Tahoe shows.

''After I see Ben and Kim off to school in the morning, I'll acquaint you with the shop and discuss the repairs that take priority.'' Since she'd had their ten horses boarded in Carson City for the winter—another decision her children still hadn't forgiven—she decided any mention of the barn could wait.

He leveled his gaze on her. "Sounds good to me."

There was something about the way he looked at her—as if he knew her thoughts... She shook her head. Time to get back to the coffee shop.

She made it as far as the door before she remembered her manners. "Thank you for fixing the sink so quickly."

"You're welcome."

"I'll see you later. Come on, Cutty. Let's go."

After shutting the door, she stood on the porch step to breathe in deep draughts of air. Anything to settle her nerves. Until now she'd never experienced a reaction like this in her life.

She studied the forested landscape her husband had loved so much, especially at twilight.

She felt close to Matt in this place, carrying his baby—and yet she recognized the beginning of a new distance. And it was because of Josh Walker. A stranger. A man she'd known less than twenty-four hours.

"HELLO, HARVE."

"Josh! I wondered when you'd get around to calling me. Did your cover story work? Are you the new handy-man at Moon Lake Resort?"

Josh had just finished a surprisingly delicious roast beef dinner, with homemade pecan pie for dessert. Wendy was waiting on the last remaining customers, which meant that right now was a good time to make contact with his supervisor.

He'd purposely chosen to use the pay phone inside the front door of the coffee shop so he'd be visible to her. She was still suspicious of his reasons for wanting a job that didn't pay a salary. It was important that she at least believe he had a fiancée and was missing her.

But in case Wendy had to use the cash register before he broke off his conversation, he turned his back for privacy, facing the mountain road.

"You're speaking to him. Give my regards to Brenda and Henry. They outdid themselves in the reference department. Buy them each a box of chocolates, will you?"

"Of course. But they've performed these services often enough before. What made today so different?"

"Because until my new boss vetted them, I didn't stand a chance of being hired." In fact, if she could find a legal way to get rid of him tonight, he had a gut feeling she'd do it. "Mrs. Sloan is nobody's fool."

"That's the reason I've always felt it was wise to stick to the truth as much as possible. Besides, Henry thinks of you as a son. He knows how to sound convincing when he talks about you."

Josh made a sound in his throat. "Well, like I said, they both outdid themselves this morning."

"That's good to hear. I take it everything is straightforward—no surprises."

Through the glass, Josh could see Wendy's pregnant figure as she moved efficiently back and forth. The overhead lights emphasized the sheen of her glossy hair. His gaze was caught and held by the sheer femininity she exuded, the rich curves of her body attractively covered by a white pullover and black-on-white print smock. It ended at the knee, revealing shapely, silken-clad legs below.

"Nothing I can't handle," Josh murmured when he suddenly realized Harve had been waiting for him to say something.

She had to be tired after putting in a full day's work.

"Excellent. I'll start the letters coming. Anything else?"

In another month he wouldn't require a cane. If she were willing, he could start waiting on tables in the evenings and spare her that extra duty when one of the teens called in sick. By then, she'd be four weeks closer to her delivery date.

"Josh. Oh, Josh. I'm still here, remember?"

For the second time, Harve's voice brought him back from his errant thoughts. He looked away from the window, the better to concentrate. "Sorry, Harve. I got distracted for a minute. What did you say?"

"I said, is there anything else I can do to help you right now?"

"As a matter of fact, there is. I need a computer and I want it already programmed with a spreadsheet of a fake farm account going back ten years. It'll validate my background in case Mrs. Sloan or her son happens to pull it up on the screen.

"Send it express mail ASAP to Moon Lake Inn Resort, Route 10, Stateline, Nevada. Set me up on the Internet. Make it a USOL server."

"Don't tell me you're bored already! With all the exciting nightlife around Tahoe, I figured you could fill up your free time in any number of interesting ways."

When Josh was in college, he and his buddies would have found the casinos and revues vastly entertaining. But that was in his early twenties, when every young pup, as his grandfather was wont to call them, went through a shallow, selfish phase on his way to finding himself.

"Actually, Harve, I've discovered there's more to

occupy my time at Moon Lake than I would have guessed.''

After a silence, Harve said slowly, "Maybe I like the sound of that, and maybe I don't. You're there to get your leg healed, remember?''

"I'm fully aware of that.''

"You know something? You sound different.''

I feel different.

"It's the mountain air. You were right, Harve. Today I felt the sun on my face. Another full day of sunshine is forecast for tomorrow. Life's looking up.''

"I'm glad to hear it,'' came his supervisor's thoughtful response.

By now, the last customers had moved to the counter to pay for their meal. Josh could hear them asking Wendy questions about the various ski resorts in the area.

"I'll check in with you later, Harve. Gotta run.''

"Over and out, Josh.''

He hung up the receiver, then turned around to discover a pair of inquisitive hazel eyes trained on him. She immediately averted them before handing one of the customers some change.

As he passed her, Josh detected a faint blush on her cheeks. He didn't know if her heightened color was due to exertion or the fact that he'd caught her staring at him. Whatever the reason, her curiosity pleased him.

To save her the trouble, he cleared the recently vacated table on his way to the kitchen. It was quite a trick to stack and carry everything with one hand. Luckily he was right-handed and used his left to wield the cane.

Cutty met him at the swinging door, followed by

Ben, who took the dishes from him and hurried over to the sink.

"Thanks, sport."

"Sure."

"Josh? Have you seen my mom?" Kim stood on a stool putting away glasses from the dishwasher.

"Yes. She's still out front talking to some customers."

"I wish she'd hurry. I need her to help me with my report."

"What kind of report?"

"Mrs. Kleeve says I have to choose a hero. Then I have to write a paragraph about one and draw a picture."

Ben finished reloading the dishwasher, then turned to his sister. "That's easy! Just write about Dad!"

"She said we can't use our dads 'cause everybody would do that."

"I have an idea," Josh interjected.

Kim's sparkling blue eyes widened with interest. "You do?"

"If you're finished there, come back to the office while I fill out some papers and I'll tell you." When he'd returned for his suitcase, Wendy had told him she wanted his job application on file, plus his signature on the written contract.

"I'm all through." Kim jumped down and returned the stool to the utility closet.

"Hey—wait for me," Ben called out as he trailed them down the hall to the office.

Josh sat down and rested his cane against the desk, then smiled at Kim. By now Cutty had wriggled her way between them and rested her perky head against

Josh's good leg. "When you hear the word *hero,* what's the first thought that comes into your mind?"

"Somebody big and strong who can do anything." She closed her eyes for a minute. "Someone who's always good, and always there when you need him. Someone who's nice to children and animals."

"A hero should be smart, too," Ben asserted.

Josh sat back in the chair. "Now, I can think of someone who lives at Moon Lake who answers that description perfectly."

There was total silence while the children pondered his statement.

"Mom?" they eventually blurted out.

"But she can't be a hero. She's a woman!"

You just said a mouthful, Ben Sloan. She's a woman, all right.

Josh's attention switched to Kim. "A woman can be a hero, too. Literally speaking, she's a heroine."

"A what?"

He smiled. "Have you ever heard of Mother Teresa, for example?"

Both kids nodded. "They showed her for a whole week on the Channel One news at school."

"Why did they do that?"

"Because she helped thousands of poor people before she died."

"Was she big and strong?"

Kim shook her head. "No. She was little."

"That's right. Strength doesn't necessarily have to do with physical size. It's the size of a person's heart that determines if he's a hero—or she's a heroine."

"Mom's not very big," Kim said slowly.

"That's true. But she's stronger than any woman I know. I've watched her do everybody's work around here, including your dad's, and she's carrying a baby inside her, too.''

''Sometimes she's so smart it's frightening,'' Ben muttered.

''She loves animals, and my friends say she's the nicest mom.''

''That's because your mother has character, Kim.''

The expression on her cute little face had grown solemn. ''What's that?''

''When your father died, she didn't quit like some people do. She just kept on being your mom, going along the way he would've wanted her to. That's character. It's a rare quality.''

She cocked her head. ''What was that word again? Hair-row—''

''Heroine. Here. I'll spell it for you.'' He jotted the word down on a piece of notepaper and handed it to her.

When she took it from him, her whole face was beaming.

''Thanks, Josh.'' Before he could react, she gave him a quick kiss on the jaw, then slipped the note in her Levi's pocket. ''Don't anyone tell Mom about this.''

''Don't tell me what?''

At the sound of Wendy's voice, all heads lifted. Josh realized it was up to him to save the moment.

He studied her classic features. The blush he'd seen on her cheeks earlier had disappeared. ''The children are afraid you'll be upset when you read on the application that I enjoy an alcoholic beverage now and again. But as I explained to them, I only do that when I go out with my friends, or for a special dinner with my fiancée.''

His comment seemed to take her aback. She frowned at her children. "Instead of bothering Josh, you two should be at the house getting your homework done."

"We know, Mom. We just came in here to tell him good-night. Come on, Kim." They started out of the office.

"As soon as I turn off the lights and lock up, I'll be right there," Wendy called after them.

The click of the back door sounded clearly. For the moment, he was alone with his new employer. He sensed that she was more than aware of it. And from her taut position against the doorjamb, he also knew she felt distinctly uncomfortable about it.

"When I go home, I'll talk to the children," she began, speaking quickly. "We'll lay down some ground rules about their interaction with you. But that won't be enough unless you set boundaries for them, as well. Children will take all the attention you give them, and then some. Especially my children. They're missing their father." Her voice stumbled on the last word.

You're missing him, too.

"Mrs. Sloan—Wendy. I'm not an expert where children are concerned. But I lost someone very dear to me when I was Kim's age. It was a traumatic time, so I have some understanding of what you're all going through.

"Since I'll be staying around here for a while, I'd like to be a friend to everyone. Ben and Kim are charming, delightful children. As for the application, I'm glad they told me how you feel about your employees smoking or drinking.

"Just so you know, I still have to take painkillers once in a while at bedtime. For that reason, I haven't touched alcohol since my accident. While I work for you, you have my promise I won't be drinking on or off the job. As for smoking, I've never tried it.

"I got over my party-animal tendencies in college. At this point in my life, I prefer an early night. If there's anything else you're worried about, please ask me now."

She shook her head. "Thank you for being frank with me. Normally I wouldn't ask personal questions like that. But we had trouble with another employee about his drinking, so…" She shrugged. "Anyway, thank you."

"Thank you—for hiring me." Maybe it would be overstepping his bounds to mention something he'd been thinking about, but since her phone call this morning, his protective instincts had kicked into high gear.

"Mrs. Sloan…I realize you hired me to help maintain the resort's facilities. However, since I won't be going into town in the evenings, I'd be more than happy to stretch my duties around here at night."

A confused expression broke out on her face. "What do you mean?"

"I could turn out lights and lock up the coffee shop. Maybe combine it with a nightly security check of the property. You might as well use me while I'm here. Plus, it'll be a good way to exercise my leg before I go to bed."

Her unmistakable tension betrayed how hard she was still fighting him. "Why don't we talk about it tomorrow?" she finally suggested.

Once more she'd surprised him by not responding with an outright no to his offer.

"You've got the keys I left for you?"

"Yes. Thank you."

"Good. Then I think that's everything." She wanted him to go.

He'd prefer to stay here and get to know her a little better. Of course, that wasn't possible. But there was always tomorrow night. *Tomorrow night.* For once he'd forgotten to be depressed and was actually looking forward to another day.

Reaching for his cane, he rose to his feet. She stood aside so he could pass. In fact, she gave him such wide berth, he had the distinct impression she didn't want him to accidentally brush against her. A tantalizing thought.

"Good night, Josh." He watched her affix a patently false smile. "Just remember one thing. If by morning you've had second thoughts and want to change your mind abou—"

"I signed that contract for a month's probationary period." He cut her off before she could finish. "Your signature is right there beneath mine. Under the circumstances, I intend to stick to our agreement." Not even a Biblical-sized catastrophe could drive him away now. "Good night."

WENDY STOOD FROZEN to the spot until the back door closed and she couldn't hear his footsteps.

Thank God she was finally alone, with no children to notice every little detail and ask her what was wrong.

She'd hired other people for temporary work before. Other men. More often than not, Matt had asked her to handle that part of their business, because he trusted her instincts. The one time they'd had to fire a stablehand for disorderly conduct, Matt had been the one who'd given him the job in the first place.

Hiring Josh Walker was nothing new. She had the most valid of reasons for doing so.

But her feelings about him—the way she felt when she was around him—were foreign to her. He made her more aware of herself as a woman. Worse, she felt this awareness of him....

It seemed such a betrayal of Matt's memory. How could she even notice another man this soon, especially when she was carrying Matt's child? She buried her face in her hands, horrified by her shameful weakness.

That was why she'd been so ambivalent about hiring Josh, she admitted. But they'd both signed the contract, so it was little wonder he'd sounded testy just now.

The poor man had no comprehension of what she was feeling—the confusion, the grief and guilt...the attraction. While she'd been watching him out of the corner of her eye, he'd gone to the pay phone to call his fiancée. No doubt he was begging her to come home as soon as possible.

Wendy could imagine how restless he'd become since his accident. Did his fiancée have any idea how devoted he was to her? Most men finding themselves alone, whether single, engaged or married, would leap at the opportunity to avail themselves of the nightlife around Tahoe.

"Listen to me go on and on." She said the words aloud. "What an idiotic fool I am." Tears burned her eyes. "Damn, damn, damn."

Making a determined effort, she turned out lights and locked up. By the time she reached the house, she'd decided that if it helped Josh fill the hours until he was reunited with his fiancée, he could take on all the work he wanted. Heaven knew there was more than any of them could accomplish.

She ought to be grateful for his offer. Since Ben's birth, she'd always slept with one ear open to listen for the children. Since Matt's death, she'd kept the other ear open, as well. She'd become chief defender of the castle.

With Josh's arrival, she now had backup support. Why not be thankful? Why wallow in her own confusion?

He'd said he wanted to be a friend to the family.

That might be possible with the children. However Wendy didn't hold to the philosophy that a man and woman could remain friends. Either sex, or romance, or both, got in the way. If neither of the above happened, then one of them moved on to another relationship. In her view, it was the natural order of things between men and women.

Since Josh would be getting married in the near future, Wendy would strive to attain a pleasant working relationship. What else could she do?

Her awareness of him was a given. She knew herself well enough to understand that this awareness wasn't about to go away. So...it was just another problem she'd have to tackle. Like the problem of getting the resort sold as soon as possible.

Her baby deserved to come home from the hospital to a nursery. That meant she needed to start looking for a nice little house in Sacramento.

Maybe she could get a rental with an option to buy. If she called her sister tonight, Jane could check the local newspaper and see what was listed.

Tomorrow morning, the first thing she'd do was phone the Realtor and tell him to speed things up. So far the For Sale sign in front of the coffee shop had produced zero results.

He'd actually tried to talk her out of putting up a sign because he said it just brought in a lot of curiosity seekers who had no intention of putting down earnest money. He'd insisted that the best way to get a good price was through a private deal.

So far he'd been wrong on both counts, but she was still hoping to get lucky. It was possible the perfect buyer would come along tomorrow and solve her financial problems.

"Hi, kids. I'm home!" she called out as she entered the house. Cutty came streaking down the hall to greet her. Wendy leaned over to scratch her behind the ears. "How are you, girl?" The dog rubbed against her legs affectionately.

"Kids?"

"We're in the kitchen doing our homework!"

That would be a first. They were up to something.

Since Josh Walker had walked into the coffee shop, she'd seen a noticeable change in her children. A little while ago, there'd been a definite air of secrecy when she'd caught them talking to him in her office.

After hanging up her parka in the front hall closet, she walked through the living room to the kitchen.

"Need any help?"

Kim sat on her chair eating a cookie. "Ben's making a trilobite. What's a trilobite?"

"I think it's a fossil."

Ben flicked her a glance. "You're pretty smart, Mom. It's a marine anthropod fossil."

"Ah...I forgot." She smiled. "Can I see it?"

He shut his loose-leaf binder. "Not until parent-teacher conference."

Wendy frowned. She'd forgotten about that. "When is it?"

"April sixteenth. Here's a handout."

"Mine's on the same night," Kim said, handing Wendy a similar notice.

Fortunately, the grade school and the junior high sat next to each other. She wouldn't have a great deal of walking to do.

Another parent-teacher conference to live through...

Wendy liked talking to their teachers. She just hated the lineups. But they were a fact of life and couldn't be avoided.

"If everybody's ready, let's turn in and I'll read another chapter of *The Hobbit*."

That suggestion seemed to meet with everyone's approval. They moved out of the kitchen and down the hall to their bedrooms. "The Dark Rider's scary."

"No, he's not!"

"He is, too! When Mom was reading to us the other night, I saw you hide under the covers."

"I just did that to make you afraid."

Kim turned to Wendy, hands on her hips. "Ben got scared, didn't he, Mom?"

"I can't speak for your brother, but I know I wanted to crawl under the blanket."

"See! Mom even admits it."

"That's because you're girls. Guys don't get scared. Ask Josh!"

Ask Josh.

It's not Dad anymore, is it, Ben? It's Josh.

Dear God.

What have I done?

CHAPTER FIVE

BEN AND CUTTY CAME RUNNING up to the truck before Josh had pulled to a stop in front of the garage. The boy wore dress slacks with a jacket and tie. It looked as if he was going to church, but this was a weeknight.

Josh's watch indicated ten after six. He'd returned from town later than he'd meant to. Besides doing some personal errands, it had taken him time to find a good Chinese restaurant, and his fourth therapy session had run longer than planned.

The therapist, Diane Collins, had spent another half hour talking about his progress and the things he should start doing. He'd had enough therapy in Ohio to know she was a real professional. He could trust her judgment.

But as he was leaving her office, she detained him further by revealing that she was divorced and would enjoy showing him around Tahoe the next time he came in for a session. Josh told her that if he weren't already engaged, he'd have taken her up on her invitation.

It was a lie, of course.

Though she was an attractive brunette, he'd felt no accompanying interest or curiosity. Without that necessary spark, he could never pretend to feelings he didn't have. His phony engagement was coming in handy for a variety of reasons.

However, right now his mind was on other things. He had plans for tonight....

So far, Wendy Sloan had been a pleasant person to work for. In the two weeks since his arrival, she'd proved to be fair and congenial. She'd even allowed him to start closing up at night and taking on more responsibilities. But she'd drawn a circle around herself that wouldn't allow him to come any nearer.

It maddened him when she left notes about the day's work schedule on the bench in the garage. That was how she avoided conversation with him. He was positive she had an agenda to stay out of his way as much as possible.

Up to now, her methods had been successful.

Every night, after the last diner had left the coffee shop and the family had cleaned up the kitchen, she'd disappear with her children. He could never get her alone. She refused to linger.

But tonight, all of that was about to change. He'd come home from town prepared.

Josh rolled down the truck window. "What's up, sport? I hardly recognized you without a T-shirt and cowboy boots."

Ben made a face. "We have to go into town tonight for parent-teacher conferences. Ada's staying late to serve dinner."

With that revelation, Josh just saw his plans go up in smoke.

"Mom asked me to watch for you and tell you that a whole bunch of boxes were delivered for you while you were at the therapist. They're in the back office. She also said Ada's closing up tonight, so you're free to do whatever you want."

Do whatever I want. He grimaced. Once again,

Wendy had used Ben for the messenger rather than seek Josh out herself.

At least Harve had pulled through.

''I'll be right there.''

Fighting a keen disappointment that his plan had been sabotaged, he climbed from the cab and reached for the sacks of food.

Ben made a noise. ''Something smells good. What have you got in there?''

Josh had to think fast. He'd bought enough food for the whole family, but he'd planned to ask her to eat alone with him once the restaurant was closed.

''I brought a special dinner for everyone to enjoy.'' Egg rolls, Char-Shu, Mongolian beef, almond chicken, French-fried shrimp, ham-fried rice. The lot.

It wasn't really fair to do this to Ben, but Josh had been thwarted on too many other occasions. Now was the time to make a move, illegal or otherwise. ''I guess if you're all going out, I'll have to eat it by myself. I can put the leftovers in—''

''No way! We'll hurry and be back real fast!''

Not if I know your mother, but I'm counting on you.

''Hey—you're walking a lot better,'' Ben observed as he followed Josh through the coffee shop to the kitchen. ''It doesn't look like you even need your cane anymore.''

To Josh's surprise, he discovered only a minor aching in his leg. Normally he required painkillers after a therapy session. Realizing he ought to be thankful for that much progress, he said, ''That's because my leg's getting better every day. Coming to work for your mom has been good for me.''

''I'm sure glad you did.''

''That makes two of us,'' Ada chimed in.

Josh smiled at both of them. "You know how to make a guy feel important." He put the sacks in the large refrigerator. Turning to Ada he said, "I hear you're running the late show tonight. As soon as I wash my hands, I'll come and help."

"I won't say no to an offer like that!"

"Glad to hear it. I'll be right back."

Ben walked him to the bathroom, with Cutty in close pursuit. "I wish we didn't have to go anywhere tonight," he grumbled.

"What's the matter? Afraid your mom'll hear what the teachers have to say?" Josh teased as he washed his hands.

"Nope. I'm getting four *A*s and three *B*s this term."

Ben was a remarkable boy in more ways than one. "Good for you." He reached for the towel to wipe his hands. "That ought to make your mother happy."

"Not really. She'll want to know why I didn't get all *A*s."

Josh nodded. "I know what you mean. My grandpa used to say the same thing. 'Josh, my boy—if you're smart enough to get a *B*, then you're just plain stupid if you don't go for the *A*.'"

They came out of the bathroom laughing, but their laughter was cut short when they discovered Wendy waiting for them in the hall. Josh could smell a flowery fragrance, and in the dim light, her eyes seemed to have taken on a darker green hue.

She was dressed in the same attractive black-on-white print smock she'd worn a couple of weeks ago. This evening, however, she'd worn it with a long-sleeved, black blouse.

It was the first time he'd seen her with makeup, which she didn't need. Where he'd thought her lovely before, tonight he found her positively stunning. The whisper of temptress and mother-to-be, all wrapped together in one mysterious package.

To Josh's way of thinking, Wendy Sloan embodied the essence of what womanhood was all about. He'd thought the same thing the first night he'd watched her approach his table.

"I—I didn't realize you were back from town already," she stammered before averting her eyes. "Did Ben tell you about the boxes that came?"

He took a fortifying breath. "Yes. When you hired me, I asked my farm manager to ship my computer out here. What I didn't realize was that there wouldn't be an operational phone line for Internet service in my cabin." The lies were starting to compound. "That was my mistake. I'll send everything home tomorrow."

"Please don't do that! There's space on the other desk in the office. We used to have a computer but the hard drive crashed and I haven't had the money to replace it yet."

"Cool!" Ben interjected. "I'll help you set it up when we're back from parent-teacher conference."

Josh's scheme to get himself under the same roof with her a little more often couldn't be working out better. "You've got a deal."

"Ben!" his mother reprimanded. "Josh's computer is off-limits, do you understand?"

He shrugged his shoulders. "Well, sure. I only meant—"

"I know exactly what you meant." She cut him off before he could say another word.

The back door opened. "Mom?" Kim called out. "When are we going? I've been out in the car waiting.

Mrs. Kleeve'll be upset if we're late. I thought we were going to stop at Mad Mack's for a hamburger first!''

Ben shook his head. ''We're going to eat here after the conference. Josh brought home a special dinner for all of us!''

Wendy's head lifted. Her stunned eyes met his. ''You bought us dinner?''

''It was meant to be a surprise. I didn't know you had other plans.''

Kim skipped in place. ''We'll hurry, won't we, Mom? Did you bring onion rings?''

Josh's lips twitched. ''No, but I bought something I think you'll like.''

Wendy looked flustered. ''Well—in that case—''

''Come on, Mom. The sooner we go, the sooner we can get back!'' Both children grabbed hold of her arms.

''I'll see you later then.'' *Try to squeeze out of this one, Mrs. Sloan.*

A dazed-looking Wendy gave him a little nod before the kids dragged her off.

Oh, yes, things were definitely improving.

I'll see you later then.

Those words, casually offered, continued to whirl in Wendy's head all the way to the children's schools in town. Why was it that when Josh said anything, it always sounded so…so personal?

For a moment there, she'd actually felt like a breathless teenager who'd been asked to the prom by the cutest boy in class. Her reaction was absurd! Embarrassing!

Josh had brought some food for them. He was a nice man. It was a thoughtful gesture. Why was she turning it into a federal case?

''Do you think he brought us fried chicken?''

"I have no idea," Wendy muttered as they got out of the car. Several people she knew waved to her.

"Stay, Cutty. We'll be right back."

"She'll need air. Crack the window, Ben."

"Sure thing."

"We've gotta go to my school first." Kim skipped ahead, making it difficult for Wendy to keep up. Luckily, Mrs. Kleeve's room was located on the main floor near the south entrance.

As they walked through the doorway, only one set of parents was ahead of them. While they chatted with the teacher, Wendy took the opportunity to stroll around and look at the children's latest creations.

A big, laminated poster of Uncle Sam held place of prominence on the back wall. It said, America Needs Heroes.

Each student had drawn a picture of a hero and had written something beneath it to validate his or her choice.

Wendy couldn't recall Kim working on that project. Maybe it was something they'd done in class.

As her daughter pulled her along, Wendy noted that most of the black-and-white drawings depicted the sports figures of the day. She counted at least seven creative facsimiles of Mark McGwire and Sammy Sosa, three of Tiger Woods, four each of Michael Jordan and John Elway. Only a few were distinguishable. The rest needed names for clarification.

Another group displayed music and television stars. She could barely make out Garth Brooks, John Denver, Leonardo DiCaprio.

While Ben mocked the less imaginative write-ups with just enough volume to irritate his sister, Wendy searched for her daughter's signature. She knew Kim hadn't missed a day of school since her cold in February.

Finally she came to the last picture. It had been framed. The likeness of a pregnant woman with a rolling pin in her hand stared back at Wendy.

As soon as she read the words, "Mom, My Heroine," her eyes blurred with tears. She had to blink a couple of times in order to read the paragraph below.

Kim squeezed her hand in excitement. "I was the only one who got an *A*. Do you like it?"

Swallowing hard, Wendy looked down at her daughter. "Do you remember what happened at the end of *How the Grinch Stole Christmas,* when the Grinch heard all the people in Whoville welcome Christmas morning?"

Kim's earnest eyes gazed up at her. "His heart grew three sizes."

"That's what mine just did. Oh, my precious girl—" Wendy clasped her daughter in her arms. "Thank you for that wonderful gift."

"You're welcome." She rose up on tiptoe and whispered, "Josh helped me."

Josh?

Suddenly it felt as if all the air had left Wendy's lungs.

"Mrs. Sloan? I'm ready for you now."

Wendy straightened, then moved toward Mrs. Kleeve in a daze. When had Josh and Kim spent time together?

"I've been looking forward to our talk. Your daughter's not only an independent thinker, she was the one student who caught the essence of what I'd hoped to put across. Kim's a very special young lady. With you for a role model, I'm not surprised."

"I don't deserve your praise, but thank you anyway, Mrs. Kleeve."

With a benevolent smile, the teacher handed her Kim's report card to sign. "Except for Math, I've given her Very Commendables in all her subjects."

"I'm afraid Math was never my forte, either. We'll keep working on it."

"Please do. I'm glad you came. Kim could hardly wait. You know…"

Ben and Kim both started making sounds suggesting that they wanted to leave. The reason for their impatience was no mystery. Someone much more fascinating than their teachers and friends had dinner waiting for them at home.

At the first opportunity, Wendy cut short the conversation with Mrs. Kleeve and said goodbye. The three of them headed out the door and down the hall to the exit.

"Why don't we just go home now? You saw my report card, Mom. There's no reason for you to talk to my teachers. The ones who gave me an *A* will just say they want me to keep up the good work. And the ones who gave me a *B* will say I need to apply myself— whatever that is—to get an *A*. Same as last year. No big deal."

He was right, but Wendy wanted to show she was supportive of the school's programs.

"Your Earth Sciences teacher gave you a bad grade in citizenship. I need to see him about that."

"But I told you the reason the other day!"

"Ben—I wasn't born yesterday."

"Hey, Mom. I told you the truth. Honest! You can ask Eric. This term Mr. Bybee gave everybody in the class a zero because no one would tell him who jammed up the VCR.''

"Do you know who did it?''

"Yeah. *He* did. The kids in the front row saw him put the volcano cassette in the wrong way. After that, he couldn't get it out and he blamed us. But you can talk to him if you want.'' He shrugged with apparent nonchalance.

"Okay.'' Wendy believed her son. "I still need to put in an appearance, though.''

"Just don't talk to any of your friends,'' Kim begged as they crossed over to the next building.

"Look, Mom! Cutty's waiting for us, poor thing.'' Their dog's snout poked through the crack in the window.

"She can wait a little longer,'' Wendy said, trying not to chuckle.

But between her children's cajoling, an aching back and the long lines in the junior high gym, she decided to admit defeat. With luck, no one important would see them duck out.

"Okay. Let's go home.''

Though the joy generated by that pronouncement didn't surprise her, she worried over the children's excitement. What would happen when they moved to Sacramento—or Josh left for Ohio? Were her kids depending on him too much? Developing unrealistic expectations?

"We'll see you at the car,'' Ben shouted.

Of course, they *were* hungry, and any dinner not cooked at home would be a real treat for them. But Wendy had a hunch that if Josh had bought them mud pies, they'd be just as enthusiastic.

"Hold on a minute, Mrs. Sloan.''

Wendy turned around. She saw a bald man leave the gym and come toward her. "I'm sorry. Have we met before?"

"No. I'm Mr. Finch. The school hired me after the fall parent-teacher conference."

"Oh, yes. The new computer lab teacher. Ben talks a lot about you. He thinks you're cool."

The older man laughed. "The feeling is mutual. I've been watching for him. When I saw all of you leave— and I certainly don't blame you with this crowd—I decided to catch up with you."

"Uh-oh. Was that *A* on Ben's report card a mistake?"

"No. Quite the opposite, in fact. He really knows his way around a computer. His instincts are excellent. I just wanted the chance to tell you what a great son you have."

Only a couple of weeks ago, a stranger had said the same thing.

"Well, thank you, Mr. Finch. Next to his horse, I think the computer is now Ben's greatest love."

"I'm glad." For a brief moment he eyed her with what looked like compassion. "I hope his class project produced results for your sake."

She wasn't sure she'd heard him correctly. "Results?"

"The ad for a handyman to help around your resort? It was an impressive piece of work. Of course, I made sure he worded it to protect you. In one week, there were over a thousand visits to his web site. Out of those, there was bound to be a good response."

What?

Suddenly, she was struck by the memory of Ben running into the house to tell her a man at the coffee shop was looking for a job. "He's really cool, Mom. He looks like Mel Gibson."

She took a deep breath. Until she had a detailed explanation of what Ben had been up to, she preferred not to embarrass him or herself in front of his teacher. "Actually, we did hire someone."

A broad smile lit his face. "That's wonderful news. He was so worried about your situation. I feel you're lucky to have a son like him. In the same circumstances, I don't believe too many students would have shown that kind of caring or resourcefulness. One day Ben's going to go places. Mark my words."

Wendy could only agree with Mr. Finch. Her son possessed many talents, especially the one for taking matters into his own hands.

Most of the time, she secretly applauded his drive. But in his determination to find a handyman to forestall the sale of the resort, he'd really outdone himself. He'd placed that ad without her knowledge or consent. Presumably the teacher thought she'd given her approval.

"You're very kind. Good night, Mr. Finch."

"Good night, Mrs. Sloan."

As she left the school and headed for the car, she mulled over several questions.

Had Josh come across Ben's ad on the Internet and responded to it? If so, had Ben sworn Josh to secrecy? She'd always thought it a lame excuse that Josh had claimed to see the Help Wanted sign in the coffee shop window. It hurt horribly to think she might have stumbled on to a cover-up taking place under her very own roof. Though she couldn't excuse the lie, she understood Ben's part in it. He was fighting to hold on to his heritage. Deep down, she loved him even more for trying to keep his promise to his father.

But Josh was a thirty-five-year-old male who knew better than to take advantage of a twelve-year-old boy's vulnerability!

An honorable man would have been honest with her. It seemed that he had betrayed her trust, and without trust, all contracts were null and void.

She gritted her teeth.

Over the last few weeks, unusual things had been going on in the Sloan household. There'd been a prevailing spirit of…excitement. Funny how everything, even information gleaned from the children's teachers, seemed to lead back to Josh Walker. Her thoughts leaped ahead faster and faster.

Today Josh's computer had arrived. Already Ben saw himself the lucky beneficiary of such a windfall. He wouldn't display this attitude unless Josh had been encouraging him—would he?

Until now, she had to admit, Josh had done nothing overt to betray her trust. He'd been given glowing references. He could fix anything. No job was too difficult. Nothing was beyond his scope. She never heard him complain. Not once did he use his leg as an excuse. Ada sang his praises. The children quoted him on everything.

But knowing about the ad made her feel differently about Josh's showing up for a job; it made his fortuitous appearance rather suspect. She needed to get to the bottom of this right now.

For the first time in their lives, she wondered if the situation was so big, so emotionally fraught, that Ben would have trouble being honest with her. That left Kim, his innocent confidante. She would know the truth.

What if the truth reveals that Josh found the job over

the Internet, and then lied to you about it for Ben's sake? If that's the case, you'll have to let Josh go tonight.

She had no choice.

A man who would align himself with Ben behind her back would undermine her in other ways. A person like that had no sense of integrity. But somehow that picture didn't mesh with her impression of the man who'd already made himself pretty indispensable around the resort.

The thought of dropping him off at a hotel in Stateline, never to see him again, brought her no joy. Being disappointed in someone she'd come to respect was a much bigger blow than she'd realized. Her problem now was to figure out a way to get at the truth without direct confrontation.

Throughout the drive home, the children were so excited about the evening ahead of them, they didn't notice her preoccupation, which was just as well. There would be unpleasantness soon enough. She dreaded the task ahead of her.

When the resort finally came into view, Wendy couldn't see any cars in the parking lot. That meant dinner was over and Ada had gone home. But something didn't seem right. As she pulled into the driveway, she realized the outside lights weren't on.

"How come the coffee shop's dark, Mom?"

"That's what I'm wondering. Maybe there was a power failure."

They drove around to the garage area, where the truck stood parked in its usual spot. "The floodlights are working back here!"

"You're right, Ben. I guess a fuse went out."

"Josh'll fix it," Kim announced as they jumped out of the car. "Can we go to his cabin and get him?"

"That won't be necessary." They heard his deep voice from a short distance off. Wendy whirled around to face him as he emerged from the shadows.

But it was a Josh without a cane....

Instead of jeans and a T-shirt, he wore black trousers and a maître d's black jacket and shirt. He looked completely different from the man they'd left less than two hours ago.

Not only did Cutty stay her distance, the children's silence meant they were equally stunned by the change in him.

He smiled at them. "Welcome to the house of the rising moon. If you'll come with me, please, your dinner awaits you." His formal way of addressing them added a note of authenticity that held even Wendy spellbound. Kim giggled nervously as they followed him at a respectful distance.

Except for the hall light, the rest of the place was shrouded in darkness.

When they reached the dining room, Wendy received another shock as her gaze swerved to the scene in front of the hearth.

Several tables had been pushed together. On top of an unfamiliar white, banquet-sized cloth, a veritable feast awaited them.

Candlelight combined with the glow from the fireplace to create an exotic ambiance. Vases of greenery, decorated with glittering silver moons and stars, were arranged in the center of the table. At each place stood a tall juice drink with a colored paper umbrella and a slice of lime.

"Ooh," Kim sighed ecstatically.

"Man—this is really awesome."

Ben only used that word when he was truly moved by something.

Wendy was so impressed, "awesome" didn't begin to describe her reaction. Particularly when she had such a weighty matter to resolve before the evening was over.

Josh pulled out a chair for her. His eyes narrowed as they played over her face. For some reason, her heart began to pound. Slightly breathless, she sat down, but she was so aware of his nearness, she barely had the presence of mind to murmur a thank-you.

He seated Kim next to her, and Ben stationed himself on the opposite side of the table. That left the last chair for Josh, who took his place directly across from Wendy.

"At the house of the rising moon," he intoned, "we do things a little differently. The fortune cookies are opened first to help provide interesting dinner conversation. May I suggest we begin with the youngest person at the table."

Kim smiled in delight as she opened her cookie. After studying it, she read aloud, "You're due for good luck any day." She looked at her brother. "What does yours say?"

"There's money in your future. The wise person will save some of it." Ben laughed, raising his dark-blond head. "Cool."

"Now you," Josh said to Wendy in a quiet voice.

She'd felt his gaze on her the whole time. Her fingers trembled as she broke open her cookie. "You must prepare for something momentous coming your way."

Ridiculous as it was, the words seemed to reflect her

own emotions, the sense of anticipation she'd recently felt.

"Did they know you were going to have a baby?" Kim asked in all naiveté.

Ben made a mocking sound. "Of course not!" He turned to Josh. "What does yours say?"

Josh opened his with great solemnity. "The wise man suggests all persons assembled at the table eat their food now before it grows cold."

"Yippee!"

While the children started passing the dishes around, Wendy burst into laughter. "Let me see that."

She heard his low chuckle. "I don't think so." He held the paper a little out of reach. Their eyes met in shared amusement. "Maybe later."

Maybe later.

Her heart raced again.

What was that supposed to mean?

What do you *want* it to mean?

Maybe she was experiencing a moment of temporary insanity. Blame it on the enchantment Josh had created. She'd almost forgotten; before this night was over, she might have to ask him to pack his bags.

Though she'd been hungry earlier, now her appetite had deserted her. Not so her children, though, who'd already started on second helpings.

After all the trouble Josh had gone to, she determined to be polite and took small portions of everything. But she couldn't swallow a bite. Instead she sipped her virgin strawberry daiquiri.

"No room in there?" His mild inquiry appeared to be for her ears alone.

"I'm sorry." She refused to meet his probing gaze. "Everything looks delicious, but I just can't."

"Don't worry about it. If the drink tastes good to you, then I'm glad."

He sounded so sincere, she didn't want to entertain any negative thoughts about him.

"I-It does. You shouldn't have gone to so much trouble."

"I wanted to. It's my way of saying thank you for hiring me. How did the conferences go?"

She almost dropped the glass. "According to Kim, you're the reason she got an *A* on her report."

After a long silence, he said, "All I did was tell her a woman could be a hero, too. She took it from there."

Wendy put an arm around her daughter and gave her a squeeze. "I loved it. Unfortunately, I didn't get to see Ben's science project. All his teachers met in the gym. I took one look at the long lines and decided to leave."

"Yeah," her son concurred as he finished off the last egg roll. "But it's no sweat if you're getting above-average grades. Like I am in science and computers and—"

"Ben," she broke in. She stared across the table at him. "Did I tell you Mr. Finch caught up with me before I left the building?"

Ben's eyes rounded in surprise. He seemed to have trouble swallowing. "What did he say?"

"That he was very proud of the ad you ran over the Internet to try and find a man to work for us. He said he gave you an *A* on the project."

An embarrassed look crossed her son's face. "I've been meaning to tell you about that," he mumbled.

"It would've been nice to be consulted. But that's all water under the bridge now. Apparently a thousand or more people saw it. According to Mr. Finch, it was well written. Maybe tomorrow you could run off a copy for me.''

Josh sat there without comment. As for Kim, she wriggled in her seat, proving she'd known about her brother's secret.

''It wasn't any good,'' Ben retorted in a dull voice.

His comment came as a surprise. ''Why do you say that?''

''It doesn't matter how many people visited the web site. Nobody wanted the job. We didn't get one letter sent to our PO box. Not one. It was a stupid idea.''

''But that doesn't matter 'cause you saw the sign in our window, huh, Josh?''

''I surely did, Kim. That was my lucky day.'' The corners of his mouth lifted.

''It was our lucky day, too. My fortune cookie even said so. We hope you never leave, right, Ben?''

''Right. Cutty doesn't want you to go either, do you, girl?'' The dog barked.

No response to the ad. Wendy's heart ran away with her.

She pushed back the chair and got to her feet. The action pulled another muscle. A gasp escaped that she was positive everyone could hear. ''Excuse me for a minute. I have to visit the ladies' room.''

When she reached the bathroom, she hugged the door, faint with relief that Josh hadn't known anything about Ben's ad. It meant he was who he said he was.

It meant...

How could it possibly mean anything to you? she asked herself. *In a few months you'll be in Sacramento giving birth to Matt's son. By that time Josh Walker will be long gone and married to his fiancée.*

While she stood there trying to come to grips with a flood of new emotions, she heard voices in the hall.

"Come on, guys. I'll walk you to the house."

"What about Mom?"

"I think she got overtired today. When she's ready to leave, I'll make sure she gets home safely."

"Don't you want us to help with the dishes?"

"That's a very nice offer, Kim, but tonight's my treat from start to finish."

"Do you think you should walk all the way without your cane?" she heard Ben ask.

"Probably not. Thanks for reminding me, sport. It's in the office."

"I'll grab it."

"I loved the Chinese food, Josh," Kim burbled. "Thank you, thank you! We had the best time. Will you save me the umbrellas?"

"Who else would I give them to?"

"Yay!"

"Here's your cane."

"All right. Let's go."

"Come on, Cutty."

The minute Wendy heard the back door close, she broke down sobbing.

CHAPTER SIX

"WENDY?"

"I'm in the kitchen."

Josh saw her standing at the sink, her back slightly bent because of the baby. "You weren't supposed to touch the dishes." He knew he sounded exasperated, but he couldn't help it. The second he'd left the restaurant to walk the children home, she was hard at work once again.

"After that wonderful dinner, it was the least I could do," she called over her shoulder. "Besides, cleaning up didn't take long. I'm almost finished. By the way, I put the cloth and table decorations in the pantry."

He rested his cane against the cabinet and grabbed a dish towel to wipe the glasses. Except for some utensils that needed to be put in drawers, everything else was done.

He went to the dining room to clean up there. Naturally, the room was already prepared for the breakfast crowd because she'd gotten there ahead of him. When he saw that she'd even moved the tables back where they belonged, his irritation turned to anger. She was risking her health—and her baby's. At this stage in her pregnancy, she shouldn't be doing heavy labor of any kind.

He walked to the front door to make sure everything was locked up tight. Once he'd turned off the gas log, he walked back to the kitchen, determined to have a talk with her. She was cleaning the countertops.

"This was my responsibility." He struggled to keep himself under some semblance of control. "From now on, I want it understood that I take care of any messes I create."

Her head lifted. She stared into his eyes. "Don't you understand what you did tonight? Everything was magical. It was something we've all been needing since my husband died. Neither the children nor I will ever forget any detail of it." She smiled. "Especially the sight of you without your cane, dressed like the maître d' of a fabulous five-star restaurant—but standing in the middle of a forest."

Her words broke the tight bands of tension constricting his chest. "You think it could become a trend?"

"It's perfect. Where'd you get it?"

"I borrowed it from a maître d' in South Lake Tahoe."

"Thank you for going to so much trouble. It reminded me how important it is to spread a little joy and sunshine once in a while. We haven't allowed ourselves to have much fun...or enjoy much luxury in the past few months. It was a fabulous evening. Under the circumstances, you wouldn't begrudge me this small contribution as payment, would you?" she half whispered.

"Of course not," he murmured. "I have to admit this was the most fun I've had since before my accident."

Her expression sobered. "That must have been an awful experience."

"I've had better moments, but the inactivity following my hospital stay was worse. I'm afraid it sent me into a depression. Nothing seemed to pull me out of it, not even my trip. But I'll always be glad I took it. Otherwise I would never have known about Moon Lake.''

He wished he could tell her the truth—that, as she'd originally suspected, her son's ad was the sole reason he knew of its existence.

''Wendy—'' He cleared his throat. ''It's important for you to understand that working here, being here with you and your family, has made a new man out of me. My depression is gone.''

''Th-that's wonderful.'' She didn't seem to know how to handle his confession.

''More wonderful than you could possibly imagine.''

She bit her lip. ''Josh? I know this isn't any of my business, but do you mind if I ask you a personal question?''

''Fire away.'' He'd been waiting two weeks to have this kind of conversation.

''Why would your fiancée leave at such a critical period of your convalescence? With your depression and everything…''

He'd wondered how long it would take for that subject to come up. He knew that meant more lies. As long as he worked for the Bureau, he had to do things their way.

''Lisa's a freelance journalist who spends a lot of time out of the country. We met at a party about a year ago and started to date on an exclusive basis. But it didn't take either of us long to realize that she craves adventure, and I'm more of a homebody.

''Because of the attraction between us, we both made compromises to accommodate each other's needs. Everything seemed to be all right and we got engaged. Soon after that, I had my accident. At first I was told I might lose my leg."

Wendy gasped and briefly touched his arm.

Her compassionate gesture almost made him forget the cover story he'd learned by rote. But he managed to resume. "When I heard that, I'm afraid I wasn't fit company for anyone. Lisa tried her best to handle it, but my black state of mind took an emotional toll on both of us.

"Thankfully I found a surgeon who operated on my leg and saved it. He said that if I followed his instructions and underwent intensive therapy, I'd eventually be able to get around almost as well as I did before the accident.

"Knowing it would take months for that to happen, I urged my fiancée to accept any overseas assignments until I could walk down the aisle with her."

Wendy's chin lifted. "You've obviously made great progress in your recovery, Josh. But you know you overdid it tonight by not using your cane. It would be terrible to suffer a relapse now!

"I-if I were your fiancée and found out you'd done anything to hamper your recovery, I'd not only be hurt, I'd be furious!"

Her impassioned delivery had brought color to her cheeks. With those words, he realized she would have stayed with the man she loved and forced him to work his way out of the darkness.

More than pleased by her reaction, he said, "Your point is well taken. Why don't we make a deal? I'll agree to take care of myself. In return, you have to do the same thing."

She frowned. "What do you mean?"

"You could hurt the baby moving tables around. That's what I'm here for."

"They're not heavy."

"I'll bet your doctor would have a fit if he knew."

She looked as though she was going to fight him on it. Then she let out a sigh, leaning her hip against the counter. "You're probably right. I suppose I'm so used to doing everything around here, I don't consider the consequences."

"Surely your husband must have insisted you take it easy during your other pregnancies."

"Of course he did. Matt was wonderful to me."

This was the first time she'd been willing to talk about her personal life.

"How long did you have to look after him before he died?"

She bowed her head. "Six months before his death, he was diagnosed with lung cancer. The pain didn't put him in the hospital until the last month."

Obviously exhausted, she yawned.

"You should be in bed. Until the baby comes, you ought to sleep in more. Take naps. Take whole days off when you feel like it."

She shook her head. "I'm afraid that's a luxury no working woman can afford."

"You could if you were given the proper help. I've got some ideas I'd like to talk over with you."

"No, Josh. I'm already feeling guilty about the extra time you've put in around here. Since I can't pay you a salary, I refuse to add to your workload."

He'd anticipated this. "Not even if my ideas produced revenue so you could pay me?"

That got her attention. She stared hard at him.

"What ideas? You realize this place could be sold by next month." She yawned again.

"Maybe. Maybe not. But it's getting late. We can talk about it tomorrow. Come on. I know you're exhausted. I'll walk you home."

She needed no urging. As they went out the back way, he locked the door and flipped the switch for the floodlights in front of the coffee shop.

Tonight marked a subtle but distinct change in their relationship. For one thing, she kept pace with him while he used his cane. For another, they moved along the path in companionable silence, without the tension so evident before.

Exhilarated, he breathed deeply of the cool mountain air, feeling a sense of well-being he'd never experienced in his life. The pregnant woman at his side was the reason for it. With that knowledge came the illumination of certain truths, both thrilling and terrifying in their implications.

"WENDY? WHEN YOU find a minute, could we talk? I'm in the back office setting up the computer."

At the sound of Josh's low voice, she jerked around, almost dropping her rolling pin on the floor. After dinner last night and their subsequent conversation, it was inevitable that she'd fallen asleep with him on her mind.

But her sleep had been fitful. No psychiatrist could have made sense of her dreams. She'd awakened feeling tense, nervous. Unlike her children whom she'd never seen in better spirits.

They chattered about Josh all the way to the bus. As soon as Ada arrived—another member of the Walker fan club—she added her two cents' worth. It sounded more like five dollars, Wendy thought irritably.

Somehow, everything combined to make her feel more out of sorts than ever. Thank goodness she had an appointment with her OB this afternoon. She needed to get away from Moon Lake for a little while.

"Yes, of course," she answered Josh. "I'll be there as soon as I put these in the oven."

"I can do that for you," Ada offered. "You go on and take a load off your feet."

Ada had never acted so worried about Wendy's condition before. More of Josh's influence, no doubt.

"I appreciate your concern, Ada, but I'm not bed-ridden yet."

"You will be if you keep up this pace!" Without asking Wendy's permission, she whisked the pies out of her hands. "Go on. Josh's waiting for you."

Even for Ada, this was going a little far. Did her strange behavior have something to do with those ideas Josh had referred to last night? Had he already discussed them with the older woman? She'd never seemed so anxious to get Wendy out of the kitchen.

"Thank you, Ada," she said with sarcastic sweetness.

It seemed to go right over her cook's head. But annoyed as she was by Ada's behavior, she couldn't quell this growing sense of anticipation. She quickly washed her hands and went in search of Josh.

She saw him before he noticed her. The desk she'd told him to use stood against the far wall, so his back faced the doorway.

Today he wore a khaki shirt and jeans. He was all male. Powerfully built. Dark.

She'd grown up with smaller people. Blondes. She'd

married a blonde. Her children were blond. Josh's size, his brown hair and olive skin, provided a distinct contrast, one that drew her gaze more often than she liked to admit.

"I'm ready to talk now if you'd like."

His head swerved around. In less than an instant she felt the sweeping assessment of his eyes. Every cell of her sensitized body seemed to respond.

Without words he got up and pulled out her chair. Once she was seated at her desk, he took his place again, extending his injured leg in front of him.

"As you know, I've spent most of my time working on the cabins. Except for another coat of varnish to the exteriors, which I'll apply when the weather gets a little warmer, I can attest that they're in excellent condition."

"I know. I made an inspection while you were at the therapist's. You've done a fantastic job. Because of your efforts, I'll get a better price when the time comes. I'm indebted to you, Josh."

"Let's not talk about debts. As I told you last night, I'm a new man, so let's call it even. Look, Wendy—" He sat forward, eyeing her intently. "I realize the ski season brings in a great deal of money, and you've already lost that crowd. But it's not too late to recoup."

She shook her head. "I don't know if you've noticed, but the phone doesn't ring as often. The number of people driving by to ask for lodgings has dwindled. Neither the Chamber of Commerce nor the big hotels in the area refer people to us anymore because they know we've closed down the cabins. Word has gotten around.

"Even if we opened them again, it would take several years to build the business back to what it was. I simply don't have the money to run an ad campaign."

"You don't need money," he declared.

"I don't understand."

"With my computer, we could put an ad on the Internet. Didn't you tell us last night that Ben's teacher said his web site had produced at least a thousand visits in one week?"

"Well, yes—but he didn't get one written response."

His unwavering gaze met hers. "Try putting yourself in a man's place. One who wanted steady work and had a wife and family to support. Would you have responded if there was no salary offered?"

"No. Of course not."

"But think about those thousand visitors. People are surfing the net, trying to find different places to take a vacation. Moon Lake offers something unique for the whole family. Maybe we could take a look at Ben's ad. With a little change in wording, we could run our own ad over the Internet. We'll set up an e-mail address and see what happens."

His idea sent a spurt of adrenaline charging through her body. "Josh, even if we did get a good response, we'd need help in the kitchen."

"I've been thinking about that. You shouldn't be working right now. We could ask a local employment service to find someone to replace you full-time. I could pay that person's salary until we started generating money."

"No!" she said vehemently. "I couldn't let you do that."

"Then ask the bank to lend you enough money to buy extra food and pay someone a salary. If you told them how you plan to generate business and showed them some figures, I'm sure they'd agree to it.''

Maybe it was crazy, but his idea actually sounded plausible. Unable to sit still, she got to her feet. ''But the resort is up for sale.''

''That's true. If you really want to sell it, then you'll get an even better price if it's a going concern. On the other hand, you may be so pleased with the response, you'll decide to put off selling altogether.''

''No. The only way this could possibly work would be to have a man like you living on the premises year-round. But you're getting married soon.''

''Not until fall at the earliest,'' he interjected in an oddly defiant tone.

She realized it was still a touchy subject for him. ''Your fiancée might not want to wait that long.'' *I know I wouldn't.* ''As for my baby, he or she will be here before I know it. With an infant at home, I couldn't deal with trying to hire a new manager, even if I *could* pay him a decent salary.''

''But I could. Let me take care of finding and training someone to replace me. In the meantime, your ad will produce more e-mail than you'll know what to do with. I've used the Internet many times to sell used farm machinery or hire extra hands for the harvest. Believe me, it works!''

She shook her head again. ''In theory, it all sounds possible. Practically speaking, I—I just don't know.''

''At least talk to your banker. Tell him our idea. See if he thinks it's at all feasible.''

''I might,'' she whispered, feeling on the verge of tears for no apparent reason. ''Thank you more than I can say for your interest and concern. Now, if you'll excuse me, I have to get back to the house.''

Wendy needed to get away from him. When she was around Josh, things seemed to happen. Exciting things.

If he stayed at Moon Lake, if he were there all the time, she had no doubt that anything was possible.

Therein lay her problem.

He'd be gone soon. In a particularly important way, he was like her husband, Matt, who'd been one of a kind. No other man would be able to fill Josh Walker's shoes. Josh hadn't *replaced* Matt at Moon Lake and with her family, but he'd brought something new into their lives. Something that was his alone. There couldn't be two Joshes living in this world. She felt the truth of that statement clear through to her bones.

She should do what she'd set out to do before Josh came to Moon Lake. Sell the resort and move to Sacramento. The sooner, the better.

But two weeks later, her hopes were deflated. After her regular doctor's visit, she met with the Realtor and discovered that he still had no good news for her.

"There've been a few expressions of interest, but I wouldn't have insulted your intelligence by telling you about them. A good buyer takes time, Mrs. Sloan. I'll let you know the second something concrete is in the offing."

At the last minute, she told him about Josh's suggestion that they reopen the cabins. Her Realtor applauded the idea. "If your resort is fully operational, a potential owner can't argue with success. They'll see their investment already working for them. If you want maximum money for the place, then it's the only avenue to take."

Wendy left his office deep in thought. She couldn't imagine the bank lending her any more money. But Josh's admonition to find out if his plan was feasible prompted her to consider a visit. Since she'd never take money from Josh, everything hinged on the bank's giving her a loan. She could stop by there today and end all this speculation.

The post office was closer, so she went there first. For once there were no bills, only the usual junk mail. As she started to toss it in the nearest waste bin, her eye caught sight of a thin letter wedged between two credit card offers. The blue aerogram bore a Guatemalan postmark. Mr. Josh Walker.

When she reached the car, Wendy finally gave in to her burning curiosity and turned the envelope over. In place of a return address, his fiancée had written, "Call me the second you read this. I'm coming home as soon as possible, darling."

The words seemed emblazoned on the paper. Their message was unmistakable.

How perfect her fiancée's timing had been! His trial month would be up tomorrow.

Josh's days at Moon Lake were well and truly numbered. Tonight could be his last night. Forget the bank!

Flooring the accelerator, she sped out of the parking lot. By the time she got home, she felt distinctly ill, but she had a plan.

"Please don't be in there, Josh," she prayed as she hurried through the back door of the coffee shop. To her relief, no one was about except the cook.

"Ada?"

The older woman darted her a glance. "Hi. How did your appointment go?"

"The doctor says I'm fine. Everything's normal."

"Are you sure?"

"Yes. Why?"

"I don't know. You look flushed."

"I always get this way by my seventh month," she lied. "Ada, something's come up and I'm going to drive the children to Sacramento. We'll be leaving as soon as they get home from school. I'll be back day after tomorrow, and I'll see you Monday morning. I'm going to close the place until then.

"Would you mind stopping what you're doing and just putting everything away in the fridge? While you're at it, leave a sandwich for Josh."

"I can do better than that."

"Thanks, Ada. You can take the rest of the day off—with pay. I'll put the Closed sign in the window right now. If you want, I'll drive you home on our way out. Meet me at the car in half an hour. I'll phone Cindy's mother to tell Cindy not to come in."

"Fine." One eyebrow dipped. "Whatever you say. You're the boss."

JOSH FINISHED repairing a step at one of the cabins. It had come loose over the winter and was one of his few remaining jobs. Satisfied he'd made it solid, he picked up his tools and headed for the garage. It was already dinner time. He frowned when he realized that Ben and Cutty hadn't paid him their usual after-school visit.

As he approached the back parking area, he noted that Wendy's Toyota was missing. She must not have come back from town yet. He figured the children had gone to their friends' to play until their mother returned. Maybe she was collecting them now.

He put everything away in the garage, then walked over to the coffee shop. Even before he tried the handle of the back door and discovered it locked, his instincts told him something was wrong.

Using his key, he let himself inside. The place was

completely quiet. He made a quick tour. The Closed
sign had been propped in the window.

His mind reeled with possibilities, none of them
good. Wendy had been at her doctor's appointment that
afternoon. Maybe the OB had found some kind of
problem. It wouldn't surprise him, he thought grimly;
she worked too hard. And the nature of restaurant work
forced her to be on her feet much longer than Josh
deemed wise. Perhaps she'd developed a problem that
required hospitalization. He broke out in a cold sweat.
Anything could have happened.

Forgetting to use his cane, he rushed to the back
office, where Wendy kept a sheet of important phone
numbers. He'd call Ada. She would know what had
happened. As he reached for the receiver, he glimpsed
a note addressed to him in Wendy's handwriting. He
snatched it from the desktop and read it, his eyes nar-
rowing in disbelief.

Dear Josh,
I decided to follow doctor's orders and take a day
off. The children and I will be in Sacramento tonight and tomorrow. But we'll be back Sunday. I
gave Ada the time off. That goes for you, too.

For your information, a letter came for you. I
taped it to your monitor. Keep in mind that tomorrow ends the month's trial period we both
agreed upon. You're perfectly free to return to
Ohio at your earliest convenience, with my blessing.

If you want to leave Sunday, we'll be back
early enough to say goodbye and give you a small
bonus for your invaluable services. Naturally, I'll
drive you to the airport.

I think you already know that you surpassed my expectations with the work you've done. Everyone will miss you, including Cutty.

Ada left your dinner in the refrigerator. She said to warm it in the microwave.

Sincerely, Wendy

What in the hell?

Josh spun around and pulled the letter off the monitor screen. He ripped it open to discover a blank piece of paper inside. That was when he saw the handwritten message on the back of the envelope. He read it twice.

Lord. His eyes closed tightly.

When he'd managed to recover some control, he lunged for the receiver.

Pick up your phone, Harve!

On the third ring there was a click. "Josh? You must've received my note. That was quick. I didn't expect your call until tomorrow at the earliest."

"I didn't exactly expect the kind of message you wrote on the outside of that letter!" Josh muttered angrily.

"Take it easy." Harve chuckled. "I was only trying to make your engagement look authentic."

In frustration, Josh raked a hand through his hair. "Consider your mission accomplished."

You did it so well, in fact, Wendy assumes I'm going to take off for Ohio on Sunday to join my nonexistent fiancée.

Hell.

As far as he knew, she hadn't done anything about getting a loan. If she'd seen that letter, he suspected she might wonder how long he intended to stay around. If she thought he was going to leave Moon Lake soon, she probably wouldn't pursue the idea of a loan. Heading for Sacramento out of the blue like this could mean only one thing. She planned to start looking for a house in California.

In all fairness to Harve, he'd just been doing his job. But that note might have done permanent damage to Josh's plans.

"Josh? You still there?"

"Yes."

"What's up?"

"I'm thinking."

"Oops. I don't like the sound of that."

Harve understood Josh better than any other person. As his superior, he had the right to personal information. But the precarious situation with Wendy was still in its earliest stages. Until there was a significant breakthrough in their relationship, Josh preferred to keep it to himself.

"Do me a favor, Harve," he said sardonically. "Next time, don't write anything on the outside of your letter."

"Okay, Josh. Listen—someone will phone you instead. Take care of that leg."

"Harve!"

Too late he heard the click of the connection being ended.

Josh cursed inventively before slamming down the receiver.

It took a full minute of standing there in the semi-darkness to realize he wasn't mad at Harve. No, his current state of misery could be blamed on someone else.

What the hell was he going to do with himself until Sunday morning?

Josh had thought he understood the meaning of loneliness. Like every human being, he'd experienced moments of it on occasion.

But the dead silence within the coffee shop, which normally teemed with life and love, created such a devastating sense of emptiness, he knew something unprecedented was happening to him.

Moon Lake no longer represented merely a place to hide until he could return to his former life. Somehow, some way, Moon Lake seemed to have *become* his life. More than that, it felt like the life destiny had always meant him to live.

He had the strongest impression that up until now, he'd simply been marking time....

He shook himself out of his reverie and called Harve back to apologize for snapping at him. His supervisor merely chuckled and told him to forget it. No sooner had Josh hung up than the phone rang. Probably one of the children's friends. They inevitably called the coffee shop when they couldn't reach the kids at the house. If Eric and Misty didn't know about this quick trip over the border, Wendy's precipitous flight had to be a result of that damn letter.

Once more he picked up the receiver. "Moon Lake Resort."

"Josh?"

"Ben?" It was a relief to hear the boy's voice, but he spoke so softly Josh could hardly understand him. "Where are you calling from?"

"My aunt's house."

At least they'd gotten there safely. "What's wrong? Why are you whispering?"

"Mom doesn't know I'm calling. She'd kill me if

she knew. Are you really going back to Ohio on Sunday?''

Josh had been right. Wendy had made a false assumption about his leaving Moon Lake. If she felt she couldn't carry out her plans without him, had she gone to Sacramento to discuss other alternatives with her family? "No. I'm not going anywhere, Ben," he said quietly.

"Honest?" the boy cried with tears in his voice.

That display of emotion brought a lump to Josh's throat. "I'd never lie to you."

"But Mom said your fiancée was coming home and—"

"Your mom's a sweetheart, Ben. She doesn't want to keep me from my fiancée. But the fact is, I spoke to Lisa a few minutes ago. We still have some serious problems to work out. Until they're resolved, we won't be getting married.''

"Really?" The change in his voice spoke volumes.

"When you plan to live with someone forever, you've got to be sure it's right for both of you. That's the part we're still working on. For the time being, I'm happy at Moon Lake.''

"I'm happy, too. I mean—"

"I know what you mean," Josh said quietly. "See you on Sunday, sport.''

"Yeah." The boy's happy laughter was exactly what Josh needed to hear.

He suddenly discovered that he was starving for one of Ada's meals. He hung up the phone and hurried to the kitchen.

Later on tonight, he'd fool around with an ad for the

Internet. First thing in the morning, he'd head to town. He had a certain errand in mind. Once again his world was filled with purpose. Those long, dark periods of depression seemed a thing of the past.

CHAPTER SEVEN

THE CHILDREN SAW the basketball hoop mounted on the back of the garage before Wendy did.

"Cool! Mom! Isn't Josh the greatest?"

The exuberant outburst produced an excited bark from Cutty. The children scrambled out of the car. She knew where they were headed and couldn't have stopped them if she'd wanted to.

Matt had been planning to put a hoop there. He and Ben had talked about it several times, but her husband hadn't gotten around to it. Not when he had so little strength toward the end and there were more important things to worry about, things that took precedence.

It was just like Josh to do something thoughtful for the children before he left. With spring in the air, his timing couldn't have been more perfect. The kids would enjoy tossing baskets until moving day.

Wendy was glad she'd gone to visit her family. It had helped clear her head. Everyone except Ben and Kim was ecstatic that they were moving to Sacramento. But to Wendy's surprise, her kids seemed to be handling the inevitability of it better than she would have expected.

Not when she first told them about Josh's fiancée coming home, of course. Then the silence in the car had made it seem as if she'd just announced the end of the world. But being with their cousins had apparently made the difference. They'd become animated again. To Wendy's everlasting relief, they'd finally stopped bringing up Josh's name every five seconds.

That was good. When they'd first arrived, Wendy's sister glanced at her curiously each time the subject of the new handyman came up.

On Saturday, they all went over to her mom's, then her brother-in-law, Bob, took all the kids to the movies. That left Jane and Wendy free to go house-hunting in the afternoon. There were quite a few rentals available; she jotted down phone numbers for several and would make a decision in a few days. Everything was overpriced. California real estate was notoriously expensive.

None of the rentals had an option to buy. But that was all right. She could worry about purchasing a home after the birth, once she was back on her feet. Until the resort sold, she couldn't make a down payment, anyway. After visiting the Realtor, she'd realized that selling Moon Lake might take a while. Not too long, she hoped. The small amount of insurance money she still had left wouldn't last forever.

"Let me help." His voice resonated through her body. She caught her breath sharply.

While the children had run to his cabin to find him, Josh had emerged from the garage, wearing his usual jeans and a T-shirt. Before she could react, he'd pulled the two overnight bags from the trunk.

"Th-thank you. Especially for putting up that hoop. The kids are overjoyed."

"You're welcome." He shut the lid. "How was your trip?" She felt his eyes range over her. It wouldn't take too close a look to see she hadn't slept well. Part of her had wondered if Josh might be gone before they returned. He could easily have left a note and called for a taxi. But another part of her—

Forgive me, Matt.

"We had a wonderful time." So what if that was a slight exaggeration?

"I'm glad to hear it. I don't know of anyone who deserves a break more than you do. Are you going to the house now?"

Was she? Wendy had no idea. His nearness drove every thought from her head. This morning she seemed to have trouble functioning, let alone deciding which foot to put in front of the other.

"I think I'd better open up and start breakfast first."

"The coffee's percolating. Fortunately you're here to do the omelets. In the meantime, I'll take these to the house and put them on your porch." Without waiting for a reply, he walked off with both cases under one arm, his other hand on the cane.

She stared after him until she reminded herself that he could turn around at any time and catch her looking.

As she reached the back door of the coffee shop, she could hear the children calling out for Josh. It went without saying that nothing in their world would be quite right until they found him.

In the beginning, she'd thought they might behave this way around any man who showed an interest in them. But their behavior with their uncle Bob, whom they adored, and who loved and cared about them, hadn't been the same at all. No, there was some-thing…special about Josh. They knew it, and so did she. Much as they loved Bob and Jane and their grand-mother, they couldn't wait to get back to the resort.

She ought to be happy her children had come to accept their father's death, that they'd made it past the worst of their grief. She *was* happy. Unfortunately, they were about to face another loss.

And Wendy couldn't protect them from it.

A steady stream of customers kept her busy until the breakfast crowd tapered off around ten-thirty. While the children helped her in the kitchen, Josh waited on tables, something she only allowed him to do occasionally. Since he seemed so insistent, she decided to let him.

She knew exactly what this was about. He was leaving—and working up to his goodbyes. They all understood that he'd be gone very soon. This was his way of doing all he could to help before she was left alone to deal with everything herself.

When he brought the last of the dishes into the kitchen, she asked the children to stack them in the dishwasher. "Josh? Could I talk to you for a minute in the office?"

Josh murmured his assent and ambled out of the kitchen behind her. He winked at Ben, whose face broke out in a conspiratorial smile. He saw Wendy in that smile. She had two attractive children whose pleasant natures he'd found appealing from the start. As far as he was concerned, the Sloans represented family life at its very best.

He'd missed the children while they were gone. He'd missed their mother. It had satisfied something inside him to hear them call out his name this morning. Even Cutty had come running up to him.

Slowly he followed Wendy into the back room. The scent of her shampoo lingered in the air—strawberry, he thought. He lounged against the doorjamb, waiting for her to make the first move. He enjoyed watching her. She had a beautiful body he found even more enticing with pregnancy. After a moment, she turned. For the first time all morning, she really looked at him. This was progress.

"Obviously you found my note. A-and the letter."

"I did."

She rubbed her palms against her hips nervously. "I hope you'll forgive me, but I couldn't help seeing what was written on the back of it."

He smiled. "Everyone at the post office must have read it, too. You don't have to apologize."

"I meant what I said in the note."

He noticed how hard she fought to keep her voice steady. She wasn't as much in control as she wanted to be.

He knew she would always have feelings for her husband, but it was Josh she was aware of right now. The chemistry between them was undeniable and growing stronger.

"You said a lot of things," he baited her softly. "Which one are you referring to?"

Her lower lip was caught gently between her teeth. He couldn't make himself look away....

"That you'd fulfilled your part of our bargain. With your fiancée coming home, you don't have to stay here any longer. You can go."

"Is that what you want?"

She let out a strange little cry. "This has nothing to do with *me*."

"Then you're not displeased with my work?"

Color washed up her neck and cheeks. "You know better than that!"

"Do I?" He continued to tease, enjoying her vehement reaction more than she'd ever know. "Then why do I have the feeling you're trying to get rid of me?"

"Josh…"

He loved the way she said his name in that husky beseeching voice. But he wasn't about to make this any easier for her.

"I simply assumed that you'd want to go back to Ohio. I-if I were in your shoes, I couldn't get there fast enough."

"That's because you don't understand the situation. Until my leg's healed—and we've sorted things out—I prefer we remain apart." At the moment, he scarcely felt any guilt about continuing the lie.

Wendy blinked in confusion. "But she obviously wants to be with you."

"Not until I'm ready."

Her face seemed to close. "I think you're just saying that because you feel some kind of obligation not to let me down."

"You're wrong, Wendy."

Her breasts rose and fell swiftly. "What do you *really* want to do?"

If only you knew. "Why, nothing."

Torment had turned her eyes a stormy green. "Then you're planning to stay here?"

He folded his arms. "Unless you're asking me to go," he said calmly. "Our bargain was two-sided. I'm perfectly satisfied with my half."

She averted her eyes. "You don't understand. The Realtor said it might take longer than he thought to sell the resort. I looked at rental houses while I was in Sacramento. In the next few days, I'm going to be making a decision about which one to take."

Not if I have anything to say about it. "Then I'll be around to help you move, if that's what you'd like."

She fidgeted with a sheet of paper. "No— I mean,

I hate the thought of moving, but naturally I'd be grateful for your help.''

He straightened from the door and took a step closer. Her instinct was obviously to back away. ''Did you get a chance to stop by the bank after your doctor's appointment?''

''No.''

Just as I thought. ''Before you dismiss the idea of a loan altogether, you might take a look at this ad I've worked up, in case you want to put it on the Internet. Look at this draft of the business plan we discussed, too. Study the figures.''

He had to move past her to reach it. In the process his arm brushed against her belly. There was instant electricity between them. He couldn't describe it any other way.

He'd never dated a pregnant woman, never put his hands on one. The small mound was much harder than he'd imagined it would be. Suddenly he couldn't fathom the concept of a life growing inside another human being. He'd never really thought about it before, just taken it for granted. There were a dozen questions he'd like to ask her.

Not so fast, Josh. This wasn't a surveillance mission where you swooped in and flew low to surprise the enemy.

She took the papers from his hand, then found a chair—as far away from him as possible. He could tell that her fingers were shaking.

An unexpected tap on the door startled both of them. ''Mom?'' Kim called out. ''Some more people just came in. Are we going to serve them breakfast or lunch?''

''Lunch. I'll be right there.''

Josh moved to the door and opened it for her. Of necessity, she had to pass by him. He stayed where he was, craving the feel of her body against his.

This time her sweatered arm grazed his chest. It took everything he had not to reach out and pull her toward him. He ached to touch her, to feel her mouth respond to the pressure of his. This longing to wrap her in his arms, to kiss her, had been building for weeks. Better give her a head start before he forgot the rules.

A good-sized lunch crowd kept them busy for the next couple of hours. When everything had finally been put away, Kim emerged from the pantry carrying the small paper umbrellas, of all things.

"Josh, I can have these, right? And the fortunes, too?"

He chuckled. "Of course."

Her blue eyes sparkled up at him. "I know what yours says."

He'd forgotten about that. "Go ahead and read it."

She took her role very seriously. "You are about to embark on a great love affair."

Josh's eyes sought Wendy's, but he saw that she'd discovered something to straighten in one of the drawers.

"What's an affair?" Kim asked.

"You know," Ben chimed in while he changed Cutty's water. "All that love stuff on the soaps."

Josh tousled her blond curls. "A real love affair means a marriage that gets better and better with time."

"When are you and Lisa going to get married?"

He crouched down to meet her eyes. "When I'm ready, and not before."

"Then you're not going back to Ohio yet?"

"No." He shook his head.

"Yippee!"

"All right, you two. Let's go home and get ready for church."

Ben frowned. "Ah, Mom! Do we have to? Josh's going to play basketball with us."

"I'll be here when you get back."

"Do you want to come with us?"

Kim was a darling. But her innocent question had caught him off guard. He hadn't been inside a church since his buddy's funeral. It would be hard to hear the music and not remember things he wanted to forget.

"I think we'll let Josh enjoy his afternoon the way he wants," Wendy commented as she started to herd her children out of the kitchen.

"Can I go with you next week?"

"Okay." Kim beamed. "You can sit by me."

His heart felt a tug. "I wouldn't sit anywhere else."

Ben paused at the door. "Do you mind if Eric plays ball with us, too?"

"The more the merrier."

"All *right!*"

Wendy acted as if she wanted to say something, then thought better of it. He knew exactly what was going on inside her. *Panic.*

A tide had been gathering momentum. Now it seemed to be carrying them places without their permission. She could sense it was going to be a wild ride and was fighting it.

Josh had reached the point of no return long ago. All he had to do was wait it out. But that took self-control. Until he met Wendy, he'd always figured he possessed a normal supply....

"MRS. SLOAN? Nice to see you again. What can I do for you?"

She pulled out the ad and the business plan Josh had prepared and handed them to the bank loan officer. "I have a new manager living on the premises full-time. He's not drawing a salary, just room and board.

"If we reopened the resort right away using the Internet for advertising, we could generate the figures you see there within a month's time. If you compare them to the same period last year, when my husband was still alive, you'll see it can work.

"I'm here to seek a small, short-term loan. The money would go for more food supplies and a salary for an additional cook.

"My Realtor feels that if I can make the resort fully operational again, it'll bring me a better price when it's sold. At that time I'll be able to pay off the loans. What do you think?"

While she held her breath, he pulled up her original loan on the computer and made a few notes.

It had taken her two weeks to find the courage to come here today. Though she didn't think they'd actually lend her the money, Josh had made everything sound possible. The figures he'd arrived at would be difficult to dismiss out of hand.

If there was any chance she could hold on to Moon Lake a little longer in order to get a higher sale price, she felt she owed it to the children, as well as to Matt's memory. Matt would want whatever was best for his children; she knew that without question.

At least if the bank turned her down, she could feel satisfied that she'd tried everything. In case of failure, she had her backup plan to move to Sacramento. All she needed to do was make a phone call. Any one of those three rental houses could be theirs by tonight. It would be a simple enough thing to hire some movers to pack up their furniture. A local housecleaning service would do the rest.

That left Josh.

He'd mentioned helping her with the move, but she could never bring herself to involve him that way. No, if she and the children were leaving Tahoe, then she'd tell him she no longer required his services. Josh would be able to return to his farm and get married. With his leg improving every day, there was no reason he couldn't do light farming chores again. Whatever, it really was none of her business.

Josh isn't your business.

It wasn't working, anyway. Ever since he'd come to Moon Lake, she'd lost her ability to concentrate. Lately she'd found herself listening for his footsteps. Every morning she awakened feeling a sense of anticipation—because she knew she'd be seeing him soon. Then, there was her heightened awareness of his presence whenever he came anywhere near.

She supposed this reaction was simply human. If she were an onlooker, she'd probably say it was inevitable. Although she'd buried her heart with Matt, his death had made her as vulnerable as the children, especially to someone like Josh, who'd come along at the darkest time in her life to help shoulder some of her burden.

What threw her into turmoil was this involuntary physical attraction, which obeyed no laws, respected no boundaries. Such as his engagement, for instance...

If he'd been someone like the bank loan officer, someone balding with a middle-aged paunch, she probably wouldn't be having these troubling thoughts.

Face it, Wendy. You may be pregnant and feeling

the weight of too much responsibility, but your body appears to have a drive all its own.

The unkind jokes she'd heard all her life about lonely widows were no longer funny. There was no way to prepare emotionally for the death of a spouse. People, family, had told her she was one of the lucky ones who'd been given advance warning of her husband's death.

She supposed she *was* lucky. Everyone had been able to say goodbye. Yet confronted with the stark reality of his passing, she hadn't been prepared at all.

It was a little like going into labor. Nobody had ever told her what it would really be like. Nobody could. Certain life experiences couldn't be understood vicariously. You had to live through them yourself. Was it any wonder people sometimes lost perspective? Or that judgment became impaired? Maybe that was all part of surviving a husband's death....

She could still hear her son begging her to give the stranger in the coffee shop a chance. Ben had been so desperate to hold on to his old life, he would have done anything to persuade her. Who could blame him? Hadn't Wendy been just as desperate when she'd actually hired Josh?

On the surface, it had solved some practical problems for them. With hindsight however, she could see that her decision had been fraught with pitfalls. Since his arrival, certain forces had been at work, creeping up on her and the children. Invisible. Insidious. They were like little tentacles that reached out here and there, quietly attaching themselves with surprising tenacity.

"You didn't indicate exactly how much you wanted to borrow."

Wendy had been so deep in thought, it took her a

second to realize the banker had just spoken. "I'm sorry?"

"How much should I make the check out for?"

Good heavens—could it really have been this easy? But that meant… She put a hand to her throat. It meant so many things. She could scarcely contain her chaotic emotions.

"Ten thousand."

He nodded. "I'll be back in a moment with papers to sign and the money."

Twenty minutes later, she left the bank so dazed by this stunning turn of events, she almost forgot to stop by the post office.

This time she was careful to look through everything before she tossed the junk mail. Not that she expected to find another letter from Josh's fiancée sandwiched in.

What did catch her eye was a letter with a New Orleans postmark, addressed to Cutty. What on earth? She slit open the envelope and pulled out a two-page typed letter.

To Whom It May Concern:
My name is Dr. Thomas Welch. I'm a surgeon from New Orleans.

Recently I saw your advertisement on the Internet.

Wendy shook her head. Ben's ad had produced some mail, after all.

After giving it a great deal of thought, I decided to write to you. I own Belle Maison, a large plantation with a stable, located on the Mississippi.

The property has been in my family for generations. I don't live there year round, but it has been James McGee's home for fifty-seven years.

He has been the family's general handyman for as long as I can remember. He does everything, including opening the place up when I give parties.

Jimmy, a widower, is the soul of integrity. Sadly, he has never been on a vacation, never traveled farther than New Orleans itself. That has been his choice, of course.

The other day we were talking, and I told him I'd be leaving for a medical convention in Reno, Nevada, next month. He asked where it was. When I told him about the magnificent Sierra Nevada mountains, he said, ''I've never seen mountains. I'd surely like to visit some before I die.''

That's the only time I've ever heard him express an interest of that nature. When I asked him if he'd like to go to Reno with me, he said yes. Jimmy's been overdue a long vacation for years. The only problem is, he wouldn't know what to do with himself. All he's known is work.

When I saw your ad, I couldn't help but think he might enjoy spending some time working for you. He'd be able to experience the mountains firsthand, yet he'd be around horses—his greatest love. I might add that he's a congenial, lovable man. One of my best friends.

If you haven't filled the position yet, would it be possible to arrange a meeting with you when we fly out? Jimmy might like it. Then again, he might not want to stay in a place that's unfamiliar. But if it turned out both of you were amenable, we could talk more.

I've enclosed some pictures of Jimmy and me.

Engrossed by the touching account, she studied the half-dozen snapshots taken around the plantation and on horseback. The letter was as touching as it was unexpected.

"Wendy?"

When she heard that familiar male voice, she raised her head abruptly. "Josh! I didn't know you were in town."

"I had no idea you'd come, either," he murmured. "I just finished another therapy session and decided to drop by to see if you were here."

Wendy didn't care how much he downplayed his troubled engagement; she suspected he was missing his fiancée terribly. He'd experienced months of loneliness. Though he'd deny it to her face, she knew he'd driven over here hoping to find another letter from Lisa.

Stop it, Wendy.

His gaze dropped to the letter she held. "Have you received bad news?"

She shook her head. "Not at all. Someone answered Ben's ad. You'll have to read it."

He nodded. "Is something else wrong?" he probed. "Did you have to visit the doctor all of a sudden?"

Josh was so much more protective than Matt had been, she hardly knew how to respond. He probably behaved this way because he'd never been married and never had a wife who was pregnant.

"No. Nothing like that. I—I decided to go by the bank and see if they'd give me a loan."

"And?" he asked with more intensity than usual.

"Ten thousand dollars has now been deposited in the resort's bank account. Your figures convinced them. I didn't have to lift a finger."

She detected a satisfied gleam in his eyes.

"Congratulations! This calls for a celebration."

"I don't know," she said in a shaky voice. "Now I've got to make it work!"

"Follow me to that malt shop on the way out of town and we'll get down to business."

When she hesitated he said, "One day I plan to take you out for a proper drink, but not until after the baby's born."

After the baby's born?

"That would be nice, Josh. But I have a better idea. The children and I will give you an engagement party. We all want to meet Lisa."

She saw an enigmatic expression cross his face before she turned to walk out of the building ahead of him. He might not like her mentioning his fiancée, but Wendy needed to keep the other woman in the forefront of her mind.

When they reached the outside, he said, "If we leave now, we'll have time for a milkshake before you have to get home for the children."

Much as she craved his company, she knew it would be wrong. "Thank you for the invitation, Josh, but I have another errand to run. I'll see you back at the resort. We can talk after dinner."

With a nod, he helped her into her car, courteous as ever. But she had the strongest suspicion she'd offended him, the last thing she wanted to do.

He might not think anything of going to a restaurant with his boss. Unfortunately, she hadn't viewed Josh as a mere employee for quite some time.

Now that he'd be working at the resort a few months

longer, she needed to keep any contact between them strictly professional.

If she didn't lay the ground rules today, she could kiss any peace of mind goodbye. Josh Walker couldn't mean anything to her this soon after Matt's passing. He just *couldn't!* The trick was to convince herself of that fact, and go on convincing herself until she believed it.

JOSH FINISHED HIS second whiskey, then reached for his cane and walked out of the hotel bar to the public phones. Harve didn't pick up. "Hell. Why aren't you there?" He left a message saying he'd try to reach him later.

After replacing the receiver, he followed the signs to the indoor pool and rented a suit. His therapist had told him swimming would be another effective way to exercise his leg. Why not get started now? Later, he'd follow up with a steak dinner.

Until he'd worked some of the alcohol out of his system, he wouldn't be driving anywhere. Besides, he'd made a promise to Wendy. At the time, he'd thought he could keep it....

After wearing himself out, he lay down on a lounger. Several nice-looking women paraded past him, but he wasn't interested. His eyelids felt heavy. He turned over on his stomach. It didn't take long until he was fast asleep.

When he suddenly came awake again, he saw that it was after nine o'clock. Muttering an oath, he jumped up from the lounger and grabbed a quick shower. After downing a meal in record time, he headed for Moon Lake.

He'd been closing up the place every night, but this evening he'd arrived back too late. Quiet reigned. Ten o'clock was bedtime in the Sloan household. He wouldn't be able to talk to her until tomorrow. *Hell.*

Before he went to his cabin, he walked to the front of the coffee shop and tried once more to reach Harve on the pay phone. Finally his supervisor answered.

"Josh? Sorry I missed your call earlier. I figured it was important. Since I was at a dinner, I had Agent Wood phone the resort."

"That means she pretended to be Lisa!"

"Who else? Standard operating procedure. Are you all right? What's going on?"

He expelled the breath torturing his lungs. "Harve— I'm in trouble."

"Has somebody discovered where you are?" With that question, all levity vanished.

"No. It isn't that kind of trouble."

"Thank God."

"It's worse."

"What could be worse? Unless there's been further damage to your leg."

After a pause, he murmured, "I've met a woman."

"Is that all?" Harve chuckled.

He grimaced. "This one's different."

"Josh? I feel like we're dancing around each other. If she's coming on too strong, I can send you somewhere else first thing in the morning."

"You don't understand, Harve. I'm the one who's coming on too strong."

"You're right. I *don't* get it. Let's start over again. From the top."

"Josh?"

When he heard Wendy call out from the rear of the coffee shop, he almost dropped the receiver.

"I've got to go, Harve. Talk to you later."

He met her in the back office. She'd changed into oversized blue sweats, probably her husband's. The knowledge sent a stab straight to his gut.

She looked younger, and with her hair attractively disheveled, he thought he'd never seen anyone as sexy or adorable. The urge to draw her into his arms was overpowering.

"Forgive me if I was intruding."

"You could never do that."

Her breathing sounded shallow. "When I heard the truck, I came to tell you that Lisa phoned. It wasn't until after I went home that I realized I hadn't put her note back here where you'd find it." She tossed it onto the desk.

"That's very thoughtful of you, but it could have waited until tomorrow."

"Not according to her. She was horribly disappointed to learn you weren't home yet. She told me to tell you to call her back no matter what time it was."

Wendy sounded upset, almost angry.

Was it because she'd expected him to be here to close up? Or was there another reason... His pulse raced crazily. Dared he believe that?

"I'll do it in a little while. Right now I'd like to talk about our next plan of action." He pulled out a chair for her.

"I can't stay. The children are waiting for me to read to them."

It was an excuse. He could feel it.

"Then we'll talk tomorrow about hiring a cook."

"I already took care of that in town. An employment agency is going to send out some applicants over the next few days."

So that was where she'd gone in such an all-fired hurry.

"That's good. I'm going to arrange for the ad to go out over the Internet first thing in the morning. Pending your approval, of course."

She refused to meet his gaze. "That would be wonderful."

Before she bolted, he said, "You were going to tell me about the letter that came in response to Ben's ad."

"It's at the house. I'll have him show it to you tomorrow. Good night, Josh."

Oh no, you don't! "I'll walk you home."

She made a sound of exasperation. "But I promised your fiancée you'd call her! I'm afraid she'll think I didn't relay the message."

"I'll assure her you did. She won't mind, I promise. In any case, I'm tired. It's been a long day for both of us. Shall we go?"

CHAPTER EIGHT

"ADA? OF THE THREE applicants, who do you like best?" Wendy put the last pie in the oven and set the timer. Thank heaven that was done. She had a splitting headache and a slight fever.

"Vera Cline. Josh was the most impressed with her, too."

"Well, then," Wendy murmured dryly.

If Josh said so, it was good enough for Ada. But in this instance, Wendy happened to agree. Not only did Vera have waitressing experience, she'd been a cook at a major Las Vegas restaurant before she and her husband had moved to South Lake Tahoe.

"Josh made it clear to Vera that because you're pregnant, you're not to be bothered unless it's an emergency."

Wendy shrugged lightly. Josh seemed more concerned for her welfare than she was herself.

"He told her she'd have to wash dishes and clean up," Ada rattled on while Wendy put away cutlery. "That sounded fine to Vera. After working at the Edelweiss where they serve two hundred people per sitting, day and night, she said Moon Lake was going to be heaven."

Vera really was the perfect candidate. Her references were glowing. She had a pleasant, open personality and her situation was convenient: she lived nearby and her three children were grown.

If the house hadn't been close to the coffee shop, Wendy could never have carried on her job all these years. Childhood sickness and unexpected problems guaranteed there were many times she'd had to drop everything in Ada's lap to see to Ben and Kim's needs.

Of course, hiring Mrs. Cline meant giving her insurance benefits and paid vacations. Wendy did the same for Ada. It added considerably to her expenses, but in order to get people of their caliber and keep them, she had no other choice. Assuming Vera lived up to their expectations, Wendy would demand that when the resort sold, the new owner retain her and Ada as part of the conditions of sale.

"Then I'll give her a—a call and tell her t-to report Monday morning." The sneezing had started.

"The sooner the better. Josh came in a little while ago and told me another family of four has reserved a cabin for next week. At this rate, you're going to be filled to capacity in no time. Those people who say the Internet is nothing more than a waste of time don't know what they're talking about."

Wendy hadn't seen Josh yet to hear the news. This morning she'd felt too ill to get out of bed. For once, the children had made their own breakfasts and gone out to the bus without her.

"You know something?" Ada eyed her frankly. "You don't sound good. Go home and take care of yourself. If things get too busy around here, Josh'll help me."

"You know something?" Wendy repeated with a wan smile. "I think I will." No doubt the decision to reopen the resort had brought on extra stress, thus the cold. "See you later, Ada. Thanks for all your help. I don't know how I would have managed all these years without you. Especially this last year," she added. She'd barely finished her sentence when she started sneezing again.

"That goes both ways. You and Matt were willing to take a chance on me when I had no experience."

"Well, you've got it now. And as far as I'm concerned, you're in charge of Vera's training. You two can schedule your shifts and days off the way it works best for you. I trust your judgment completely."

Wendy left the kitchen, but not before she saw the gratified smile on the other woman's face. Keeping Ada happy was of primary importance to Wendy. She'd found out a long time ago that working together as a unit was the key to the resort's success. To her surprise, Josh had fit into that unit as if he'd always been a part of it.

Out of breath when she reached the house, she grabbed a quilt and lay down on the couch. Cutty promptly curled up at her feet. Using the remote, Wendy turned on the TV. She couldn't remember the last time she'd watched a soap opera. A year maybe? From the day Matt was first diagnosed, nothing on TV had been able to hold her interest.

It appeared the characters on *Days of Our Lives* hadn't changed. Stefano DiMera was still orchestrating everyone's lives with his outrageous schemes. The very attractive John Black didn't look any older.

The conversation droned on. Her heavy eyelids closed. If they ever had to replace him, she knew a man...

JOSH HAD KNOCKED on the door more than once. Except for Cutty's barking, there was no answer.

"Wendy?" he called out, knocking harder this time.

He had good news for her. When he'd seen the kids headed to the bus stop alone, he asked them where their mother was. They'd said she was sick.

Not liking the sound of that, he waited with them until the bus came, then hurried to the coffee shop. Apparently Ada hadn't seen her yet, either.

He ate breakfast without enthusiasm, then started his work removing shutters from the cabin windows. Normally he quit for lunch around two, but by noon he gave it up and returned to the restaurant. Ada told him about Wendy's cold. He called the house. When there was no answer, he packed up soup and sandwiches and went over there.

"Wendy?"

Alarmed by her lack of response, he found her house key on his ring and unlocked the front door. Cutty met him at the door. The TV was on.

"Wendy? It's Josh!"

Standing in the foyer, he saw movement out of the corner of his eye. She lifted her head from the couch. "Josh?" She'd obviously been asleep and sounded badly congested.

"Forgive me for intruding, but when I tried to get you on the phone just now, you didn't answer. Ada and I both got worried about you. May I come in for a minute?"

"What time is it?"

"Twelve-thirty."

He heard a groggy moan as she sat all the way up and smoothed the hair out of her eyes. Her flushed face attested to fever.

"Yes. Of course."

This was the first time she'd invited him inside. It seemed he'd been waiting forever to cross over her threshold.

The house was actually a glorified cabin with Western decor. He liked the predominantly red plaid of the upholstery. A hand-carved hutch displayed her china and crystal. Books lined a whole wall. There was a black-and-white portrait of a man—it had to be her husband—and a pair of large framed photographs of Lake Tahoe taken in summer and winter, which he found glorious. She'd created a lovely, warm atmosphere. He had to applaud the rightness of placing Matt's picture in its prominent location near the hearth. This man had been her husband, was her children's father, and he deserved to remain in their memories.

He shut the door. "Where shall I put your lunch?"

She stared up at him in surprise. "On the coffee table. Oh, Josh, you shouldn't have gone to the trouble."

He put everything down and handed her the chicken soup, kept hot in a large crockery mug. "If I were ill, I have no doubt you'd do the same for me. Have you called your doctor?"

"No. He won't prescribe medication because it could hurt the baby. I just need to take it easy and drink lots of fluids."

"Do you have a steamer?"

"Yes."

"Where?"

She shook her head. "Don't worry about it. I'll get it later."

"I think you need it now."

He was afraid she'd argue about it and felt relieved when she finally said, "It's in the children's bathroom under the sink. Second door on the left down the hall. Don't mind if there's a mess.''

He reached for his cane. Cutty trotted behind him.

Everything looked clean and tidy. He found the vaporizer easily, and within a couple of minutes had it set up on the end table next to the couch.

''Thank you,'' she said as steam started to infiltrate the room. ''The soup is delicious, but I don't think I could manage anything else.''

He looked down at her. ''Mind if I stay and eat a sandwich with you?''

After a slight pause, she whispered, ''No. Of course not. Pull up a chair.''

This felt good. So good, in fact, he knew it would be hard to go back to work. With the slightest encouragement, he could curl up on that couch and hold her all day. But so far, Cutty was the only one who had the privilege of getting close to her.

''I saw Ben and Kim off on the bus this morning. While we were waiting, he told me about the letter from that doctor in Louisiana.''

She nodded. ''If I was going to bring up the horses from Carson City, I might be interested in meeting this Jimmy. We usually hire a stablehand for the summer.''

''But not this summer.'' He bit into the other half of his sandwich.

''No,'' she said quietly after another sneezing episode.

Josh frowned. The children would be disappointed. This morning their conversation had focused exclusively on the horses. It was obvious they couldn't wait to go riding.

''May I ask why?''

''They're a lot of work. We have enough to deal

with as it is. I've told the man who's boarding our horses to allow them to be ridden. The revenue from renting them helps pay his fees.''

''Then I need to change the ad on the Internet. It says horseback riding.''

''I'd forgotten about that...''

Josh could see she'd finished her soup; at least she still had an appetite. He leaned over to take the mug from her.

''Thank you. I haven't been this pampered in ages.''

''A mother-to-be deserves a lot of spoiling. Tell me something—does the ban on horses include Rusty and Magpie?''

She darted him a rueful glance. ''I can see you've been briefed.''

He smiled. ''Ben tells me there are some wonderful trails. Since I can't do any serious hiking yet, the next best way to explore the area is on horseback. He has a trip all planned out for us.''

''No, Josh! I thought I'd made it clear to Ben that we're not going to have the horses here, not even the children's.''

Josh felt a sense of shock. In an instant her whole demeanor had changed. Apparently the subject of the horses caused her a lot of pain. The children had told him their father often rode with them in the summer.

Ben was Matt's son. She was still in mourning. Some people stayed in that mode all their lives. His grandfather had been one of them. Dear Lord.

Josh had stepped over a line, and she was letting him know it.

''Forgive me for upsetting you. Please be assured that the next time Ben mentions the horses, I'll remind him that any and all decisions are yours.''

He rose from the chair and gathered up the lunch dishes. "If you need anything else, phone the coffee shop and let Ada know."

"Josh? Wait!" He heard his name called out between sneezing attacks.

Much as he'd like to do just that, he couldn't. He didn't dare. Otherwise he might say something to jeopardize their friendship. That was what she wanted. All she wanted, despite the attraction between them.

She's still in love with her husband.

How could he expect anything more of her when the baby she and her husband had made together was growing bigger every day?

Now that Josh had practically forced her to reopen the resort, he owed her his help, not more complications. By the time he got back to work, he knew what he had to do.

"MOM?" BEN SOUNDED UPSET. "Do you know where Josh went?" Both children ran into the kitchen. "The truck's not there. I was going to shoot some baskets with him."

"He's probably at therapy, Ben."

His frantic concern echoed Kim's. Yesterday her daughter had dashed into the house after school, asking the same question.

Last night Ada had wanted to know why Josh had started eating dinner in town.

No one was happy, least of all Wendy.

Three days ago, she'd driven Josh from her house with harsh words he could only interpret as a rebuke. The second they'd left her lips, she'd wanted to die. She'd tried to call him back so she could explain.

But it was too late. He'd been out the door like a shot.

Until she could find him and tell him what had provoked her outburst, nothing would feel right again. Not for her kids—or her.

Unfortunately, she'd been weak and feverish until this morning. By early afternoon, she'd rallied enough to wash her hair and do a little cooking. The poor kids had been feeling abandoned, by her and now by Josh. Her fault, she knew. It was time for some damage control.

Tonight she'd be waiting for Josh when he returned from town.

As for the children—

She put milk and cookies on the table in front of them. "Guess what?"

"What?" Kim asked in a lackluster voice.

"Your favorite movie's going to be on at seven. I thought we'd make some popcorn, light a fire and watch it."

Kim's face brightened. "You're feeling better, huh?"

"I am!"

"If it's *The Parent Trap,* no thanks." Ben shoved away from the table and ran out of the kitchen, leaving his milk and cookies untouched.

Wendy had gone for some counseling after Matt's death. One of the things she'd learned was that if a daughter lost her father, she still had her mother as a role model.

But when a son lost his father, he also lost the person who would guide him into manhood, by encouragement and example. Ben's struggle would be harder.

"Stay here a minute, sweetheart. I need to talk to your brother."

"How come Josh doesn't like us anymore?"

Wendy's eyes closed tightly. "Of course he likes you! Why would you ask a question like that?"

"When we were on the bus, Eric asked Ben if he could come over, and Ben said Josh didn't want any of us around."

"That's not true." She kissed the top of Kim's head. "I'll be right back."

When she entered Ben's room, she found him face-down on the bed with his arm around Cutty. His shoulders shook. He was trying to stifle any sound. She hadn't seen him like this for months now. Not since midwinter, when he'd accepted his father's death and let him go.

This active grief was for someone else....

With a heavy heart, she sank down on the bed and stroked his hair. "Want to talk about it?"

"No."

"Not even if I tell you the reason you haven't seen Josh lately?"

"I already know the reason." His words were muffled.

"You *think* you know the reason. But I told Kim you're both wrong. Josh likes you two so much, he wanted to bring the horses up from Carson City. I told him no."

By now Ben had turned over. His pained eyes stared at her with a mixture of incredulity and confusion.

"Josh took it to mean I didn't want him telling me how to run my resort. He was totally wrong in that assumption, of course. But I was feeling sick, and he left the house before I could explain my reasons.

"Because he respects me, and is such a good man, he's been trying very hard not to interfere in our personal lives. Do you understand what I'm saying?" This was all true, but there was more. She couldn't share it with her son, though. Josh's fear of horses, and the reason for it, had been told to her in confidence. It wasn't that she wanted to keep secrets from her son. But if Ben knew the truth, he might bring up the subject at a later date and cause Josh embarrassment—or pain.

Ben and Cutty both clambered off the bed. The tears were gone. "Yeah."

"So give me a chance to talk to him, and you'll find out nothing's changed. He thinks you kids are great."

"Did he tell you that?"

"Many times. Now, I have something else I want to say. You've heard it before, but you need to hear it again. Josh won't be here forever. There's a woman he loves very much. They're going to get married."

"How come you keep mentioning it?"

"Because through the years, you'll meet lots of people you like. Some will remain in your life. Others will move on."

"You mean like Dad."

"No!" She shook her head, perplexed. "No, sweetheart. You loved him. He'll always be a part of your life. I'm talking about people you like. Remember Allen? Your good friend in fourth grade? Remember when he had to move to Florida? That's the kind of feeling I'm talking about. There's a world of difference between liking someone, and the kind of love you had for your father."

"I know the difference," he said. Ben sounded so much like Matt, it was uncanny.

"Good."

A long silence followed.

"I don't want Josh to go away, Mom."

Oh, Ben. "Well, he's not leaving tonight."

"I hate his fiancée."

"You know better than to talk that way."

"I don't care." New tears welled up, and he brushed at them with the back of his hand. "I hope they break up."

This had to stop!

"You know what?" She fought to keep her voice steady. "A lot is going to happen in the next couple of months. Josh will be leaving. We'll be moving closer to Grandma. You'll make new friends...."

"But most important, the baby's going to be born. You'll have a new little brother or sister. You and Kim will be so busy arguing over whose turn it is to hold the baby, you won't have time to miss anyone."

She could tell she wasn't getting through. "Ben, I'm going to need your help."

"I'll help you," he muttered, not looking at her.

"Thank you for saying that. Now, I've got an idea. How would you and Kim like to go to the doctor with me next time?"

"Why?"

"Well, afterward I thought we could go to a show and have dinner. It'll be something to look forward to. What do you think?"

"That'll be cool," he said without enthusiasm. "When are you going to talk to Josh?"

Wendy sighed. "The next time I see him. Maybe you ought to get started on your homework so you'll be able to watch the movie with us. And it's not *The Parent Trap,* it's *The Borrowers.* Okay?"

"Okay."

For the rest of the afternoon she kept busy doing laundry and cleaning the house. Ben finally sauntered into the kitchen and began his homework at the table. After a casual dinner of salad and scrambled eggs, they fixed popcorn, then settled down in front of the TV.

Wendy grimaced. On the surface, their family looked like the picture of domestic bliss. But underneath, everyone was suffering varying degrees of turmoil.

Half an hour later, she could no longer sit there watching a movie she'd already seen half a dozen times. When she said she needed to go to the office for a few minutes, Kim protested, but Ben calmed his sister. He knew exactly what his mother planned to do.

WENDY WAS THE LAST person Josh expected to see when he walked into the office to check his e-mail. It seemed like weeks instead of days since he'd left her house, feeling as though more than his leg had taken a hit. Tonight he'd eaten his third meal in town, but that was getting old fast....

According to Ada, Wendy had been too sick to get up. He was surprised to find her here this soon after her illness. She looked pale. But her paleness only emphasized the purity of her skin and features. He could tell she'd just washed her hair. It gleamed like gold in the shadowy light.

She wore a blue top that outlined her shape. Her pregnancy was definitely more pronounced. He noticed everything about her. But that was *all* he could do. New rules had gone into effect. He had to forget about touching her the way he did in his dreams.

"I'm glad you're back, Josh. I need to talk to you." She didn't sound nearly as congested.

He sat down, rested his cane on the desk and propped his leg in front of him.

"Would you like me to turn on the computer so you can see how many reservations have come in?"

"No. That can wait. What I have to say can't."

The intensity of her tone alerted him. She'd had three days to decide she'd made a mistake in getting the loan. All bets were off, and she was letting him go.

That look of pleading from those clear green eyes meant she'd been working herself up to this moment for a long time.

"Go ahead. Tell me."

She cleared her throat. "If you recall, when you applied for this job, you gave me two references." He nodded, wondering where this could be leading.

"The farmer I talked to—"

"My neighbor, Henry Kendal."

"Yes. That was the name. Anyway, while we were talking, he told me something in confidence."

Josh clasped his hands behind his head. Henry could have convinced her of anything. He should have been an actor rather than an FBI agent. "If it was so disturbing, why didn't you tell me about it right away?"

She shook her head. "Because I didn't think the subject would come up."

He was trying hard to read between the lines but wasn't having much success. "And now it has?"

She rubbed her arm with a well-manicured hand. "Yes. Because of the horses."

His brow furrowed. "If Henry told you I've never had any experience around them, he'd be right."

She glanced away. "That was part of it."

He leaned forward. "And the other part?" Her agitation was a total mystery to him.

"When Ben made the suggestion about bringing the horses back here, he had no way of knowing—I mean he didn't realize that you—" She broke off.

"That I what?" He waited. "Wendy, look at me." She finally lifted her eyes to his. "What's the other part?"

"Mr. Kendal said that when you were a boy, you saw your grandmother get thrown and die. He said you've had a fear of horses ever since. I was horrified when I realized Ben had been making all these plans to go riding with you. I—"

He stared at her, hardly daring to believe what he was hearing. "You mean *that's* why you were so upset the other day?"

"Yes. Of course. Don't worry about the horses, Josh. I'd never expect you to take on a project involving horses when such a tragic memory is associated with them."

Lord. He'd thought—

He bowed his head. It didn't matter what he'd thought. Her anger had erupted out of concern for his feelings. She'd acted to protect him!

His elation was so great, he actually felt light-headed.

"It's true I watched her get thrown. The accident broke her neck. She died right there in front of me. The experience was very traumatic, but I survived. Children have amazing resilience.

"Sadly, my grandfather never got over it. He was the one who made sure I never went near a horse. His fear kept me away from them—not my own." He shrugged. "I've always wanted to try riding, but some-how the occasion never presented itself. I guess I've been too busy with crops to have energy left over for livestock.

"But Ben convinced me that I've got to see the Tahoe Rim from the back of a horse. Since he's an accomplished rider, I figured he could teach me. I was actually looking forward to it."

This time when he smiled at her, she smiled back. The sensation produced a high greater than pushing Mach 3 in an F-16.

"I'm glad her death doesn't still haunt you. What happened to your parents?"

The thing he'd been waiting for had happened. She wanted to know something personal about him. He'd almost given up hope.

"My parents were killed in an auto-train accident soon after I was born. I was lucky because I had wonderful grandparents. Henry probably told you they spoiled me rotten. It's all true. I could do no wrong in their eyes. What they didn't know about me would fill a book."

She smiled again. "Well...Henry said a few things."

Josh chuckled. "I knew there had to be more. So, am I going to hear about them?"

Her glance slid away. "He didn't like the idea of your coming out to what he called 'sin country.'"

At this point Josh broke into full-scale laughter. He hadn't laughed like this for so long, he thought he'd forgotten how. "Did he think I'd gone to work for a gambling casino featuring Les Girls?"

"You're close," she admitted, then started laughing, too. "That's when I told him about Moon Lake and the horses." Now it all made sense. "I liked him. I really did."

"Everyone likes Henry."

When her laughter subsided, she said, "He misses you."

"I miss him, too."

"I got the impression he's anxious for you to work things out with your fiancée."

Josh was getting to the point where one of these days he was going to blurt the truth. "Naturally Henry wants to see me married," he said in as matter-of-fact a voice as he could muster.

Her hand betrayed a tremor. Something else was wrong.

"Josh, you've probably noticed—Ben has developed a pretty critical case of hero worship. I'm not accusing you of encouraging him, consciously or otherwise. It's just that his dad's been gone long enough for him to want another strong male in his life. Kim and I don't fill the bill.

"He knows you're getting married, but he's in denial about it. Do you understand what I'm saying?" Her voice trembled as she spoke.

"Of course." Only too well.

"The trouble is, the last few days you've been unavailable to him. So he thinks you don't like him. I explained that you were simply trying to be professional and not intrude in our personal lives. I also reminded him again that you'll be leaving, that you're marrying…Lisa soon and going home."

He turned on the computer. "I'm glad you told me everything. Now that I know, I won't actively avoid him, but I'll make sure I'm so busy, he'll get bored and find something else to do." He knew it was what she wanted to hear.

"Thank you. I think it's for the best. One more

thing—Kim's crazy about you, too.''

And what about you, Wendy?

"I'll keep that in mind. Now, are you ready for this?" He clicked on to the program he'd installed to keep track of reservations. "Two cabins are fully booked for the second week of May. Four for the third and fourth weeks. Five are fully booked for the month of June. At this rate, all six cabins could be booked before long.''

"Oh, Josh!" There was another note in her voice beyond excitement. It revealed the depth of her love for Moon Lake.

"The reservations are pouring in. I wanted your permission to line up some teens from your old list to do housekeeping and run the front desk. Shall I call the phone company in the morning to get the cabin phones operational again?''

"Of course. Thank you.''

"You, more than anyone, know this is when vacations are planned. It was our good fortune to put out the word in time. In fact, we've done such a good job, we could accommodate more guests if I weren't living in one of the cabins. That's what I want to talk to you about.''

"You're the most generous man I've ever met, but I draw the line at your pitching a tent," she said wryly.

"How about the loft?''

She blinked. "You mean the barn?''

"Why not? It's perfect, even has that small bathroom.''

"But there's no hot water.''

Lady, if you only knew how many cold showers I've taken since I met you...

"Cold is invigorating. Besides, the weather's getting

warmer every day. All I need is a sleeping bag and a cell phone.''

"No.'' She shook her head. "I refuse to let you do that.''

"If we can accommodate four more people a day, my cabin alone will pay off the short-term loan before you know it. In a way, I'd almost prefer to be somewhat separated from the guests.''

"You're making that up.''

"No. I crave my privacy like anyone else. Since we're not offering horseback riding—for the moment, anyway—no one will have reason to go near the barn.''

"But what about your leg? Can you climb a ladder?''

"It'll be good exercise.''

"You'll have to walk farther.''

"That's the whole point. Besides the distance is negligible. And there's always the truck.''

"I can see you have this all worked out,'' she said in a voice of quiet frustration.

"Only in my head. If you truly object, then I'll stay put. But after what you told me about Ben and Kim, I've been thinking a move to the barn would make me less accessible to your house.''

"Knowing them, they'd find the idea romantic and decide to move into the loft with you.''

Josh tried in vain to stop a certain fantasy that flashed through his mind just then. "You could make the barn off-limits,'' he murmured.

"That goes without saying. But, Josh—you have to have a bed!''

"How about a camp cot? I'll pick one up in town, along with a sleeping bag.''

"You need other things. A dresser. A closet.''

He grinned. "A place for everything and everything in its place? My grandmother used to say that, but it wasn't something I worried about."

"You sound as bad as Ben when we're housecleaning on Saturday mornings."

"That's one of the interesting differences between the sexes."

"Interesting is right, when a woman walks in on the mess!"

Josh laughed to cover a tumult of emotions. If she ever walked in on *his* mess, he would know she wasn't thinking about her husband.

He heard a sigh of resignation. "If you want to move out to the barn, it's all right with me. But I want it understood that this was your idea, not mine. If it doesn't work out, don't be afraid to tell me you're moving back to the cabin. I refuse to jeopardize your comfort for the sake of a few more guests!"

"Agreed. I think I'll do it tomorrow while the kids are at school. They won't even notice."

"Until they can't find you," she whispered anxiously.

He didn't answer but merely said, "Come on, Wendy. Let's get you home."

CHAPTER NINE

"LOOK WHAT I'VE GOT!"

Ben glanced up from his tackle box. "Hey—what are you doing with Josh's cane?"

"Ada said he left it for me today 'cause he doesn't need it anymore."

"That's awesome! How come you get it?"

"'Cause I asked for it first."

"Let me see it!"

"No!" Kim moved it out of reach. "Mom says to get our church clothes on and meet her at the car. We've been invited to dinner in town."

"I'm going over to Eric's. We're planning our fishing trip for tomorrow."

"Where are you going to fish?"

"Above Moon Lake. Don't you dare tell Mom."

"I won't. Come on—we have to get ready for dinner!"

"Not me. I don't like that doctor. Didn't you hear the weird way he talked?"

"Mom says that's a Southern accent."

"Yeah, well it drove me up the wall. Yesterday he kept calling me 'son.' He walked around the place as if he owned it or something. What a jerk!"

"I liked Jimmy."

"Yeah, he was nice. But I don't know why Mom let them come here when she's not going to hire him. She wouldn't let Josh bring up the horses, so there's no point.''

"Mom says that we all have to be nice to them 'cause he bothered to answer your ad.''

"Well, I'm not going to dinner with them. You can if you want.''

"Okay. But you're in big trouble. Bye.''

Maybe Josh had been invited, too. Ben decided to find out before he got on his bike. His mother had forbidden them to go to the barn, but they could call him on his cell phone if there was an emergency.

Josh answered right away, and that made him happy.

"Hi, Josh. It's me.''

"Ben?'' Josh sounded really serious. He'd been that way all month. Maybe because it was the end of May and the resort was so busy now.

"Yeah.''

"Is it your mother? Is there a problem with the baby?''

The baby? Ben had forgotten all about that. He felt a fleeting guilt. "No. I just wondered if you'd been invited to dinner, too.''

It took Josh so long to answer, Ben wondered if he'd even heard.

"Dr. Welch invited your mother to dinner again tonight?''

"Yeah. He wants Kim and me to come.''

"You don't want to go?''

"Heck, no! He'll just talk to Mom all night and ignore everybody else like he did the last time. He's taking her on a boat ride tomorrow on Lake Tahoe. I can't figure out why she's going when she's been there a million times. He's such a loser!'' Just then he heard footsteps on the front porch. "Hey, Josh? I gotta hang up now."

"All right. But do me a favor?"

"Sure."

"Go with your mom, sport. The baby's coming. She needs you and Kim to look after her. That's what family's all about. You know what I mean?"

"Yeah. Okay. Bye, Josh."

He hung up and flew to his room to get dressed.

"Ben?" his mother called out.

"I'm in here, Mom! I'll be ready in a minute."

"Kim told me you weren't coming."

"I was just teasing her."

"That teasing has got to stop!"

"Okay."

"When we get in the car, I want you to apologize to her."

"All right."

"I want you to be nice to Dr. Welch, too."

"I am nice."

"Ben, I've always been told by other people what a polite, wonderful son I have. I'd like Dr. Welch to feel the same way about you."

"Why? Do you like him or something?"

"Yes. Of course."

"Well, I don't."

"I can't believe I heard you say that."

"Mom, he's just so phony."

"The man is intelligent and interesting. You could learn a lot of history just listening to him. He comes from an entirely different culture than ours."

"You can say that again."

"He'd like us to visit New Orleans after the baby's born. Think how fascinating it would be to stay on a real plantation. He'll show us around the French Quarter. Jimmy will take you horseback riding. Think how much fun that would be.''

Something was wrong with his mom. She'd been going out with the doctor while Jimmy stayed in town at the hotel. She wasn't acting like his mom anymore. He felt sick to his stomach.

AT THE FIRST SIGN of lightning the next afternoon, Josh motioned to the families out on Moon Lake to bring in the boats. What had started as an overcast morning was building into a violent mountain storm. Thunder shook the ground.

A cold wind had sprung up. Even Moon Lake had whitecaps. There'd already been a twenty-degree drop in the temperature, and you could smell rain in the air. The guests needed to get to their cabins before the cloudburst started in earnest.

By the time the last canoe and kayak had been brought in, raindrops had begun pelting him. Once all the boats were turned over, he headed for the truck. But he was drenched when he climbed inside the cab.

Normally he found storms exhilarating. But Wendy had left early for Lake Tahoe with Dr. Welch; Josh had seen them pull away from the coffee shop in his rental car. They could very well be out on the water right now. Storms of this magnitude had swamped sightseeing boats before. He wouldn't rest easy until she was back at the resort, safe and sound.

In fact, he wouldn't have any peace until Dr. Welch left Nevada. Ben's phone call yesterday confirmed Josh's suspicions that the divorced surgeon was attracted to Wendy. When a man went in pursuit of a beautiful woman, the signs were unmistakable.

While Josh had shown Jimmy around a few days earlier, it had twisted his insides to watch Wendy smile and respond to the doctor's Southern gallantry. Jimmy McGee was a quiet, shy man—a true gentleman. Unlike his boss, in Josh's opinion. He didn't care for Dr. Welch, and that was putting it mildly.

Jealousy was a new emotion for Josh. To win Wendy's trust, let alone her friendship, had been like walking through a minefield. One misstep and it would have been all over. Yet the good doctor had no qualms about running roughshod over the same ground to get whatever he wanted.

And Josh knew exactly what the other man wanted.

Ben was right. Dr. Welch was a jerk. The boy's instincts were precise—the man was out hunting, and Wendy was his prey.

She didn't appear to mind. It was making Josh feel crazy, especially now as he drove blind through the rain, worrying about her safety.

If he hadn't been so familiar with the resort, he wouldn't have been able to reach the coffee shop. This was the ˙kind of monsoon downpour where you couldn't see one inch in front of your face.

"You're sopping wet!" Vera cried out when she saw him enter the kitchen.

He poured himself a cup of coffee. "Sorry to make a mess of your floor. I'll clean it up in a minute. Have you seen Mrs. Sloan?"

"No. She said not to expect her back until evening."

He gritted his teeth. "Where's Kim?"

"At Misty's."

"And Ben?"

"I believe he's at Eric's."

It appeared to be a typical Saturday with one difference. Wendy wasn't where she was supposed to be. Home. With her family. With him.

Lord. He was starting to sound like Ben.

"After I mop up this water, I'll be in the back office doing some paperwork."

"I'll take care of the cleaning. It's almost four, and you must be starving. I'll bring you lunch. There's one piece of apple strudel left."

So far, she was the only bright spot in this miserable day. "You're an angel, Vera."

A HALF HOUR LATER, he'd given up all hope of being able to concentrate. He phoned harbor security on Lake Tahoe for information. Apparently a couple of small sailboats had gotten into trouble during the storm, but there were no accidents or problems reported involving the large sightseeing crafts.

Relieved by that much good news, he pushed himself away from the desk and got to his feet. Too bad Ben wasn't here. With the rain beginning to let up, they could throw some baskets. That way they could both release some of their pent-up energy.

Come to think of it, Ben might like a ride home from Eric's. They could stow his bike in the back of the truck. Afterward, they could swing by Misty's and pick up Kim. During the drive, Josh could count on the children to give him an unabridged account of last night's activities. Until Josh knew exactly what had gone on between Wendy and the doctor, he wouldn't be able to settle down to anything constructive.

To his disappointment, he got the answering machine at both houses. Josh left the message that if they wanted a ride home, to call.

Still at loose ends, he went out to the front desk to

see if the storm had made Jonathan late for work. He and Ross were two high-school students who took turns running reception and the cash register from three to eight during the week. When it wasn't busy, they could study.

The second he saw Jonathan, the younger man gave him the high sign. So far so good. The coffee shop was full of customers, some of whom had probably stopped to get out of the rain. Everything seemed fine. But Josh wouldn't be satisfied until the whole family was home and Dr. Welch had made his exit.

No sooner had he returned to the back office than the phone rang. He picked up before the second ring. "Moon Lake Resort."

"Hi, Josh."

"Hello, Carol. Are you ready for me to come and get Ben?"

"You mean the boys aren't there?" she cried anxiously. "I thought I must have misunderstood when I heard your message."

Josh's hand tightened on the receiver. "I was told Ben was at your house."

"I haven't seen the boys since early morning. They had plans to fish at Moon Lake."

"That's what they told you? That they were fishing at the lake?"

"Yes. They packed a picnic and said they'd be home around three. I watched Eric leave with his pole and tackle box. All this time, I thought they were with you. Does Wendy know?"

He closed his eyes. "No. She went to town early and isn't back yet." Josh didn't even want to think about her reaction. "Until the storm hit and everyone ran for cover, I was out at the lake most of the day helping guests with the boats and life preservers. I didn't see either of the boys there. Maybe they changed their minds and went over to Andrew's house."

"No. Andrew's family is in California this weekend."

"What about Bryan?"

"I'll call him right now."

"I'm going to do some phoning, too. We'll stay in close touch."

"Okay. Thank you, Josh," she said, her voice shaking.

But an hour later, after dozens of phone calls, neither of them had turned up any information. Apparently the boys had chosen another spot to fish.

Although it wouldn't be nightfall for several more hours, the low clouds and drizzle made it feel like nine o'clock already. They should have been back three hours ago. Anything could have happened to them during that storm. Josh's stomach had a crater in it a mile wide.

In the past, his professional training had enabled him to distance himself from fear and other negative emotions while he carried out a mission. But there could be no lying to himself about this particular situation. Ben was someone vitally important to him. No matter how hard Josh tried, he couldn't compartmentalize his feelings in this instance.

After another phone conference, Eric's parents drove straight to the coffee shop. The three of them pored over a map of areas where the boys could have gone on foot.

The steep terrain of the mountain above Moon Lake was dismissed out of hand. That area had always been off-limits to the children. The rock ledges were too slippery and dangerous to climb on. The stream feeding into the lake flowed too swiftly, especially during late-spring runoff.

Josh supposed some well-meaning neighbor might have given the boys a lift to another part of Tahoe. But he and Steve Irvine decided to proceed on the assumption that Ben and Eric had remained closer to home.

Having decided on some specific spots, Josh phoned in a missing person's report to the sheriff's office; a search of the places they'd targeted would begin as soon as possible. After that, Josh and Steve got in the truck and drove around the area, hoping to see the boys walking along the highway. They questioned everyone they saw, tourist and local.

Another hour passed. The hope of finding them before dark was diminishing. They returned to the coffee shop to start phoning neighbors who would help with a search.

Josh had been expecting a phone call from the sheriff. When his cell phone rang, he was surprised to hear Kim's voice on the other end. At least she hadn't gone fishing with them.

"Hi, honey. Are you still at Misty's?"

"Yes. We just got back from dinner and a movie. Is my mom home yet?"

He groaned inwardly. "Not yet. Neither is Ben. You wouldn't happen to know where he and Eric went fishing, would you? We're all kind of worried because they should've been home hours ago."

"Ben told me not to tell."

Josh's heart pounded heavily. "If he's in trouble, then he'll be thankful you told me."

"Okay. He said they were going to fish above Moon Lake."

Josh passed on what he'd learned to the Irvines. With those words, everyone's worst nightmare had just been realized.

"Thanks, honey. Stay put at Misty's until you hear from your mother. All right?"

"Can't I come home?"

"Soon, honey."

"Okay."

In an instant, Josh had related the news to the sheriff, who said he'd notify the search-and-rescue team in South Lake Tahoe so an official search could get under way. By this time Carol had fallen apart. Her husband had his hands full trying to comfort her.

There was more bad news when the sheriff said that all the rescue units in the Tahoe area were out on other emergencies. Because it was dark, a search of that rugged terrain might have to be put off until morning.

Josh moved out of hearing of the others. "Does that include all air rescue units, too?"

"Afraid so."

"This is Special Agent Quincy with the FBI, air surveillance department. I'll let you get in touch with my supervisor, Harve Pearson in the Cleveland office." He gave Harve's private number. "If there's an extra chopper, I can fly it. I'll cover any additional costs."

"Hold on a minute."

While Josh waited, he made the decision that if the sheriff couldn't come up with one, he'd phone Harve who would authorize something through the department.

"Yup. We've got a chopper."

"Can you get a couple of men to go with me?"

"We'll put a team together."

"Good." He swallowed hard. "Sheriff—I'm undercover right now. It's absolutely vital you keep this information confidential. It could endanger many lives, not just mine.''

''No one's going to hear a thing from me.''

''Thank you. If you'll give me directions, I'm on my way.''

WHEN TOM WELCH pulled into the parking area in front of the coffee shop, Wendy insisted he stay in the car. ''Thank you for the last three days. I loved showing you and Jimmy around Tahoe. But I do need to go in. The children will be waiting for me.'' And Josh, too, she hoped.

''I hate to say good-night, but I understand. Will you join me for breakfast in the morning before we have to leave for the airport?''

''I'm afraid I can't. That's the one day of the week I have to be on duty here.''

''Then I'll phone you to say goodbye.''

''Do that,'' she murmured as she slid out of the car and shut the door.

Attractive and interesting though he was, the more time she'd spent with him, the more she'd realized what a mistake she'd made.

When he'd first let her know that he wanted to get better acquainted, she'd thought it might be a good idea to spend some time with him and see if he appealed to her as strongly as Josh did.

Judging by the way she'd prayed for both yesterday and today to end so she could get back to the resort, she had her answer. In truth, she'd always had her answer. It felt like years instead of hours since she'd seen Josh.

These last few days had represented a sort of experiment. A foolish one that had backfired. Ben was upset, and Tom had every right to accuse her of leading him on. But he was too much of a gentleman for that.

She waved him off with unholy relief, then started for the coffee shop doors. To her surprise, Carol Irvine came running out.

"Thank goodness you're home!" .

One look at Carol's anguished expression, and Wendy knew something terrible had happened. The hole in her stomach was back, that hollow, anguished feeling she'd lived with all those months before Matt's death.

"What's wrong?"

"It's Ben and Eric! They never came home from fishing." *Dear God, no!* "Kim admitted to Josh that they went up the mountain above Moon Lake. A search-and-rescue crew has been sent out to look for them. If they find them, they'll bring them straight to the hospital."

Wendy felt Carol's arm go around her. "Come on. Steve and Josh have gone to join in the search. I waited here to drive us to the hospital."

"But Kim—"

"She'll stay with Misty overnight if necessary. Everything's under control. Ada and her husband are inside. Let's go!"

"BEN? DO YOU th-think we're g-going to d-die?"

"Nope. Josh'll find us."

"W-what if h-he d-doesn't?"

"Of course, he will. Josh can do anything!"

"B-but w-we l-lied about w-where w-we were g-going."

"Kim knows. She'll tell Josh."

"H-how d-do you know?"

"Because Josh'll get it out of her."

"I—I h-hope s-so."

"I know so."

Ben believed that with all his heart. But it was night now, and nobody would search up here before daylight.

Eric's head was in Ben's lap. He was probably looking at him, but it was so dark, Ben couldn't see his friend's eyes. It was freezing out here on the ledge.

The sound of rushing water a few feet below them made him shiver all the more. He'd taken off his jacket to help keep Eric warm and ward off shock, one of the first things he'd learned in Scouts.

Ben figured Eric might have broken his leg or his foot. He sure as heck couldn't walk. Until morning, they were stuck on this ledge where Eric had fallen during the cloudburst.

As soon as it was light, Ben would try to jump to another ledge and eventually make it back home. In the meantime, all he could do was hold his friend close so they could share each other's body heat. Just the other day, the teacher had talked about hypothermia in health class. Eric was shaking so hard, Ben assumed his buddy was suffering from it right now.

"There's one more granola bar in my backpack. Do you w-want it?"

"Th-that's o-okay. Y-you e-eat i-it."

"We'll sh-share it."

He broke the bar in half and put one end in Eric's mouth. His own teeth had started to chatter. It was hard to eat and not bite his tongue.

It might start to rain again, and that would be bad. It was too late to wish they hadn't come up here. His mom had made him so mad at that man, he'd felt like doing something to hurt her. But he'd never meant to do this!

When she got home from Tahoe and found out he hadn't come home yet, she wouldn't be angry. She'd cry instead, and be frightened. It might even hurt the baby. This was all his fault. Eric hadn't wanted to come. His parents would be frightened, too.

Ben's eyes stung. He wished Cutty were here. He'd been praying a lot.

Exhausted from being in the same position for so long, he let his head fall against Eric's. Just as he closed his eyes, something woke him up.

It was like a vibration in his skull. He shook his head, then started to close his eyes again when he felt the same sensation, only stronger this time. Suddenly he thought he heard a whirring sound. A few seconds later came a kind of whipping noise. There was no doubt about it. Something was out there and getting closer. His heart leaped.

"Hey, Eric? You h-hear that?" He shook his friend's shoulders. "That's a helicopter! Someone's out h-here looking for us!"

"Yeah-h-h," Eric muttered faintly. "D-do y-you s-see it?"

"Not y-yet."

"ANY SIGN OF MOVEMENT?" Josh asked from his seat at the controls.

One of the crew members operated the spotlight while the other searched for the boys with high-powered binoculars.

"No. Looking for a needle in a haystack is nothing compared to finding someone along these ledges at night. There are too many crevices in shadow."

"We'll fly in closer so the beam can penetrate."

He dipped lower and followed the river upstream, where the boys might have tried to fish.

Josh took in the savage splendor as the light reflected the treacherous, rocky slabs that overhung the river. Darkness added its own terrible majesty. He could only imagine how traumatized the boys must be if they were still out here, at the mercy of nature in its most primitive setting.

He switched on the electronic speaker system, which would amplify his voice. "Ben? Eric? If you're out there, wave your arms so we can see you." He repeated this for the next five minutes as they systematically covered each section of rock.

"There they are!" the spotter informed them. Josh saw the boys at the same time. Ben was on his feet, waving his jacket over his head. Eric lay on his back, but he was trying to wave. They were all right!

"Hi, boys! We'll have you safe inside the helicopter before you know it. We're going to lower a basket for Eric first. Just hold on!"

For the next few minutes, Josh held his breath because it appeared that Ben was having difficulty getting Eric in position to be lifted. Both boys must be frozen to the bone. Finally Ben yelled ready, and they were able to bring him up.

"Th-thanks. I—I'm s-sure g-glad you g-guys c-came," Josh heard Eric say as one of the crew made him comfortable in back.

"We're glad you're okay, Eric. Tell me where you hurt."

While the helicopter hovered, down went the basket again. The wait wasn't nearly as long this time. When they pulled Ben inside and shut the door, Josh looked over his shoulder. Seeing both boys safe had to be the high point of his life. It made all his years of training worth it because they'd led to this one defining moment.

"Hi, sport!"

"Josh!" Ben cried out when he saw him at the controls. His eyes rounded in shock. "I didn't know y-you c-could fly a helicopter! You s-saved us!" Tears gushed down his pale cheeks. "I knew you'd c-come! I—I knew it!"

The boy's faith in him humbled Josh. "Kim told us where to find you."

Ben could still smile through the tears. "D-didn't I t-tell you, E-Eric?"

"Y-yeah."

"All right. If everybody's ready, we're going home."

Satisfied the crew had taken over to give the boys lifesaving care, Josh headed the chopper toward South Lake Tahoe. When Josh had lost his partner, depression had made him wonder why his own life had been spared. But since he'd come to Moon Lake, that depression had lifted. Right now, he gave humble thanks that he was alive to perform this particular rescue operation.

WENDY CLUNG TO CAROL'S HAND. They'd been waiting in the Emergency reception area for over an hour, but there'd been no word of the boys. Every time an ambulance pulled up, the two of them rushed over to the doors to see who'd been brought in. The agony of not knowing was tearing them apart.

More than once Carol had voiced her fear that the

boys might never be found. Wendy refused to believe it. They *had* to be out there alive!

This was all her fault. If she hadn't gone out with Tom, none of this would have happened. It had been too soon after Matt's death for her to show interest in another man. In the attempt to prove to herself that Josh didn't mean anything to her, she'd pushed Ben too far. Because of his fragile emotional state, he'd done something that could have cost him his life.

"Steve!" Carol cried when she saw her husband come through the doors with the sheriff.

"They've been found, honey!" He hugged his wife hard, then pulled Wendy into his arms. "They're both safe. A helicopter's flying them in right now. They should be here any minute."

"Oh, thank heaven," Wendy murmured over and over again. She sagged against him, limp with joy. "Carol said Josh was with you. Where is he?"

"He said he wanted to stay at headquarters where the search crew takes off, in case they needed additional help."

That sounded like Josh.

"There's the helicopter now!"

The three of them ran to the doors to watch it land on the pad. Wendy felt light-headed as she held her breath, waiting for the first sight of her son. The ER attendants rushed out with the gurneys.

They brought Eric in, then Ben. The second the pad had been cleared, the helicopter lifted in the air, no doubt to go save another life. Wendy had wanted to thank the rescue crew, but they'd taken off too fast.

"Mom!" Ben cried when he saw her.

Her heart swelled with emotion. "Sweetheart," she cried through the tears. "Are you all right?"

"Yeah." He looked drawn and pale, but otherwise unhurt. "Eric's the one whose leg got broken."

"You can talk to your boy in a few minutes, Mrs. Sloan."

Wendy nodded, so thankful her son was home safe, so grateful for a hospital that could see to his needs. Carol felt the same way. Once more the two of them wept in each other's arms. Steve stood next to them, vainly attempting to wipe the tears off his own face.

When she could pull herself together, Wendy walked over to the courtesy phone to call Misty's house and let Kim know her brother was okay. Then she called the coffee shop to give Ada the good news. The older woman's relief was tangible. She had a special fondness for Ben, and it showed.

There was another person Wendy needed to talk to, ached to talk to. She had no idea if Josh would come to the hospital or not. He might consider it another invasion of her privacy.

Wendy *wanted* him to invade her privacy. She wanted to thank him for caring enough to help with the search. Since their talk over a month ago, he'd kept a professional distance from her and the children. She'd been paying for it ever since.

The doctor came out of the cubicle and approached her. "You can go in now. Your son has a light case of hypothermia, but we've caught it early and he's going to be fine. You can probably take him home in a couple of hours. We'll see how he does."

Overjoyed with the news, she pushed the curtain aside.

Ben flashed her a wan smile. An IV had been attached to the back of his hand. She rushed over to kiss his face. "I love you, Ben. Don't ever do this to me again. What would I have done if I'd lost you?"

"But you didn't, Mom."

"We have God to thank for that."

"Josh, too!"

"Josh?"

"Yeah! He flew the helicopter that found us. One of the crew told me all the pilots were out on other rescues. If Josh hadn't come when he did, n-no one would've been able to search for us till m-morning." Ben started to sob. "He's the best, Mom! He—he saved our lives."

Speechless, Wendy reached for her son. For a long time she simply held him while she pondered his words in her heart.

CHAPTER TEN

"GOODNIGHT, ADA."

Josh walked her and her husband to the front door of the coffee shop before he locked up and made his nightly rounds of the resort. The guests were all accounted for. Everything was quiet.

His thoughts flew back to the rescue. It had felt good to be at the controls again. But tonight when they'd pulled Ben inside the helicopter, Josh had achieved a moment of epiphany. Though he enjoyed his career in the FBI and had expected to stay in it permanently, nothing could compare to the life he was living now.

Harve didn't know what was on Josh's mind. The trouble was, until Josh had some idea of how Wendy felt about him, he didn't dare talk to his superior about the possibility of retiring from the department.

Before Tom Welch's appearance on the scene, Josh had worried that Wendy might never let go of her husband's memory. Yet her sudden about-face with the good doctor from Louisiana, a man she'd only known a few days, had seemed totally out of character. Naturally, she was free to date any man she wanted, but Josh had a gut feeling she wasn't really interested in Dr. Welch.

Of course, Josh's opinions were based on his own agenda and an unhealthy dose of jealousy. The fact that

Ben disliked the man too didn't help, because the boy was every bit as prejudiced as Josh.

The only way to find out if Wendy had used the doctor as a buffer against him was to let her know he'd broken up with his fiancée for good, then see how she reacted. Would she even believe him? Wendy appeared so convinced of his love for the fictional Lisa, she might not trust his words, not for a long time, anyway.

If he could tell her the truth now—that there was no fiancée and never had been—it would force her to be honest about her feelings. But maybe she wasn't ready for that yet. And, equally important, he and other agents might still be in danger. According to Harve, the agency was closing in on the man who'd put out the contract on him, but they weren't there yet.

By now Wendy would know he'd been at the controls of that helicopter. If he did tell her the truth about his career, he would need Harve's permission first. His superior would demand to know why. Even then, Josh doubted Harve would allow him to reveal anything more than his training as a pilot, unless Josh had incontrovertible proof of Wendy's interest in him.

Josh needed that proof, but how to get it? Hell. Everything had become so complicated...

Assuming Wendy would be at the hospital with Ben for the rest of the night, he decided to check on Cutty. He drove his truck to the house and let her outside for a while. They played with her red ball before he refilled her dishes on the back porch.

As he walked around the side of the house to the truck, he spotted the headlights of a car coming his way. A moment later, he could see it was the white Toyota. His heart slammed into his ribs.

Ben jumped out of the passenger side before his mother had turned off the ignition. "Josh!"

The boy started running toward him. Suddenly he felt Ben's arms go round his waist with surprising strength for a twelve-year-old who'd just survived a grueling ordeal.

"You saved us, Josh! You saved us!" On a half sob he blurted, "You're the greatest!"

"So are you! You helped your friend hang on. I'm proud of you. Come on," Josh said in a choked voice. "Let's get you in the house. It's long past your bedtime."

With the boy still clinging to him, Josh put an arm around his shoulders and helped him up the stairs to the porch. Wendy followed close behind. Josh needed to tread carefully, in every sense. Ben was her son. This was her home.

"Good night, sport. We'll talk in the morning."

"Can't you come in?"

He would like nothing more. "Not tonight. It's late and you need your sleep."

"Please, Mom."

"Josh's right, sweetheart. The doctor said to go straight to bed. We can all talk about this tomorrow."

"Okay." Ben hugged him once more, then went inside.

Josh inhaled sharply. "Wendy? Is there anything I can do for you before I turn in?"

"Yes." She sounded breathless. "Don't go anywhere for a minute. I'll be right back."

Josh spent the longest minute of his life on that front porch. But the waiting was worth it. When she finally emerged from the doorway, her tear-filled eyes went straight to his.

He could see her throat working. Emotion held her tight in its grip. He knew how she felt because he felt the same way.

"How do I thank you?" she whispered.

"Let's be grateful they're home safe."

"Josh, you can't just stand there and say that. Not to me." Her voice trembled. "Ben told me what you did. According to the crew, the pilots never fly above Moon Lake at night. It's too dangerous. They said you performed maneuvers with an expertise no one's ever seen around here before, and these pilots are some of the best. Who are you?"

"I learned to fly in the Navy." He knew he'd have to tell her that much.

She shook her head incredulously. "I thought you were a farmer."

"I am."

"You're much more than that. You saved Ben's life without giving any thought to your own. Oh, Josh—" She couldn't suppress a sob. First one, then another, until she was convulsed with weeping.

He knew he had no right to do what he was about to, but he couldn't hold back any longer.

"It's okay," he murmured as he pulled her into his arms.

She seemed to come willingly, but he refused to lie to himself. She needed a shoulder to cry on, nothing else. His was available.

"Ben's safe now. Don't think about it anymore."

For so long, his body had ached to hold her like this. Just hold her. Feel the softness of her hair, her sweet warmth, her fullness.

He rocked her back and forth until her tears were spent.

"I—I'm sorry," she said as she lifted her head and moved away from him. The moment of weakness had passed. The strong woman was in charge again, embarrassed by her lapse. "I don't usually go to pieces like this."

Josh smiled. "It isn't every night you live through an experience like this."

"Because of you, Eric survived this with nothing more than a broken ankle. I suppose you know you're his idol, too."

"It'll pass. Good night, Wendy. Please don't hesitate to phone me at the barn if you need any help with Ben."

Josh had to put as much distance as possible between them before he did something guaranteed to change their relationship. He couldn't chance ruining things now. He'd come too far for that.

WENDY WATCHED HIM get in his truck before she closed and locked the front door.

"It'll never pass," she whispered into the darkness.

Her son loved Josh. She would never have dreamed he could feel this way about another man after his father.

An old, familiar dread crept over her. How was Ben going to handle the loss when Josh went back to Ohio to be married? Despite their grief at Matt's death, there had been a finality. They had mourned him and continued to mourn him. But Matt was gone.

Josh would still be alive somewhere, though, just out of reach. A telephone call away?

She could see troubles ahead that made her shudder. It was too late for regrets. Too late to wish she'd forced Ben to tell the stranger there was no job. Too late to turn back the clock two months or ten minutes.

Now she knew what it felt like to be held in Josh's arms.

She'd thought she was a stronger woman than that. She'd thought she was nobler.

But something so powerful had overcome her, she couldn't take that step away from him. Instead she'd remained there, silently begging him to hold her when she knew he belonged to someone else.

What made this even more humiliating was that he *knew* she knew. She was in charge, and Josh was her employee. She could always depend on him to perform the tasks expected of him, even if it meant comforting his pregnant boss.

From the moment Carol had told her the boys were missing, Wendy had looked around for Josh, wanting his strength to lean on. The whole time she'd been with Tom Welch, she'd wished she were back at the resort where she could see and talk to Josh.

Tonight's exhibition proved she had no shame. It also proved something else. Matt still lived in her heart, as an everlasting memory, as part of her life and the father of her children. But that same heart held a place for Josh, too. Caring for Josh, feeling attracted to him, didn't mean she was betraying Matt.

And she was attracted to him, oh yes. She worried about the way she looked, about what she'd wear. It was absolutely ludicrous to feel like this when Josh was engaged to Lisa.

Since she'd talked to his fiancée on the phone, the woman had taken on substance, become real. Hearing her voice should have helped Wendy dismiss the thoughts she'd been having about Josh. Instead—to her shock—Lisa's phone call had brought out an unprecedented streak of jealousy in her.

She'd never suspected she could feel this possessive about anyone except her own children. His fiancée's intrusion had brought out a primitive side of Wendy's nature. Part of her had wanted to tell Lisa she'd lost Josh by default. What was the old saying? Possession was nine-tenths of the law?

But there was one glaring flaw in that argument. No matter how many fantasies Wendy might entertain about him, he loved his fiancée or he would never have become engaged to her in the first place.

Wendy had learned enough about Josh to realize that when he made a commitment to something or someone, he did it all the way. If there were problems, he'd deal with them because that was his nature. Since his accident, he and Lisa had gone through a hard time, but Wendy knew they would survive it.

Would *she* survive it? That was the big question.

Who would have dreamed a man like Josh—a man as wonderful as Matt, yet completely different—would come into her life this soon? Both men were remarkable. Unforgettable.

She couldn't help an anguished laugh. She was going to have to let go of Josh. She had no choice in the matter, since he was engaged to someone else. More importantly, in less than thirty days her baby would make its presence known and become the focus of her world.

Feeling suddenly weary, she climbed into bed and pulled the covers up to her chin.

It might be a good idea if she started concentrating on preparations for the baby first thing in the morning. The decision to open the cabins had taken her attention away from the baby. But with Josh in charge and willing to find someone to replace him before he left, everything was running smoothly.

Under the circumstances, it was time to take charge of her family again.

While she made a mental list of things to be done, she heard noises in the hall. Soon Cutty and Ben had come into her room.

"Mom?"

"Hi, sweetheart. Did you have a bad dream?"

"No. I can't go to sleep."

"Well, get into bed with me."

He slid under the covers. Cutty jumped up on the bed and deposited herself at Ben's feet.

Wendy leaned over to give her son a kiss. "You've lived through a frightening experience. I'm not surprised you're still awake."

"Mom? Could we have a surprise party for Josh?"

She groaned inwardly.

"Could we? Please?" he prodded. "Eric phoned me while you were outside with Josh. It's the Memorial Day weekend, and we don't have school until next Tuesday, so we thought Monday night after dinner would be a perfect time. We'll decorate the coffee shop and do all the work. Mrs. Irvine said she'd help us. You won't have to lift a finger."

Taking a deep breath, she said, "I think a party would be nice, but we can't do it until school's out for the summer."

"Why?"

"Because tomorrow we're driving to Sacramento and staying for the long weekend."

Ben shot up in bed, "How come?"

"Do you remember that house a couple of blocks from Grandma's? The one with the fenced-in yard?"

"Yeah?"

"That's the house we're going to live in. Tomorrow I'm getting the keys and we'll start fixing up a nursery for the baby. We need to pick out a crib and a chest of drawers to be delivered. There's a lot to be done."

"I don't want to live in Sacramento!"

She fought for control. "Sometimes we have to do things we don't want to."

"But Josh is running everything now, so we don't have to leave."

"He's only going to be here until he trains someone else to take his place."

"Did he tell you that?"

His question was so alarming, she raised herself to a sitting position. Staring at her son in the darkness, she said, "Ben, I think you've forgotten something. I'm in charge of this household, not you. As the head of this family, I have to make the decisions I feel are best for all of us."

"I wish Josh were my dad."

"But he's not!" she countered in a firm voice. "For one thing, you have a wonderful father—Matt didn't stop being your dad when he died, you know. For another, we're moving to California. He, on the other hand, is getting married and will eventually raise a family of his own. You *must* get over your attachment to him!"

"How come you hate him so much?"

"Sweetheart—" she cried out, aghast. "How can you ask me a question like that? He's a good, kind person. He saved your life. I could never hate him."

"Then how come you're making him leave?"

"It's not a case of making him do anything! We have to sell Moon Lake. He needed something to occupy his time while his leg healed. But he always intended to go back home and marry his fiancée."

"He said he might not."

She shook her head. "Ben, wishful thinking on your part isn't going to change the situation."

"I'm not making it up, Mom! He told me that when I called him from Aunt Jane's house."

Wendy was absolutely stunned by this revelation. "You called Josh while we were in Sacramento?"

"Yeah."

"Why?"

"Because you said Josh was probably leaving that weekend to go back to Ohio. Kim and I wanted to know if it was true. But he said he and Lisa were having serious problems, and they wouldn't be getting married unless they worked them out."

Now she understood their sudden change in behavior. "That was none of your business, Ben. I can't believe you called him, let alone from Aunt Jane's house. You didn't have permission, and you know how much long distance costs."

"Kim and I are going to pay her with our allowance as soon as Craig tells us how much the bill is."

"So you involved your sister and your cousin in this, too."

His sheepish look confirmed it.

Her son was out of control where Josh was concerned. After tonight's heroic rescue, there was no telling where all this would end. That settled it; they were moving to Sacramento as soon as possible.

She lay down once more, wishing to God Matt was still there. She couldn't handle this.

"Mom?" Ben asked in a tremulous voice.

"What is it?"

"Are you going to visit Dr. Welch after the baby's born?"

Oh, Ben. "No."

"That's good. Jimmy was really nice, but I didn't like Dr. Welch. Josh didn't like him, either."

She bit her lip. "How do you know that?"

"Because he told me I should go to dinner with you. He said with the baby coming, Kim and I need to look after you because family has to help each other. I figured that meant Josh didn't trust him."

Her eyes closed tightly. "How did you happen to talk to Josh about that?"

After a slight hesitation, Ben confessed. "I called him on his cell phone. You said I could if there was an emergency."

In her son's eyes, her going out with Tom again must have constituted one. So much had gone on behind her back—all of it at Ben's instigation.

"Mom?"

What next? "Yes?"

"If Josh does get married, do you think he'll let me stay on his farm with him sometimes?"

Her breath caught, and it was a moment before she could answer. "If, one day in the distant future, he should invite you, then we'd talk about it. But if I hear that you brought up the subject to him—" She swallowed hard. "I want your promise that you'll never mention it to him. Not ever!"

He gave a deep sigh. "I promise. But I love him, Mom."

I know you do.

"I couldn't believe it when I saw him flying the helicopter. He's so awesome."

You don't need to tell me that, sweetheart.

Hot tears ran out of the corners of her eyes. She buried her face in the pillow to stifle any sound. It was going to be a long night, what was left of it.

True to her fears, she tossed and turned, periodically checking the clock. Finally at six, she slipped out of bed, where Ben was still sleeping soundly, and took a shower. After arranging her hair in a knot, she dressed in leggings and a smock top, then packed an overnight bag for herself and the children.

There was one more thing to do before she awakened Ben and drove over to Misty's house to pick up Kim. She needed to talk to Josh. But when she called him on his cell phone, he didn't answer.

She tried several times, worried that he might be sick with the same virus that had put her to bed. Or worse, he might have injured his leg again during the rescue; maybe he was sleeping off the effects of his pain medication.

Whatever the reason, she wouldn't be going anywhere until she'd spoken to him. The only thing she could do was drive out to the barn and make sure he was all right.

"JOSH? ARE YOU IN THERE? Josh?"

Wendy's voice sounded from a long way off. It was all part of the dream he'd been having. He never wanted it to end. Rolling over on his stomach, he relived holding her in his arms. Her hair smelled like flowers, enticing him to sift it through his fingers. Then he started caressing her, and could hear little satisfied sounds that delighted him.

"Josh? Josh—"

Something was wrong. Suddenly there was panic in her voice. He came awake with a start.

"Josh? Are you ill?"

He raised his head in time to see her anxious face appear above the floor of the loft.

Good heavens—she'd climbed up the ladder!

"Don't move, Wendy!"

Forgetting his leg, he leaped from the cot and raced over to the edge. Terrified she might fall, he put his hands under her arms and lifted her high above the floor until he could gather her against his chest.

Still holding her tightly he muttered into her silky hair, "Whatever possessed you to climb that ladder? Don't you know how unstable it is? What if you'd fallen?"

"I—I was worried about you. You didn't answer your phone. When I drove out to the barn and saw the truck, I knew you were here, but you still didn't answer me. I was afraid you were sick...."

At first his trembling had been caused by fear for her safety. But now that she was here in his arms, her heart pounding against his, the trembling could be attributed to something else entirely.

"You can put me down now, Josh. Holding me probably isn't good for your leg."

What leg? Right now he was feeling so great, he couldn't bear the thought of letting her go.

Though her legs were encased by leggings, he could feel their warmth through his sweats. The hard mound of her belly pressed into his stomach. That was when he felt a series of tiny jabs.

"Was that the baby?" he cried out in surprise.

"Yes. It's been active all morning."

Without conscious thought he splayed his hand across her back to bring her even closer to him. Feeling the baby's movements was the most incredible sensation he'd ever experienced. The three of them were locked together like one living entity.

"Does it ever hurt you?"

"N-not really. Oh, maybe sometimes when I'm in the wrong position, the baby will react with a little poke."

"It's…miraculous."

"It is." Her voice trailed off. "You'd better let me go now, or I'm afraid you're the one who'll end up in the hospital."

"Not yet—let me have another minute to feel that little guy."

"You think it's a boy, then?" She sounded out of breath.

He smiled against her hot cheek. "I have no idea, but if I were a betting man, I'd say yes."

The baby pummeled him several more times. "I believe he knows I'm holding you captive."

"Josh," she blurted. "Please put me down before your leg buckles under you."

"If my leg was going to do that, we'd both be on the floor by now."

"I'm too heavy!"

"You're just right," he assured her before he finally took pity and lowered her to the ground.

She immediately backed away from him, red-faced. He watched her look around the loft. No doubt she was disgusted by the sight of his clothes and personal belongings lying about in various piles. Luckily his weapon remained hidden inside his suitcase.

Her head swung back. She lifted her gaze to his. "Where's your phone?"

He liked the way she'd swept her hair on top of her head. She looked beautiful no matter how she arranged it. This morning the green of her eyes mesmerized him.

"Steve borrowed it last night and forgot to return it to me."

"I see." She seemed at a loss for words. "I'm sorry to have awakened you."

"No problem. I'm normally up by now. For some reason, I slept in."

"After last night's rescue, you should be able to take your Sunday off and do exactly what you want."

"I wouldn't know what to do with myself. Now, tell me why you tried to phone me."

"In case you couldn't find me later, I wanted you to know I'm leaving for Sacramento with the children. I'm going to rent a house I've seen and start fixing up a nursery. We'll be back late tomorrow night."

Josh's euphoria vanished. "You're renting a place this soon?"

"Yes. I didn't go into labor early with the other two, but there's always a first time. I guess I'm getting into the nesting mode. I'll feel better if our new home's in order before the baby comes."

He didn't believe a word of her explanation. She was running away again.

Was it because she was attracted to him and felt guilty, since she thought he was in love with another woman?

Josh wanted to believe that. But there was also the very real possibility that she missed her husband too much to cope with the memories here at Moon Lake.

"When do you plan to make the actual move?"

"After school's out for the summer."

"How soon is that?"

"June fifth."

Only six days from now.

"Do you have an offer on the resort already?"

"There's been one my Realtor says looks promising. It's the Majestic Hotel chain."

Josh frowned. "They'll do a complete renovation of this place. Standardize it—like all their other resorts. It'll lose its charm."

"I know." The poignancy of her response told him how much that bothered her. "But if they can give me a good price, it'll be worth it so I can stay home and raise my children."

"I would've given anything to have known my mother," he said quietly. "Your children are very blessed. You can count on my help when you get ready to pack things up."

She didn't respond to that. "I'd better be going."

He didn't want her to leave, but there was no way to stop her. "I'll steady the ladder while you go down."

She thanked him again before lowering herself onto the rungs. He held his breath until she reached the floor of the barn. Despite her advanced pregnancy, she moved with surprising agility. Once she was down, he made his descent and followed her out to her car.

The sun had come up over the horizon, promising a warm, beautiful day. But for Josh, the joy had gone out of it.

When she'd climbed into her car, she lowered the window, squinting up at him in the strong sunlight. "Please don't think that because I'm moving, I'm leaving everything for you to handle. Nothing could be further from the truth. Sacramento is only a two-hour drive, and I'll probably come up every few days before the baby's born to do office work.''

''Don't you think a four-hour commute several times a week is too ambitious for a woman this close to delivery?''

She shrugged. ''Maybe the place will change hands before the end of June. Until then, I certainly don't expect you to do my work *and* yours.''

''I asked for the job, remember?''

She wouldn't meet his eyes. ''You got a lot more than you bargained for.''

''I'm not complaining.''

''You never do. When the place sells, I plan to pay you. It won't be what you're worth, but I don't want you to think I've taken advantage of your good nature.''

''We made a bargain. I wouldn't dream of accepting your money.''

Her face closed. ''Then consider it a wedding present from the Sloan family.''

''You'd be wasting a check.'' The fact that she continually mentioned his forthcoming marriage gave him hope....

''If you won't take money, then I hope you won't say no to a party we're planning in your honor. Carol and Steve wanted to do it tomorrow night, but we'll have to put it off until next Saturday. If that's all right with you,'' she added quietly.

''A party sounds like fun. I'll be there.'' In fact it would be the perfect opportunity to do something that was going to drastically alter the situation between him and Wendy.

It was time for a heart-to-heart with Harve.

"Josh?" There were tears in her eyes. "Thank you again for saving the boys last night. When I think what might have happ—"

"But it didn't," he broke in.

"Only because you had the courage to fly up there when no one else would do it."

"No one else was available."

"Even if there'd been someone, he wouldn't have gone out before morning. It's the most rugged terrain around Tahoe. I've hiked up there—I know how treacherous it is.

"After losing Matt, I don't think I could have handled losing Ben, too. I'll always be so grateful to you," she whispered.

Josh almost groaned. He didn't want her gratitude. "You wouldn't have lost him. If I know Ben, he would've hiked out of there this morning to get help for Eric."

"Maybe. If he hadn't died of hypothermia first."

"At this time of year, I don't think that would have happened. But it's all a moot point because he's home and safe."

She nodded, then wiped her eyes with the back of her hand. "I hope you didn't hurt your leg this morning. I'd feel terrible if you'd injured it again because of me."

Wendy left him in a constant state of confusion. One minute she mentioned her husband. In the next instant, her conversation shifted back to the two of them and the intimacy they'd shared in the loft. If he didn't have answers about her true feelings soon, he knew he was going to blow sky-high.

"To be honest, I haven't thought about my leg. It

feels fine, which means no harm was done. Don't worry about it anymore.''

''I hope you're telling me the truth.''

You'd better leave now, or I won't be responsible for the consequences.

''If there was something wrong, I'd ask you to put off going to Sacramento and drive me to a doctor instead. Believe me, I want to be a hundred-percent recovered as soon as possible.''

''I'm sure Lisa's praying for that, too.''

If Wendy thought he was going to respond to that comment, then she had another think coming.

''Drive carefully.''

After a tense silence, she said, ''I will. See you on Tuesday. My sister's phone number is on that list in the office. Call me if an emergency arises.''

What if one doesn't? What if I call you for the hell of it?

''Will do.''

Unable to stand watching her drive away, he walked back inside the barn. As soon as he got dressed, he had a phone call to make. He was going to have that chat with Harve.

CHAPTER ELEVEN

"HURRY UP, MOM!" Ben called from the front room. "We're going to be late! I bet everyone's at the coffee shop already."

"We'll be right there. Kim, sweetheart—is my slip showing?"

Her daughter walked around her. "No. That dress is pretty, Mom."

"Thank you. I decided to get something new for the party while I was shopping for baby clothes in Sacramento."

Jane had insisted that the dressy black crepe with the cap sleeves provided the perfect foil for her sister's blond hair. Wendy had brushed her hair until it shone; she'd even worn makeup.

There was only one reason she'd gone to all this trouble. Only one man could have prompted her to want to look her best tonight. But it was so futile, so hopeless.

These idyllic days with Josh were numbered. The time was fast approaching when she'd have to say goodbye and wish him well in his future life.

The two days she'd spent in Sacramento away from him had been pure agony. Though she'd accomplished what she'd set out to do and had taken possession of the home they would live in, she'd counted the seconds until she could return to the resort. It was all because of Josh. She couldn't really fathom the idea that soon he'd be gone for good.

Since those breathless moments in the loft when he'd held her against him, her body had come alive in a way that had nothing to do with her pregnancy.

She wanted Josh.

She desired him, and that feeling had never gone away. Twice now, she'd felt the strong beat of his heart against hers. But those memories weren't enough. The longing to be closer to him had grown into a fire that seemed to burn hotter and more furiously. She had no idea how to put it out.

Heaven help her, but she didn't *want* it put out. She yearned to be consumed by it.

Wendy had only known intimacy with her husband. She'd never even considered the possibility of being with another man, of sharing that passion with anyone but Matt. When she'd lost him, she'd thought there could be no pain to compare to it.

That was before she'd met Josh. He had changed her. The way he talked, moved, smiled, laughed. Everything about him appealed to her so strongly, she felt she'd never be able to get enough of him. When he left, she'd be plunged into a world of pain once again. Only this time, it would be even worse, because Josh would still be alive, still within reach. Just not with her. She had no right to feel the way she did, and yet...

"Mom! What's taking you so long?"

Ben's voice jerked her back to the present. "Come on, sweetheart." She ushered Kim from the room. Ben held the front door open for them.

"Stay, Cutty." The dog sat back and watched them file out.

Wendy stepped into the balmy night air. Its softness

was intoxicating, full of hope and promise. As they walked toward the restaurant, she could feel the throb of her heart clear through to the palms of her hands.

"You should see how cool the coffee shop looks, Mom. Since Josh was in the Navy, we decorated everything in blue-and-white streamers."

"I'm sure he'll appreciate that."

"Uh-oh. We forgot his present! I'll run back for it."

"It's in the office, all wrapped," Wendy assured him.

While Carol and Steve had taken care of the food and decorations for the party, Wendy had insisted on buying the gifts and supplying a sheet cake with a helicopter motif.

In Sacramento she'd bought some little trophies marked "Hero" to give Josh and the rescue crew who'd flown with him. After searching high and low, she found a bomber-style jacket in brushed, dark-brown suede, the exact color of his hair. It had immediately reminded her of Josh. She couldn't wait to see him put it on. She couldn't wait to see him, period.

Feeling almost sick with excitement, she entered the restaurant behind her children. The place had filled up with neighbors and friends. There were a few faces she didn't recognize, most likely the rescue crew who'd accompanied Josh.

Steve Irvine stood talking to the sheriff and some of his deputies, who'd managed to make an appearance. They were dressed in uniform, which meant they were on duty and might have to leave at any time.

From her position at the buffet table, Carol waved to Wendy. Earlier they'd agreed to set it up in the center of the room, where guests could easily help themselves to drinks, along with barbecued ribs, potatoes au gratin and various salads. Wendy would bring out the cake later.

She nodded to her friend, but she could barely concentrate because she was avidly searching for their guest of honor.

Kim tugged on her hand. "Where's Josh?"

"Yeah. He's late!" Ben and Eric echoed.

"He had a lot of work to do today and probably started to get ready at the last minute. I'm sure he'll be here soon."

"We'll go get him."

"No, Ben! Why don't you guys grab yourselves a soda while we're waiting?"

"Okay."

Eric hobbled after Ben on his crutches. Not so many months ago, Josh had been hampered by a cast, too. But now he walked around the property as if he were good as new. Thank goodness he hadn't injured himself when he'd plucked her from that ladder!

Too many times she had relived the experience of being gathered against his chest. Somehow she'd managed to keep her hands from straying. But if she were ever to find herself in that position again, she doubted she'd be able to display the same self-control. And if he—

"There he is!" Ben suddenly cried out.

Wendy heard her son's voice before a roar of welcome amid cheers and clapping resounded in the dining room. She opened her eyes in time to see Josh enter through the front of the restaurant. It struck her as odd that he'd come in from that direction. But she was too distracted to analyze why.

In a bottle-green silk dress shirt and beige chinos,

his looks went beyond handsome. She could only stand there and stare.

He scanned the crowd until he saw Wendy. Then he nodded in that quiet way she'd come to recognize as his private greeting for her. His mouth curved upward. She could hardly breathe.

Slowly she smiled back at him, helpless to do otherwise. For a brief moment it felt as if there was no one else in the room.

Until she saw a tall, slender, sophisticated-looking brunette in an ice-blue linen suit. The woman came up behind him and put her arm through his. She knew he would accept that proprietary gesture only from someone to whom he had given the right.

His fiancée.

Wendy felt simultaneously hot and cold. She was dizzy and disoriented and thought she might faint.

Josh raised his free hand to quiet the crowd. "You guys know how to make a man feel good. But before this goes any further, let me introduce my fiancée, Lisa Delvie, from Ohio. I told her you were planning a party. She decided to surprise me and show up for it."

More shouting and clapping ensued as she was welcomed by the crowd, but Wendy clung to the nearest chair for support. When she saw Ben rush toward the kitchen, white-faced, she didn't need to ask what was wrong. She hurried after him with Kim in close pursuit.

By the time she caught up with him in the hallway leading to the back door, both her children were in tears.

She put her arms around their shoulders and hugged them to her, praying for a little inspiration. "I know why you're upset," she said urgently, "but you can't let Josh see how you feel."

Ben's head reared back, revealing the pallor of his face. It glistened with moisture. "How come *she* had to show up and...and wreck everything?"

"Because they love each other."

"I love him more!" Ben shouted.

"So do I!" Kim wept openly.

"If you both love him that much, you have to put his happiness above your own. That's what true love is all about." Wendy's voice trembled. She was speaking to herself now.

Ben shook his head. "I hate her for taking him away from us. She's ruined everything. I can't go back in there!"

Please God. Help me.

"What if Josh had said that the night he found out you were on Moon Lake Mountain? What if he'd said, 'I can't fly up there tonight. I just can't.'?"

Ben blinked. It meant he was half listening.

"Of course we know he didn't do that, don't we? He called for a helicopter and took off without any thought for his own safety. When no one else would dare go looking for you in the dark, he flew at his own peril to bring you and Eric back home." Tears had caused her throat to close up. She swallowed hard.

"Now you owe it to Josh to go out there and show him how grateful you are for everything he did for you, for this family."

She watched her children look at each other, then Kim's glance shifted to Wendy. "Do you think he's going back to Ohio soon?"

Suddenly the floor creaked behind them. Wendy gasped when she turned and saw Josh.

There was enough light in the hall for him to see that all three of them had been crying. She couldn't help wondering how long he'd stood there, how much he'd heard.

He reached for Kim and picked her up. "I'm not going anywhere, honey. Your mother and I have an agreement. I'll be running this place all summer."

"But you could change your mind," Ben mumbled, scraping his toe against the floor. "*She* might want you to leave."

They all knew who "she" was.

"Let's not worry about that right now. There's a great party going on in the other room. How about you kids rejoin it? Nobody's going to have any fun if you're not there. Eric and Misty told me to come and get you."

"Okay." Her biddable Kim kissed his cheek before he lowered her to the floor. After a slight hesitation, Ben brushed past them and hurried on ahead of his sister. That left Wendy alone with Josh.

He stood too close to her. She couldn't look at him.

"You warned me about the children's attachment. I'm sorry Lisa's unexpected arrival upset them so much."

Wendy struggled for breath. "You don't need to apologize for anything. To be honest, I'm glad she came. They needed a wake-up call. Now they can't deny her existence any longer." She attempted a smile. "Y-you must have been thrilled to see her after all this time. When did she get here?"

"About two hours ago. She drove a rental from the airport. Ross gave her directions to the barn."

The barn...

Images of being in the loft with him flashed through Wendy's mind.

Had Lisa climbed that ladder, too? No doubt their

passionate reunion was the reason Josh had been late for his own party.

She trembled. It *would* have been passionate. That was the way he was, about everything.

Oh, Josh—

"I'd better get out there and help."

"It's a wonderful party," he said in a husky voice. "I'm very touched by all the trouble you've gone to."

"Steve and Carol did most of the work."

"Hmm." He raised his eyebrows. "That's not what they said. It was very thoughtful of you to invite the members of the rescue crew," he added.

"We wouldn't have dreamed of leaving them out. They risked their lives, too."

"Wendy...I'm sorry if Lisa's appearance has caused you any turmoil."

"Of course it hasn't!" Her outburst sounded shrill, even to her own ears. She forced herself to go on. "I'm very anxious to meet her. You know, I expected her to show up weeks before now," she blurted, dying a little more with every word. "You should hurry back to the dining room before she comes looking for you. I'll join you as soon as I've visited the ladies'."

She disappeared so fast, Josh didn't have time to blink. But it didn't matter. He'd caught her in tears along with the children. He had the answer he'd been waiting for.

He felt as if he'd just been reborn.

As soon as he reached the dining room, he piled a plate with food, then sidled up to Agent Lisa Wood. "Mission accomplished," he whispered.

"I would say so," she whispered back. "I had my eyes on her the whole time. The second I took your arm, her face went white as parchment. That isn't something a person can fake.''

''No, thank God. She'll be back in a minute expecting introduction.''

''I know how it feels to be in love. I'll go easy on her, Josh.''

''I appreciate that. Be as noncommittal as possible. After you leave, I'll tell her we decided to break our engagement.''

''Since you trust her, why not tell her everything?''

''Because she's too near her due date for any big surprises. In a week or two, there probably won't be any reason to worry about that contract out on me, but telling Wendy about it could frighten her. Maybe even send her into early labor.''

''I suppose…''

''That's why I'm not taking any chances. Harve and I talked it over. After the baby arrives, I'll come clean with the details. At that point I'm sure I won't have to be undercover anymore. If she's willing to marry me, I'll retire from the Bureau. Until then, I intend to convince her that you and I could never have made a marriage work.''

''You don't think?'' She winked.

''Not when you're happily married to Frank.''

''I almost forgot about him.''

''I'll bet you did.'' He chuckled.

''Uh-oh. There she is.''

Josh's gaze darted to the swinging door. Wendy had walked through it carrying some presents she put on a table near Steve. Then he watched her start toward them with that determined look he recognized so well. All trace of her tears had vanished. The duty smile she wore on occasion was set in place.

She worked her way through the crowd, and with every step that brought her closer, he felt his pulse race triple-time.

"She's being very brave," Lisa said softly.

Josh's mouth twitched. "I noticed."

"Okay, you two lovebirds!" Steve suddenly spoke over a microphone the Irvines had brought for the festivities. "Lisa? If you could let Josh go for a minute, we'd like him and the other members of the rescue team to step up to the mike."

Everyone began to clap. On the periphery he saw Wendy hesitate, then search for her daughter. She grabbed Kim and seemed to be holding on for dear life.

Josh shook hands with the two other men who'd gathered near Steve.

"You've all heard the story of Ben and Eric's misguided adventure on Moon Lake Mountain. You all know the outcome." Steve's voice sounded unsteady. "If it hadn't been for these guys here, we don't know if the story would have ended as happily.

"Ben? Why don't you come up and give these guys a token of our appreciation?"

"Sure."

A sober-faced Ben handed the three smaller packages around, shaking each man's hand. Josh tried to get a smile out of the boy, but Ben purposely avoided looking at him.

In a few seconds, all three men lifted their trophies high in the air. They thanked the crowd while several cameras flashed, and more clapping ensued.

"Wendy?" Steve spoke once more. "I believe you have something else to present?"

Josh watched her urge Kim forward. As he waited

for a beaming Kim to approach and hand him the bigger present, he wished he could proclaim to the world that she was *his* little girl.

"This is for you, Josh."

"Will you hold my trophy for me?"

She nodded as he gave her the trophy before taking the other gift from her.

"We hope you like it," she said solemnly. "Thanks for flying the helicopter."

Unable to help himself, Josh leaned over to kiss her cheek.

"You're a hero," she whispered, kissing him back. "I love you, Josh."

Her gentle peck reduced him to tears. Eric chose that moment to approach on his crutches and shake all their hands.

It was providential that Josh had to open the present. It gave him something to do while he pulled himself together.

When he slipped off the box lid, he saw an expensive-looking brown bomber jacket folded inside the tissue. He could guess who'd picked it out. The size and color were perfect.

Without wasting another second, he shrugged into it, then with a grin raised his head to face the crowd. "I like it! What do you think?" But his eyes were on Wendy.

While everyone clapped and whistled, she stared at him unsmilingly, then disappeared into the kitchen.

Steve reached for the mike again. "We can't forget to thank the sheriff and his deputies, who assisted us in the search. Let's give them a round of applause."

Josh clapped hard, along with everyone else. When the din subsided, Steve said, "While Wendy's bringing out the cake, let's all sing, 'For they are jolly good fellows'!''

The party mood had taken hold and voices lifted in song. Josh decided he'd better rejoin Lisa.

She eyed him narrowly. "Mrs. Sloan has exquisite taste. If you could've had a peek at that present ahead of time, you wouldn't have needed me to tell you something that's perfectly clear."

"You know me. I like every dot connected."

"Don't we all," she murmured wryly. "Speaking of connection, here she comes bearing more gifts."

Josh turned in time to see Wendy closing in on them with their desserts. "That jacket looks good on you, Josh."

He gazed into her eyes, then took a bite of cake. "I've always wanted one like this. Thank you, more than I can say."

"You're welcome."

She gazed back without flinching. It reminded him of the first day he'd come to work for her, when she'd looked at him so impersonally. They'd come a long way since then.

"How about introducing me to your fiancée?" she asked. "Of course we've already met over the phone, but it's not quite the same thing."

She handed Lisa her dessert.

"It would be my pleasure. Lisa Delvie, I'd like to formally introduce you to Wendy Sloan, the nicest employer a person could ask for."

Wendy shook her shimmering blond head. "Don't let him fool you, Lisa. I'm a slave-driver. Ask my children and they'll tell you. It's very nice to meet you after all this time."

"Nice to meet you, too," Agent Wood responded

with a friendly smile. They shook hands. "Josh has had nothing but praise for you and your family. This has been the best place in the world for him to recuperate. The way he walks now, you'd never know he'd hurt his leg."

"I didn't see him after his accident, but I can tell he's improved a lot since he first came here. I can also report he's been faithful about visiting his therapist. You must be very gratified at his progress."

Wendy, Wendy—your acting ability rivals Henry's.

"Oh, yes." Lisa had incorporated the appropriate amount of suffering in her tone. "I'll be able to leave tomorrow with the assurance that he's in good hands."

Wendy's stunned expression satisfied something deep inside Josh. "But you just got here!"

"True. However, I really shouldn't have come. My boss thinks I'm on a flight to Paris. But when Josh told me about this party, I decided to take a detour and surprise him before I left for my next assignment."

Wendy turned to Josh. She spoke in a clear, careful voice, her face expressionless. "If that's the case, then you two don't have much time together. Please feel free to leave. Everyone will understand."

"You see what I told you?" Josh murmured to Lisa, but he said it loudly enough for Wendy to hear. "I have the world's most understanding boss. Since I know you have a long flight ahead of you tomorrow, we probably should go now. Let me thank Carol and Steve, then we'll take off."

With Wendy's shocked face indelibly inscribed in his mind, he sought out the Irvines. After thanking them profusely, he went in search of Ben, but the boy was nowhere to be found. He must have gone off with Eric and the girls.

He shook a few more hands, then scanned the room one more time for Wendy. She, too, seemed to have disappeared.

He took Lisa's elbow and escorted her out of the restaurant. As soon as he felt the balmy night air on his face, he made a noise of contentment.

"Look at all those stars. Trillions and trillions of them. Have you ever seen a sky like that before? What a gorgeous night!"

"Too bad you can't spend it with her," Lisa murmured when they'd both climbed in the truck. "She's in agony, Josh. It's going to be a long night for her, knowing we're out at the barn."

"Can't be helped. I don't dare rush things. My broken engagement will have to come up naturally in conversation. And I won't be able to let her in on the real story until I have permission from Harve. Now let's talk shop."

"Not a good idea. I need a break. Besides, I've never seen you this happy before. Why spoil it? I've done you a favor, so you can do me one."

He started the engine. "What's that?"

"Take me to some shows. I've never seen any Nevada nightlife."

"Believe me, it's overrated. Why don't we compromise and see a movie instead?"

"Do you know what's playing?"

"I don't have a clue."

"Let's find a newspaper. I wouldn't mind a romantic comedy."

"Sounds perfect."

WHILE WENDY COVERED the small portion of uneaten cake with foil, Kim wandered into the kitchen looking depressed. "Misty wants to sleep over at our house tonight."

"Don't you want her to? It's all right with me."

"I guess."

Half a minute later, her grim-faced son came into the kitchen. "Eric wants me to sleep at his house tonight, but I don't want to. Where's Josh?"

Wendy had been driving herself crazy asking the same question. Lisa was lovelier and nicer than she could have imagined. Much as she wanted to hate the other woman, she couldn't.

When she thought about the two of them together, the pictures that filled her mind tormented her so badly, she knew she'd never fall asleep tonight. It seemed her children had demons of their own to battle. Her heart ached for them.

"How long's she going to stay?" Ben asked next.

"Lisa said she'd be leaving for Paris tomorrow on another assignment," Wendy said as matter-of-factly as she could.

"Tomorrow she's going to be gone?" The joy in his voice needed no translation.

"That's what she said."

"All right! I've got to tell Eric. Can he sleep over at our house tonight—instead of me going over there?"

Why not? School was out for the summer. There wouldn't be too many more nights like this.

Within a few days, the moving van would cart everything off to Sacramento, signaling the end of an era.

Then a new version of hell would begin. No longer would she have Josh in her life. She contemplated the empty years without him and it made her feel physically sick.

"Wendy? We're leaving now."

She jerked her head around. "Good night, Carol. Thanks for everything."

"Thank you for letting us hold the party here. I'd say it was a great success. Josh looked happier than I've ever seen him. His fiancée seemed nice. Did you see that marquise diamond she was wearing? It was a pretty shape, wasn't it."

"Yes." Wendy didn't know how she managed to get the word out.

"We've cleaned up the dining room—it's ready for customers. Are you sure it's not too much for Eric to stay over tonight?"

"Heavens, no! I want the children to enjoy their friends as long as possible."

"Steve and I can't bear the thought of you leaving Moon Lake. It won't be the same around here without the Sloan family. We love all of you. Eric's been upset ever since he found out you were going to move."

"My children are still in denial about it. This is a hard time for all of us, but we'll make it through somehow."

"Wendy... I can't even imagine how you feel right now. If you need to talk—or if you need someone's shoulder to cry on—please call me. I'm here, day or night."

"You proved that when Matt died. Thank you, Carol. Your friendship means more to me than you'll ever know. I love all of you, too. Go home and relax. You've done enough. I'll talk to you tomorrow."

"I was going to tell you the same thing. You and the baby should have been in bed long before now."

"I know. I'm a mess."

"Actually I think you look beautiful."

"Then you must need glasses. I'm swollen, puffy,

hot all the time, and I walk bent over because my back aches.''

"I remember those days. Steve and I are still trying to decide if we want to go through that again.''

"Really?''

"Yes. Sometimes I get this feeling that there's one more to come. Steve says we'd be crazy when our daughter's on the verge of marriage. Can you imagine a child and a grandchild, all at the same time?''

"Stranger things have happened. Finding out I was pregnant with this one was the biggest surprise of my life!''

"You must feel so close to Matt these days. Uh-oh. I can hear my husband calling. See you tomorrow.''

Wendy swayed on her feet. She had to clutch the edge of the counter to prevent herself from falling.

Carol meant well, but she was so far off track, it was laughable. Matt might have made her pregnant, but he had died with no knowledge of it.

It was Josh who'd made her pregnancy seem real.

He acted more like a father-to-be than any man she'd ever known—including her husband. Josh was the one who'd felt her baby move and been thrilled by it. From the very beginning he'd hovered, always watching to make sure she didn't exert herself. Every time she came home from her doctor's appointment, Josh asked her about it.

He was always there when she needed him.

His curiosity about her condition delighted her. His protectiveness humbled her.

Only God knew her secret.

Since that moment in the loft, she would always think of this baby as Josh's.

Tears rolled down her cheeks. Lisa was the luckiest woman alive to be loved by him.

I've got to get over him. I have to.

After a long cry, she closed up and left the restaurant to go home. When she entered the house, she saw three kids and a dog lying on the floor in front of the TV watching *Back to the Future*. Eric lay in the easy chair with his leg propped up.

Wendy slipped into a nightgown and robe, then stretched out on the couch to watch the movie with them. Anything to take her mind off Josh.

As she reached behind her to switch off the lamp, she noticed the trophy sitting on the end table. Kim had brought it home for Josh. Wendy remained half-turned, unable to move as she stared at it.

"Mom? Are you all right?"

"Yes, Kim. I'm just tired."

"Josh says you work too hard."

Wendy closed her eyes. Once Josh had left for Ohio, she wondered how long it would take before his name was no longer the most used word in her children's vocabulary.

CHAPTER TWELVE

"Hɪ, Jᴏsʜ."

He had just swallowed his last bite of dinner. "Hi, honey. How's my favorite girl?"

Kim smiled. "I'm fine. Mom said to give you this. She was afraid it might get packed with all our things." She handed him his trophy.

"Thank you for taking care of it for me. Where are you off to in such a big hurry with that other present?"

"Hailey Clegg's birthday party."

"Do you need a ride?"

"No. Misty's mom is driving us."

"Next time, ask me. I enjoy feeling as if I'm part of your family."

"Mom says not to bother you 'cause you have too much work to do as it is."

"I like to be bothered by you guys. You know that, don't you?"

"Yes." She flashed him another sunny smile, so much like her mother's it made his heart leap.

"Where's Ben tonight?"

"At Scouts."

Thank you for the information, sweetheart. That's all I needed to hear.

He kissed her cheek. "Have a good time at the party."

"I will." She kissed him back, then ran to the restaurant doors.

Three days of waiting to find Wendy alone had tested his patience long enough. This morning he'd seen a truck from a local moving company in front of her house. He'd seen the movers stack dozens of packing boxes on her porch.

Since she refused to let an opportunity arise for them to talk privately, he'd have to create one. This was as good a time as any. With the kids out of school, maybe it'd be his only chance for a while.

He refused to wait any longer.

He took his dishes to the kitchen, praised Ada's cooking, then headed for Wendy's house. En route, he waved to several guests out for a walk. It was another glorious evening. The pungent smell of fresh pine brought all his senses to life.

He could barely recall the man who'd arrived here more than two months ago in a dispirited state, broken inside and out, grieving for his friend. Embittered by events he couldn't change.

He took the porch steps two at a time and realized he hadn't done that since before the shooting. Lately he never thought about his leg. It had stopped hurting. He hadn't been forced to take a pain pill in ages.

But his euphoric mood vanished when he discovered Wendy's front door wide open and the screen door unlatched. *Anyone* could walk in on her unannounced. Normally Cutty would be here to guard the house, but Ben had probably taken her with him.

One of the children must have gone off without locking up, and Wendy wasn't aware of it. Her car was parked by the garage, so he knew she was somewhere on the premises.

"Wendy?" He knocked on the screen door.

When there was no answer, he tried again. Finally he went back down the stairs and started around the side of the house.

"Wendy? Where are you?"

"Josh?"

She sounded surprised—which drove home the point that he was the last person she would have expected to drop in on her.

Out of the corner of his eye he saw her through the screening of the back porch.

"I had no idea you were here!" She paused. "Is there a problem you need to discuss with me?"

He had to make an effort to control his emotions. "Did you know your front door is wide open?"

"Yes." She looked puzzled. "I wanted to start packing the books in the front room and felt like some fresh air."

"Then what are you doing back here?"

"Trying to find the little stepladder so I can reach the top shelves of the bookcase."

He muttered a curse; he couldn't help it.   .

"Josh? What's wrong? Why are you upset?"

He took a deep breath. "I came to offer my help with the packing. When I couldn't rouse you and saw that your front door was open...naturally I was concerned about your safety."

"You worry too much about things like that, but I appreciate your thoughtfulness."

Thoughtfulness be damned!

"Obviously you've never lived through a bad experience," he said. "But it could happen, even in a place as quiet as Moon Lake."

"I realize that. But tonight's so beautiful...."

''Now that I'm here,'' he said brusquely, ''why not let me pull the books off those top shelves? You know as well as I do that your doctor wouldn't want you getting up on a stepladder for any reason.''

''Josh.'' She sounded impatient. ''When I hired you to help around here, the job description didn't include packing up my household. You work hard all day every day. I don't expect you to give up your nights, too.''

''Night's the worst time for having nothing to do. I like to stay busy. You'd be doing me a big favor.''

''Then why don't you go back to Ohio and be with your fiancée?'' she cried out. ''Lisa could see your leg's been healing perfectly. Yet you didn't seem to care that she was leaving again. It must have hurt her dreadfully. If I'd been in her shoes, I'd—''

''You would've what?'' he interjected softly.

''I-it's none of my business. I'm sorry I'm so outspoken.''

''Don't apologize. I want to hear. What would you have done in Lisa's place?''

After a long silence, she said, ''No matter how much pain was involved, I would've had it out with you once and for all. No one can go on living in that kind of limbo and survive for long. I-it would tear me apart. I honestly don't know how Lisa's stood it up till now.''

''As I told you earlier, we've had…certain problems to resolve.''

''But you can't resolve anything if you're never together!''

''Sometimes being apart crystallizes things for you.''
Every time you go to Sacramento, the sun disappears from my world.

''Love can't thrive under those conditions!''

''Lisa said the same thing.''

Josh heard Wendy's breath catch. He'd caught her off guard and decided to take advantage of it.

"That's why she flew here. To have it out with me once and for all, just like you said."

She leaned against the screen door. "Did you decide to get married right away? Because if you did, you know you can leave tomorrow. Ross and Jonathan will run things around here." She was talking faster and faster. "They both told me they want all the work they can get before college sta—"

"Wendy," he interrupted.

"Yes?" she whispered.

"Lisa decided she didn't want to wait until the doctor gave me a clean bill of health. She returned the ring before she got on the plane."

"What?"

In that one word, he heard every emotion driving her.

"She accused me of using my leg as an excuse to keep her away. She was right, of course. But I didn't know I'd been doing that until she pointed out something that made a lot of sense."

"What?" Wendy whispered the same word again, more quietly this time.

"The details aren't important. Suffice it to say I've changed a lot since the accident. Too much, in fact. She's called off our engagement."

If Wendy could see her own face. The compassion in those soulful green eyes.

"You must be devastated. I know what it's like to lose someone."

"If anything, I'm relieved. As I've told you before, my old life doesn't hold the same interest for me anymore. Lisa's a wonderful woman who deserves to be happy with the right man. I'm not that man.''

''That's easy enough for you to say!'' Wendy fired at him. ''She has to be going through hell!''

Wendy, what other woman in the world has a heart as big as yours?

''No doubt. But she flew all the way out here to give the ring back, which tells me she's been contemplating this for some time.''

''She's very lovely, Josh. As first impressions go, I liked her a lot.''

''Everyone likes Lisa.'' She was one of those superwomen agents Josh admired so much.

He hoped she got out one day soon—before she was taken out.

''What can I do for you? How can I help you?'' she asked gently.

Josh lowered his head. If Wendy had any idea how long he'd been waiting to hear those words...

''I'm feeling at loose ends tonight, and there's something important I want to discuss with you. Why don't you let me box up your books while we talk.''

''All right,'' she said shakily.

She let him in through the back door. Another first in the long, torturous road toward a relationship with her. This was progress. He couldn't complain.

After locking the door behind him, he followed her to the front room, unable to take his eyes off her bare legs. She was dressed in sandals and a sleeveless lime-green dress that came to the knee. He hadn't seen that outfit before. Maybe she'd bought it, along with the stunning black dress, when she'd purchased his jacket in Sacramento.

Even in her advanced stage of pregnancy, she had a

gorgeous body and shapely limbs. Her hair had grown longer. It danced above her shoulders like the finest silk. Her delicious scent, her grace, everything about her drew him with a power unlike anything he'd ever experienced.

So far she'd taped one box together. The rest sat in a pile on her living-room floor.

She had an impressive collection of books. They filled a whole wall. He saw a little bit of everything— the classics, bestsellers, art books, college texts. There were several encyclopedias, one set scientific.

He saw a series dealing with World War II planes; he'd love to browse through it. There were other series of plays by Shakespeare and Molière. Cookbooks, gardening books, self-help books on how to build everything from a new shower to a sun deck.

Two shelves contained children's books; the *Chronicles of Narnia,* the *Lord of the Rings* trilogy, the Dr. Doolittle series, at least a dozen old Oz books, vintage Nancy Drew mysteries, a Texas Blue Bonnet series.

There was a shelf of romances, mysteries and fantasy novels. Some travel books. Books on local history. And so much more…

Josh had always been a reader. Wendy's children didn't know how fortunate they were to be surrounded by so many books.

"Do you care where I start?"

"No. And don't worry about sorting them in any particular way. The new house is quite a bit larger than this cabin. After we've moved, the children can go through each box and we'll decide what goes where."

He began his task, delighting in this precious time with her. Behind him he could hear her taping another box together.

"What did you want to talk to me about?" Obviously her curiosity had gotten the better of her.

"Has the Majestic Hotel chain made you an earnest money offer yet?"

"No. But my Realtor says they'll be presenting me with one before the end of the week. He thinks I ought to accept it, that I can't do any better."

"That's not necessarily true."

"I know. But as my attorney pointed out, it could be a year before the perfect buyer comes along. I don't have the luxury of waiting, and at least these people are willing to retain Ada and Vera at the same wages and benefits."

"What about the horses?"

"According to the Realtor, they're planning to convert the barn into more guest units. I'll probably end up having to sell the horses to Mr. Lott in Carson City. He has first option to buy."

"The horses add something special to a place like Moon Lake."

"I know."

He finished filling the box, sealed it, then turned toward her. She had perched on the couch next to the coffee table where she was putting another box together.

"How would you feel about hiring a full-time manager who'd live here year-round on a permanent basis? That way you wouldn't have to uproot your family."

She let out a half-angry laugh. "That's like asking how I'd like to win the ten-million-dollar lottery. Even if I *could* afford to pay that person, let alone what he or she's really worth, finding someone like that would take longer than waiting for the right buyer to come along. As I told Ben months ago, there's no such person.''

''You're wrong.''

Something in his tone must have gotten through to her because she slowly lifted her head and looked at him with an incredulous expression.

''I farmed because my grandfather taught me to farm, but I love this job. It's grown on me—so much that I don't ever want to give it up. I've become a changed man out here. I was drawn to this place from the moment I drove through these mountains. I have no desire to go back to my old life.''

''Josh...'' He was afraid for a moment that she might faint.

''I wouldn't blame you for thinking I'm not capable of being totally rational right now. But I can assure you of one thing, Wendy. Working at the resort felt right from the moment I ate my first piece of your cherry pie and fixed the pipe under the kitchen sink. It's always going to feel right. I know it in my gut.''

''But—''

''Don't move to Sacramento, Wendy. Don't sell the resort. Take it off the market and let me see what I can do to make this place pay for itself. I'll get the horses back here. Ben will help me. They'll bring in the revenue you've been missing.

''Since the party the other night I've been thinking what a great place the coffee shop is to entertain. We could open it up on weekends for special occasions like wedding dinners, anniversary parties. Events like that will gross you extra money and help pay off your loans faster.''

She moistened her lips nervously. ''It all sounds as if it could work. But you're forgetting one thing. I could never pay you the salary you deserve. When you said you'd work without pay, I was at a very low point. I hired you because I knew it would only be temporary. A-and because I could sense you needed it so badly.''

''I did. I still do.''

''Don't you understand I could never live with myself if I allowed you to work for me, and never paid you what you're worth?'' she cried out. By now she was on her feet. ''I've already felt horrible about using you as much as I have. To go on using you would be criminal!''

''Then let me invest in the resort. Or make me a partner so I can stay here and you can feel good about it.''

''A partner?'' Her voice had risen.

He raked a hand through his hair, afraid he might have said the wrong thing. ''Wendy, if you won't let me stay and work under the conditions we agreed to in the beginning, then what kind of arrangement *could* we come up with?

''No matter what happens now, I'm planning on selling the farm.'' This was the truth. He'd held on to his grandparents' place as an investment, and had rented it out. Now he could put that investment to use.

''It's worth close to a million,'' he continued. ''There are people waiting in the wings to purchase it. I have other assets, as well. If you'd prefer, I could buy your resort outright and pay you a salary so you could stay here for the rest of your life. But my intention isn't to own a place like this. Only to live here and do work I enjoy.''

She stared at him as if she'd never seen him before. He could tell he was going too fast, but now he had to finish what he'd started.

"When I asked for the job, I told you I didn't need the money. The fact is, I'll never need the money. But I do need something this place gives me. Something I've never found anywhere else, or doing anything else." It was difficult to explain how much he wanted this, what a difference coming here had made to his life. It was as he'd told her—from the first moment, being here had put everything in perspective. He'd found peace and a new kind of purpose. And he'd found love....

He heard her breath catch. "You really love it here so much that you'd sell your own birthright?"

"Yes. Farming was never in my blood. Apparently my father didn't like it, either. Who knows what turn my life might have taken if my parents had been able to raise me?

"I wasn't like Ben and Kim. They know exactly where they belong and they don't want any other life. That's the difference between them and me. I've always been looking for my destiny. And lo and behold, I stumbled onto it when I drove through Moon Lake."

She wouldn't meet his gaze. "If you spoke this way to Lisa, I can understand why she was so shaken."

"Telling her anything else would have been a lie. Which would *you* have preferred?"

After a hesitation, she said, "The truth, of course. But still—no matter how much you've learned to love this area, you must feel a terrible void with her gone from your life."

"Not as much as you'd think. As I explained earlier, we had problems that distanced us even before the accident. Breaking off with her has ended the guilt." *In more ways than one,* he thought. He was immeasurably relieved that this particular lie had ended.

"I admit guilt can be a horrible thing." She sounded far away. "Still—"

"Josh! Hi!" Ben burst through the screen door with Cutty, not realizing he'd interrupted his mother. His timing couldn't have been more perfect.

"How are you, sport? Did you have a good time at Scouts?"

"No. It was dumb. They taught us how to do CPR again. We had that lesson three months ago."

Josh smiled. "Well, it doesn't hurt to have a brushup course every once in a while."

"I guess. Hi, Mom."

"Hello, sweetheart. I'm glad you're home. You still have a project to do. The one we talked about, remember?"

He heaved a big sigh. "I know. Clean up the mess in the basement." His eyes switched back to Josh. "How long have you been here?"

"Not long. But now that you've arrived, I can finally tell you how much I enjoyed the party. From what I understand, you and Eric were responsible for all those streamers. You did a great job. I looked around afterward to thank you, but you'd gone."

"Yeah, well, you were busy with your fiancée and stuff." After a tense silence, he muttered, "Did you come over here to say goodbye?"

"Ben!" his mother cautioned in a panicky voice.

Josh could have helped her out, but this was one time he refused to play into her hands. He was fighting for his life now.

"No," he merely said. "Why would you think that?"

"I...don't know."

Yes, you do. It's because you know your mother has never invited me over, so you're assuming the worst.

"Are you getting married soon?"

Josh could tell Wendy wanted this line of questioning to stop. But now that she knew he wasn't engaged, she couldn't expect him to go on lying to her children about it.

"Do you remember the conversation we had on the phone when you called me from Sacramento?"

"Yeah."

"Then you recall that I told you I wouldn't be getting married until everything felt right."

Ben nodded. "And it does now?" he asked with tears in his voice.

"No. Lisa didn't feel right about it, either. That's why she came to see me. After talking it over, we decided not to get married."

His blue eyes rounded in disbelief. "You mean... you broke up?"

"We did."

"For good?"

Josh nodded.

The transformation from pain to joy warmed his heart. A second later, Ben had grabbed him around the waist in a fierce hug. Cutty leaped excitedly against both of them. "That means you can stay here!"

"That's what I'd like to do, sport." This time he avoided Wendy's eyes as he hugged Ben back. "Now, it's getting late, and I've still got chores to do. Sounds like you do, too." Josh started moving toward the screen door.

"Yeah," Ben half laughed, half cried. "You *want* him to stay, don't you, Mom?"

Josh didn't wait to hear her answer.

"JANE?"

"Wendy?" her sister cried out in alarm. "My gosh—it's two o'clock in the morning! Don't tell me you've gone into premature labor?"

I've gone into shock.

"No. This doesn't have anything to do with the baby."

"Is one of the kids sick?"

No. Anything but. They're ecstatic. Out of their minds with joy. The second Kim walked through the door, Ben had regaled her with the news.

"No. Nothing's happened to anyone. I guess I need to talk."

"Honey…"

Her older sister sounded so sympathetic, Wendy burst into tears.

"Oh, honey," Jane soothed. "You've held up so well for the last few months, I knew there'd come a day when you'd miss Matt so much you'd feel like you were going crazy."

Wendy groaned. "This doesn't really have to do with Matt."

An unnatural quiet came from her sister's end. "Then we're talking about that handyman, aren't we? Josh Walker. Your children seem to think he walks on water." She paused. "Hmm. I wondered why you went to the trouble to buy those dresses. For that matter, I thought you've been awfully distracted lately. Did you go and fall in love with an engaged man? Is that what this is all about?"

"Yes!" she blurted out. It was therapeutic to finally admit it aloud. "Only tonight he told me he's not engaged anymore."

"And you're crying about that?"

"You don't understand!"

"You're right."

"I'm afraid, Jane."

"Of what?"

"That it's Moon Lake he cares about."

"Instead of you, you mean? How did you come to that conclusion?"

"Because he begged me not to sell. He said he wants to stay as manager of the resort badly enough that he'll continue to work for free, or become a partner, or even buy the whole place outright."

"You're kidding! He has that kind of money?"

"Apparently so."

"Then why would he be after your resort?"

"What do you mean?"

"Don't get me wrong, but there are other places for sale in the area that would be a much better investment from his point of view. I honestly don't think that's it. And don't forget, he risked his life to save Ben's. You know what, Wendy? I think the man's head over heels in love with you."

"If I thought that was true..."

"Then test him."

"How?"

"Don't sell the resort. Take him up on his offer to continue working for you without a salary. See what happens."

"That would be unfair to him. I couldn't do it and I told him as much."

"All right. Didn't you say the resort's starting to make a little money again?"

"Yes. And he's got some ideas for bringing in more revenue."

"Then pay him a nominal fee if it'll ease your conscience, and let nature take its course. In time you'll find out the truth.''

''I'm terrified.''

''I don't blame you, but I believe it's worth the risk if he's as wonderful as you obviously think he is. Your children don't want to live in Sacramento. Mom and I know you don't, either. I guess the big question is, if it turns out he *isn't* in love with you, could you bear to live around him for as long as he's manager of the resort?''

''No,'' she answered without hesitation.

''Then you're even more in love with him than I thought. One problem I see is that you signed a six-month lease on the rental house.''

''I know.''

''If I call the Realtor tomorrow and tell him you can't take the house, after all, he might be able to find a new renter soon. That way, you'll only be out a month's rent.''

''Would you do that?''

''Of course.''

''Oh, Jane, I couldn't manage without you!''

''I feel the same about you.''

''Jane? If you ever get to meet Josh, you'll understand....''

''I think I already do. And I always felt Matt was an impossible act to follow.''

''So did I...''

''Knowing you, I'd guess you're torn apart by guilt over this.''

''Yes.''

''I can understand that. But we both know Matt wouldn't have wanted you to stay single for the rest of your life.''

Tears filled her eyes. "But it's so soon after his death."

"Wendy, if this man had shown up three years from now, I can guarantee you'd feel just as guilty."

Wendy sniffed. "You're probably right."

"I know I am. It doesn't mean you love Matt any less. Now, get over your guilt and let things take their course. In the meantime, you've got to watch out for yourself and that baby. It won't be much longer now. In all honesty, I'm glad you're not going to move at this stage in your pregnancy."

"So am I."

"Listen," Jane went on. "Bob and I will come up with the kids this weekend and bring all the stuff you bought for the nursery. That way I'll have a legitimate excuse to meet Mel Gibson's double."

"Ada will tell you Josh is better-looking."

"The only matter of any importance is what *you* think."

"You already know what I think."

"We'll stay in close touch. Good night, honey."

"Good night." The second she hung up the phone, she started to cry, but these were tears of relief. She no longer had to carry her secret alone. A few minutes later, she heard a tap on her door.

"Mom?"

She might have known.

"Yes, Ben?"

"I heard you talking to Aunt Jane. May I come in?"

"Why don't you try reading yourself to sleep?" For once she wanted to be alone to give in to her emotions.

"I just wanted to know if we're moving to California or not."

Oh, Ben. "No. We're going to stay here and let Josh run the resort."

"Honest?" Her son's voice was ecstatic.

"Yes. I know how much you and Kim want to stay here. I do, too. With Josh's help, we're going to see how long we can make a go of things."

The door opened. Two figures dashed across the room to her bed. Her children's hugs told her everything they were too choked up to say. Cutty climbed onto the foot of the bed to join them.

Wendy lay in the darkness surrounded by her family. Months ago, they'd clung to her wordlessly while they poured out their grief. During that black period she couldn't have imagined a night like this, when they'd be gathered together to shed tears of happiness.

For the rest of the night, she rehearsed what she'd say to Josh, but nothing sounded right. Knowing that he was no longer engaged had changed everything, somehow.

He wasn't going to leave for Ohio and marry Lisa. It didn't seem possible that he'd actually be here all the time, the way she'd dreamed.

But she was selfish. She wanted more than dreams. She wanted the reality of a life with Josh. The reality of his kisses, his caring.... Yet until she knew how he really felt, she had to prevent herself from showing him what he meant to her.

If a man wasn't attracted to a woman, there was nothing more pathetic than to see her grovel for his attention.

Lisa had finally found the courage to let him go.

Wendy hoped that if or when she saw the same writing on the wall, she'd be able to give up as gracefully.

In the meantime, the only thing to do was wait until the birth of her baby. Life might be very different by then. Depending on Josh's reactions, she'd know whether or not there was any truth to Jane's theory.

CHAPTER THIRTEEN

AS JOSH HELPED an older couple into the boat they'd rented for an early morning of fly fishing, he caught sight of Wendy's white Toyota. She was headed toward him.

Last night he'd left her to deal with Ben. Josh knew he could count on her son to take his part in any discussion she would have held with him.

Because she'd come looking for him this early, Josh suspected she'd spent most of the night wrestling with the problem of what to do about him. She'd obviously decided and couldn't stand to put off their talk any longer.

A smile broke out on his face as he waited expectantly to find out what that decision was.

Under normal circumstances, he would never celebrate causing her a sleepless night. Not in her condition. But their relationship had reached a critical stage, and he'd been forced to make his move.

The last thing he wanted was to buy his way into the resort. Moon Lake had been the dream of Wendy and her husband. Josh had no desire to take that from her. He'd be completely satisfied if they could maintain the status quo.

But he wasn't so noble that he wouldn't stake a financial claim if that was his only option.

He walked over to the car as she pulled up. Her

lovely wan face gave testimony of her struggle. Yet he couldn't summon one ounce of remorse.

"Good morning."

"Good morning."

He rested his hands against the frame of the car. "You're up early."

She held herself taut. "So are you."

"It goes with the territory. Your job is to sleep in and take care of yourself until the baby comes."

"I couldn't. Not when I knew you'd be waiting for an answer. It's only fair to let you know where you stand."

She looked straight ahead, as if something fascinating held her attention. Above the neckline of her pink maternity smock, he noticed a small pulse throbbing, like a hummingbird's wings. With the slightest encouragement, he would have put his lips to it.

"I'm sorry if you thought I was in a hurry for a decision. It wouldn't matter if you took a week or a month to make it. I'm not going anywhere—unless you're asking me to leave," he added quietly. Might as well get that established first.

With her head slightly turned from him, he had to strain to hear her say, "Of course not."

"If that's the case," he murmured, releasing the breath he'd been holding, "can't we keep the situation the way it is?"

"No!" She swung her head back in his direction. "I don't care how much money you have. If you're going to work here, I insist you be paid a salary. I realize it won't be much money at first, but it's a question of principle."

When he nodded, she took a deep breath and went on. "Your idea about renting out the coffee shop for special occasions makes a lot of sense. Our guests normally like to grab a bite to eat early in the evening, then go to Tahoe for the nightlife. During those hours on the weekends, the restaurant could be put to good use for private parties.

"We could advertise over the Internet. If we found the right catering company, one that had its own staff, we'd have almost no work. Best of all, it would garner pure profit for us after they'd been paid."

"Maybe we ought to consult Ada and Vera first."

She nodded. "I was thinking the same thing. They're friends with a lot of people in the restaurant industry."

"Who knows? They might want to take it on themselves."

Her eyes widened. "Do you think so?"

He grinned. "You never know until you ask."

Their gazes held. Josh felt an intimate connection with her, and he knew in his gut that she was just as aware of it.

"Thank you," he whispered.

Her breathing grew shallow. "For what?"

"For letting me in the door. For giving me the opportunity to embrace a life most people might dream about, but rarely get the chance to experience."

"I should be thanking you," came her solemn response. "Your willingness to do the work around here has allowed me and the children to hold on to *our* dream a little longer."

"You have wonderful children. I can't wait to meet the third Sloan baby."

His comment provoked a little smile. "I have to admit I'm getting impatient myself."

"Mind if I ask you another favor?"

"What is it?" she asked after a brief silence.

"When the time comes, will you let me drive you to the hospital?" His question appeared to be the last thing she'd expected him to ask. "Carol told me she's already offered. But I'm closer to home, and this will be my first experience around a woman in labor. I'd like to be in on it from the beginning."

Her eyes grew veiled. "You might live to regret such a generous offer. Both times my labor started after dinner. I ended up going to the hospital in the middle of the night."

"It's an adventure I don't want to miss. Ever since I felt him kick, I've imagined a little guy who's got Ben's feistiness and Kim's charm."

"You're still convinced it's a boy, then?"

He chuckled. "Those jabs felt like a right hook. You've managed to withstand months of battering. I don't know how you do it, but I'm impressed."

"It's not that bad." But a slow smile broke out as she said it.

"You can say that to anyone but me. I was there, remember?"

A soft pink spread up her throat and face. She remembered, all right.

"As long as we're talking about plans for this place, when do you want me to see about the horses?"

She sighed. "I think we'll have to wait until August."

"Why so long?"

"Because there won't be a cabin free for you until then."

"But the whole point of my vacating it was to bring in as much revenue as possible."

"Josh, I won't allow you to live in the barn with ten horses!"

"I have to admit I didn't plan to share my lodgings with them." He grinned. "I have another idea I'd like to discuss with you."

"You can't live in a tent all summer!"

He burst into laughter.

She shook her head. "I'm sorry. I don't mean to treat you like one of the children. But ever since you moved to the barn, I've felt awful about it and I absolutely refuse to consider another unacceptable alternative."

"What would you think if I bought myself a motor home? One with a kitchen and shower. I'd park it on the other side of the restaurant under the trees, where there's access to hookups. It would have all the comforts of home, yet no one would really notice it."

"But that's no life for you!" she cried out. "For one thing, they're so claustrophobic!"

"Only if I were to spend twenty-four hours a day in it. The reason I love being at Moon Lake is that I get to work outside in these mountains from sunup to sundown. I don't require much more than a decent bed at night. A camper would be sheer luxury."

"I knew I shouldn't have let you move out to the barn," she said angrily.

"I wouldn't have missed the experience for anything. But a perfectly good barn is going to waste." As long as he'd gone this far, he might as well go all the way.

"How would it be if I got Jonathan to cover for me on Saturday, and you and I drove to Carson City with the children to see Mr. Lott about the horses? While we're there, you could all help me pick out a camper. I'd appreciate the input. We'll make it a family affair."

She stirred restlessly. "I don't know. Jane said she

might drive up from Sacramento this weekend to bring the stuff I bought for the nursery.''

Thrilled that she'd already talked to her sister about the new situation at the resort, he murmured, ''Our trip could wait until early next week.''

''Monday might be best. I have a doctor's appointment on Tuesday.''

''Monday it is,'' he said before she could change her mind.

''Josh, are you *sure* you'd like living out of a motor home?''

''I'd love it. Jimmy might like it, too.''

''Jimmy McGee? From Louisiana?''

''Yes. He said he'd enjoy working here for the summer. We could share it—that is, if you wanted to hire him to help with the horses. At least think about it.''

After a long silence, she said, ''Jimmy would be very welcome. But you'd have to promise me one thing.''

He loved her intensity. ''What's that?''

''When it starts to snow, Jimmy goes home to Louisiana, and you have to move back to one of the cabins for the winter.''

''Agreed,'' he said without hesitation. And Josh knew which cabin he wanted, too. Right now, the living-room floor was strewn with unfilled packing boxes. If he had his way, the moving company could come within the hour to replace everything and return the room to its original state.

While he stood there trying to figure out how to make that happen, he realized a group of guests had been walking toward him. He waved. ''Looks like I've got customers.''

"Don't let me keep you. I think I'll have that talk with Ada later in the day."

"Good idea. After lunch would you like me to call Jimmy and see if he's still interested?"

"Of course."

"We probably ought to start lining up a few teens to help at the stable, as well. Didn't you have a list?"

"Yes. But they might not be available anymore. We might have to rely on an employment agency."

"No problem. I'll talk to you about it later."

She nodded and drove off.

What a difference twelve hours had made.

Bless you, Agent Wood.

Later, when he'd taken care of the guests who wanted to paddle on the lake, he went back to the barn to phone his supervisor. Harve didn't seem the slightest bit surprised to learn that Josh was in love. Although he didn't like hearing Josh's plans to leave the department, he understood.

"I've been reading the signs ever since you arrived there," Harve admitted in a resigned voice.

"Was I that obvious?"

"Well…in a word, yes."

Josh smiled. "Back to business—what about that contract out on me?"

"We're working on it. Some arrests have been made. One of the gang members is willing to give us names in exchange for immunity. In my opinion we'll have the leader in custody before much longer. But even if it takes a while, the fact that you're leaving to settle in Tahoe removes you from immediate danger. However, until all arrests are made, keep your cover. As for Wendy Sloan, go ahead and tell her the truth."

"Thanks, Harve. That's all I needed to hear. Talk to you later."

"I'LL BET BEN'S EXCITED to have a bedroom down in the basement now."

Wendy eyed her sister as they finished tucking in the edges of the crib sheet. "He's so happy we're staying here, he would've volunteered to live on the back porch."

"Admit you're happy, too."

She nodded. "You know I am. Except that if Josh isn't in love with me, I'll know it soon enough. Then I'll want to get out of here as fast as I can."

"He hasn't said anything to you yet?"

"No."

"Maybe he's afraid to declare himself because this is Matt's baby. Maybe he's waiting for some sign from you."

"I don't know what more I can do without blurting out that I'm in love with him!"

"That might not be such a bad idea."

"Jane!"

"No. I mean it. Put yourself in his place. He knows that everything at Moon Lake is filled with memories of your life with Matt. It would take a courageous man to pursue you...unless he was given a few hints that you wouldn't reject him."

She averted her eyes. "I've given him hints."

"To do with his job, maybe. But I'm talking about something more personal. Have you ever asked him over here for dinner?"

"No."

"Why not?"

"Because I didn't want the children to get any ideas."

"It's a little late for that," she teased gently. "Why don't you invite him for an evening and see how he responds?"

Her heart pounded hard. "I'd love to do that. But I'm afraid the only reason he'd come is because I'm his employer."

"You're crazy! I watched him watching you at dinner in the restaurant last night. He can't take his eyes off you."

"I think you're exaggerating."

"No, I'm not. At least consider my idea. Josh is a special guy—and Bob agrees with me. Do whatever you have to do, Wendy. This is a man worth fighting for."

"But he's just broken his engagement and—"

"If you want my opinion," Jane interrupted, "I don't think he's given his ex-fiancée a thought. He's acts too...alive around you."

"Then you're seeing something I can't."

"Because you're afraid to believe it's true."

Wendy stared at her sister. "You're right."

"So," Jane's eyes narrowed provocatively. "Are you going to take my advice and fight for what you want?"

She bit her lip. "Yes. I agreed to drive to Carson City with him to see about the horses."

"That's a start."

"He also wants my help in picking out a motor home."

"This is sounding better and better."

"He included the children in the invitation."

"Well, of course he did! He loves them. A person

can't fake feelings like that. My theory is that because he was an only child, he craves the family life he's found here at Moon Lake.''

"Oh, Jane,'' she sighed. "You and your theories. You know, you're getting my hopes up.''

"Good,'' Jane said briskly. "Now that we're through in here, let's go find out how the basketball game ended. When I left them, it was my husband and son against your son and Josh, and I don't have to tell you who was throwing more baskets. I'm sure there's no contest, but I didn't tell Bob that or it would've hurt his feelings. As it is, he'll probably be cross all the way back to Sacramento.''

Wendy smiled at her sister before they left the nursery arm in arm.

"I LIKE THIS MOTOR HOME the best. There's room for six people. It's got everything!''

"The blue curtains are pretty. I hope he buys it.''

"Me, too. Josh says we can sleep in it sometimes.''

"Do you think Mom will let us?''

"I don't know. We'd better not say anything to her yet.''

"Let's wait till she goes to the hospital to have the baby. Then we'll ask Josh if we can stay with him.''

"Yeah. I don't want to go anywhere else.''

"Me, neither.''

"Josh loves Cutty, too. He'll let her sleep in here.''

"I'm glad he's not getting married. Aren't you?''

"Heck, yeah! I'm going to ask him to go on the father-and-son horseback trip with the Scouts in August.''

"I wish I could go, too. Boys get to have all the fun.''

When they heard the door of the motor home open, their heads turned at the same time. Josh stepped inside and looked around. "So you guys like this one best, huh?"

"Yeah. It's awesome!"

"That's good, because I just bought it."

"Yippee!"

"As soon as your mother returns from the ladies' room, we'll head home in it."

Kim grinned up at him. "What about Mom's car?"

"We'll pull it behind us with my fancy new trailer hitch."

"Can I ride up front with you?"

"I'll tell you what. You and your brother are welcome to take turns while your mom has a nice rest on the couch."

Kim nodded. "Her feet are swollen from sitting in the car so long," she said knowledgeably.

"Mothers-to-be sacrifice a lot to bring guys like you into the world. We're all going to have to help her more until the baby gets here."

"When my sister's born, can we take her for a ride in this?"

"Did Mom tell you she's having a girl?" Ben demanded.

"No."

"Well, it might be a boy."

"Whether it's a boy or a girl, guys, we now have something nice and roomy for the whole family to enjoy."

"Yeah," they said in unison as their mother climbed on board.

Wendy studied the furnished interior. "Well—isn't this cozy!"

Kim giggled, while Ben just stood next to Josh, grinning. Their family hadn't known this kind of happiness since Josh's surprise Chinese dinner.

After they'd arrived in Carson City this morning and made arrangements about the horses, he'd bought them a big lunch. They'd had such a wonderful time so far. She wanted it to last forever.

"JOSH SAYS YOU'RE supposed to lie down for a nap while we drive back to Moon Lake, Mom."

Wendy darted Josh an amused glance. "I think I'll take you up on your advice, Dr. Walker."

He smiled in response, and her body felt suffused with warmth. It no longer surprised her that he was so solicitous of her welfare. He was simply that kind of man.

"Kim? You can ride in front with me for the first half of the trip home. After that, it's Ben's turn. Now, while all of you get settled, I'll see that the car's been hooked up, then we'll go."

Again Wendy marveled. Anyone else might have had a fight on his hands. Not Josh. He managed the children without their even realizing it, and kept everyone happy at the same time

Ben explored the miniature fridge and stove, and Kim made herself comfortable in the front seat. Wendy lay down on her back, thankful for the chance to stretch her legs. Josh came back in the trailer just then, and their eyes met in silent greeting. His gaze broke away to follow the lines and curves of her very pregnant body, emphasized by the fastened seat belt. As he walked through to the front, she decided she must have imagined the sensuous intimacy of that look. It might only have been wishful thinking on her part.

She sighed, and propped a pillow underneath her head. Maybe by the time she got her figure back, he would have worked through the worst of his pain over losing Lisa.

Wendy didn't care what Jane said; she believed that Josh was still recovering from their breakup. But one day she would look into his eyes and read a message there about *her*...and him.

And if there weren't any?

With a groan, she turned on her side, refusing to entertain that possibility. Not today. Today she needed to cling to this new happiness with all her strength.

ALTHOUGH JOSH HAD BEEN using the resort's truck, it felt good to be driving his own vehicle for a change. He'd missed his independence in that regard.

He liked the idea that he was taking care of Wendy's family. They felt like *his* family. He couldn't imagine loving a son or daughter more than he loved Kim and Ben. They brought something to his life that nothing else had.

As for the woman who'd been fast asleep on the couch throughout the drive home, he was in love with her. It was that simple, and that complicated. Playing this waiting game was hell. Since his last talk with Harve, he'd been waiting for the right time to tell her the truth, that he was no longer undercover. But he still felt he should proceed with caution for the sake of Wendy's health and the baby's.

"Holy heck!" Ben suddenly cried out in alarm. They'd just rounded the bend in the road leading to the resort. In one quick glance, Josh saw the reason for Ben's fear.

A swarm of bikers had descended on the coffee

shop. Josh counted thirty riderless Harleys in the parking lot. If he could get close enough to inspect one of them, he'd be able to tell from the emblems if they belonged to a club out enjoying the mountains, or if they were a motorcycle gang known for criminal activity.

On the outside chance that they were members of the Hellhounds, the drug-trafficking gang who'd put out a contract on him months ago, he would proceed with extreme caution. God only knew what could be going on inside the coffee shop, let alone the rest of the resort. The guests and staff might already have been terrorized and held hostage. But Josh couldn't do anything about it until he'd made sure Wendy's family was safe.

Without hesitation, he accelerated past the restaurant to the neighbors' driveway to the north of the resort. After pulling in so the motor home couldn't be seen from the main road, he turned off the engine.

"Ben?"

"Yes?" The boy looked pale

"As soon as I leave, I want you to get your mother and Kim, and go inside the Stobbes' house. If they're not home and you can't get in, stay in here and lock the door until I come for you. Do you understand me?"

"Yes," he whispered. "Be careful."

"I'm just going to check things out," Josh assured him before he dashed through the trailer past Wendy who hadn't yet awakened. When a surprised Kim looked up from the comic book she'd been reading at the kitchen table, he put a finger to his lips, flashed her a smile, then exited.

He retrieved his gun, which he'd hidden in the trunk of the Toyota that morning, then entered the dense stand of forest separating the two properties. Stealthily he crept to one corner of the restaurant. From that vantage point he could see a couple of bikes. To his relief, they didn't belong to the Hellhounds. He moved to the back of the restaurant, where Vera's car stood next to the truck. No bikers on guard.

He called Harve on his cell phone and described the situation. "I might still need backup if they're causing trouble."

"Police are on the way in squad cars."

"No sirens, Harve. Tell them to surround the area from the woods on either side of the restaurant. Tell them not to do anything unless I fire two shots. We could have a situation here, but I'm hoping that's not the case."

"Be careful."

Ending the call, Josh let himself in the back door.

He could hear rock music coming from the dining room. It drowned out any voices.

An inspection of the office and laundry room revealed nothing amiss. He hurried down the hall to peer inside the kitchen. Vera stood at the counter filling coffee mugs on a tray.

He hid the gun in his waistband and pushed open the door. She jerked around, white-faced.

"I'm glad it's you and not Wendy!" she confided

"How long have they been here?"

"Just a few minutes. I told them I was ready to close up, but they said all they wanted was coffee, then they'd leave."

"Which might or might not be the case. I've called for the police," he muttered. "Where are Jonathan and Cindy?"

"They left about ten minutes before the bikers came in."

"You're a brave woman, Vera. But now that I'm here, I want you to get in your car and drive home."

"But—"

"Now!"

She finally nodded and left. Buying himself a little more time before backup arrived, he set out another tray with mugs until there were thirty in all. As he brewed two additional pots of coffee, one of the bikers came through the swinging door. "Need some help? Hey—where'd the waitress go?"

From the corner of his eye, Josh scanned the brawny biker's burnished forearms for the telltale tattoo of a demonized hound, the Hellhounds' gang sign. To his relief, he saw a small red flower on the guy's bicep.

After years of doing air photographic surveillance, Josh knew the names and symbols of every motorcycle gang involved with organized crime. He was ninety-nine percent sure that this one was just a riding club that meant no harm.

"She's off duty. I'm the owner. As long as you're offering, why don't you grab that tray and we'll have you guys served and on your way in no time."

"Thanks. It's been a long ride, and we still have a couple hours to go."

"Sorry we couldn't serve you a meal, but my staff goes home at nine. Where are you headed?"

"Sacramento."

"It's a beautiful night."

"You can say that again."

"I used to have a Harley. What club do you ride for?"

"We're the Scarlet Pimpernels."

"Yeah—I remember the book. And I've seen the movie. About that English aristocrat, right? Sir Percy something?"

The guy with a faceful of hair and a lion's mane to match, grinned. "That's right. Sir Percy Blakeney. He's the Brit we named our club after."

"He had a fine cause saving his French friends from the guillotine. What's yours?"

The biker grimaced. "We're sick of the Feds buying up land to prevent us from using the high-country roads to ride on. Pretty soon you won't be able to go anywhere on a bike."

"I know what you mean," Josh said. "Too much land's being tied up so that people like us who don't hike will never be able to explore it." He didn't believe this but had no trouble lying about it for the sake of peace and safety.

"Dude? You know it!"

Josh smiled and handed the biker one of the trays. "After you."

The two of them entered the dining room and started passing out coffee to the crowd. There were no other customers. And no women among the gang. Every member displayed a red flower on his upper arm. They seemed benign enough, he decided.

When backup closed in outside, they'd see Josh through the restaurant window and know everything was under control for the moment. That was the way he wanted it. No paranoia.

WHEN BEN HAD AWAKENED Wendy and told her what he and Josh had seen in front of the restaurant, she wondered if she was having a nightmare. But as she looked around the motor home to get her bearings, reality hit.

Horrified at what might happen to Josh, she gathered the children and ran to the Stobbes' house. To her relief they were home.

While her neighbor called the police, Wendy borrowed his rifle, told the children to stay put and took off for the coffee shop on a run. In the back of her mind, she was conscious of that pain in her lower back; she blamed it on her flight through the woods that separated their properties. Right now, all she cared about was Josh's safety.

Several years earlier, there'd been an incident at the restaurant when a noisy band of bikers had shown up wanting service. Frightened—because they'd seemed like a group that could easily become violent—she'd told Ada to phone Matt at the house.

He'd come running with his shotgun, but as it turned out, there weren't that many bikers. As soon as the food came, they settled down to eat. A show of force hadn't been necessary, after all

Maybe tonight was no different, but it was past closing time and Ben had said there were at least thirty bikes out front. That was more than double the previous number.

This situation could be explosive and Wendy felt she had to do *something*. There was only one problem.

Mr. Stobbe's ammo was locked up in a cabinet and there hadn't been time to get it. But no one in the coffee shop would know the rifle wasn't loaded. Victims and criminals alike had been known to bluff their way through a tense situation with unloaded weapons. She would do the same. It might buy a little time until the police arrived.

When she entered the back of the coffee shop, she could hear the din of voices, combined with the sounds of a ghetto blaster turned high. Fearing the worst, she crept down the hall and peered through the crack between the swinging door and the restaurant.

It looked like chaos to her. Bearded, tattooed men in bandanas were wandering around, holding cups of coffee, as if they owned the place. Worst of all, she couldn't see Josh. If they'd done anything to him…

Without conscious thought, she opened the door and aimed the rifle at the head of a sunburned biker standing near the kitchen. His eyes widened when he saw her.

"Shut off that radio!" she demanded.

Slowly he did what he was told. There was total silence as thirty surprised pairs of eyes turned in her direction.

It wasn't until she'd taken a few steps inside the room that she saw Josh. Relief almost overwhelmed her; her legs were trembling so much she could barely stand. He carried a tray in his hand, and she had no idea if he'd been threatened in some way.

"I don't know why you people think you deserve special treatment, but this dining room was closed twenty minutes ago. All of you can leave now, or I'm going to start shooting!"

At the sight of Wendy standing next to a biker pointing a rifle at his head, Josh's heart nearly leaped out of his body.

Lord. Brave though she was, this could end in disaster. Josh had to think fast.

"It's okay, sweetheart." He moved swiftly to put an arm around her shoulders. After pulling her into his arms, he gave her a hug, then he took the rifle from her.

"Hey, guys?" He smiled. "You'll have to forgive my wife." Staring into her frightened eyes, he said, "She always protects me if she thinks I'm in trouble. With our third baby on the way, she's twice as jumpy as usual."

The bikers began to laugh and everyone relaxed.

"Honey, these guys aren't a gang like the one that roughed me up last year in the parking lot." She'd gone limp; he had to hold her tight or she would have fallen. "They're the famous Scarlet Pimpernel Riding Club. Sir Percy here was just telling me about them."

"Sir Percy!" The bikers exploded with more laughter, making fun of their leader.

"They're on their way to Sacramento tonight. Vera let them in for coffee, and I was just going to rustle them up some of your pie. How about it, sweetheart?"

"Sure." Though she was still shaking, she'd read between the lines and played along like a pro. "Sorry about the gun, but I'd like my husband around for a long time. You know what I mean?"

They laughed and guffawed and nodded.

"Give me a second, and I'll have pie dished up for everybody."

"Want some help, honey?"

"No, Josh. I can see you're having a great time in here."

She'd said the one thing guaranteed to remove any lingering suspicions on the bikers' part.

As soon as she'd disappeared into the kitchen, Josh broke open the rifle in plain view of everyone to empty out its shells. There were none. He might have known.

"So much for my wife doing any real damage! But she still gets full marks from me."

They broke into laughter again. That touched off a series of similar stories. Soon Wendy emerged from the kitchen with a cart full of pie, and Josh helped her serve it around. In no time at all, the men had devoured every crumb and were ready to leave.

As they started to pull out money, Wendy said, "Put it away, guys. This was on the house. But the next time you pass through here, come earlier when we're serving dinner. Bring your wives and girlfriends. You'll get the best meal in Tahoe."

"All right!" Their leader spoke up, clapping the hardest.

Josh walked outside with him in plain view of any police and undercover officers. "Have a good ride," he said, shaking hands with the leader. "If you feel that strongly about preserving bike trails, then you ought to get a petition going in Sacramento to fight for your rights through the legislature. Other riding clubs in California might join you."

"Yeah." The man nodded. "You've got a point."

"Take it easy."

"You bet." He gave the thumbs-up signal and climbed on his Harley. As soon as he revved his bike and followed the others onto the main road, Josh phoned Harve.

"Crisis averted. You can call the guys off."

"I hear you almost had an incident."

Through the front window Josh could see Wendy cleaning up the dining room. He feared that a scare like the one she'd just lived through could cause her to go into premature labor. The need to make sure she was all right took priority over any other consideration.

Josh drew in his breath. "That's true enough. I'll give you the details later."

He went back in the coffee shop, to see that Wendy had already made quick work of the dining room. Everything looked ready for the morning crowd. She'd taken the rifle with her.

He locked up, switched off lights, then headed for the kitchen. She was standing at the dishwasher loading cups and plates, but she turned when she saw him. Her face had become an expressionless mask.

"Who are you?" she asked in a quiet voice.

"That's easy to answer. A man who stands in awe of you. Tonight you put your life on the line for me without any thought of danger to yourself or the baby. I'll never forget." Now it was his voice that trembled.

She shook her head warily. "There you go again. From our very first moment, you've always been ready with the right answers. You say and do everything too perfectly. Nothing is beyond your grasp. Your skills as a handyman, pilot, child psychologist, manager—*everything*—go beyond the norm.

"You certainly didn't need any help from me tonight. All I did was interfere in something you already had well under control." She shrugged, shaking her head again. "It felt like when I was in high school and we were putting on an operetta. I walked on stage before my cue. Even though the conductor didn't miss a beat, I realized my mistake."

She took a fortifying breath. "I know you carry a handgun. I felt it when you hugged me a little while ago."

Hell.

"When Ben came dashing in the house the night you showed up, and told me a stranger was in the coffee shop asking for a job, my first thought was that you were hiding from the law. Moon Lake must have seemed like the perfect resort to lie low, well out of sight. But I immediately realized my desperate son had taken one look at you, decided you could take over for his father and begged you to come work for us."

Lord.

"To appease Ben, I checked up on your references. They turned out to be so glowing, I felt guilty for having doubted you. Because I was desperate for help myself, I decided you were a godsend.

"Once you were hired, you never did anything to make me distrust you. Not until tonight, when your performance in front of those bikers convinced me you didn't want any police involved.

"Suddenly I started piecing things together. You never received any mail or phone calls from anyone except your fiancée. That's definitely odd. And you hardly ever went anywhere in the evenings. No good-looking man, engaged or not, would purposely hang around an isolated place like this, night after night, without a damn good reason.

"I began reviewing how you encouraged me to re-open the guest cabins, how you made your computer available. Naturally you'd want me to keep the place open if it meant you could hide out here longer.

"Now it makes perfect sense that you asked to sleep in the barn, away from other people. A mobile home gives you the same kind of cover."

She leveled accusing eyes at him. "You seem to have enough money when you need it. You're simply too good to be true. But something doesn't add up, so I'll ask you again. Who are you?"

Josh hadn't wanted to confide in Wendy until after

her baby was born, but obviously circumstances dictated otherwise.

"I'm Special Agent Joshua Quincy with the FBI, on medical leave to recover from a gunshot wound I received during a sting operation in Kansas right before Christmas."

He saw the way her hands clung to the edge of the counter.

"One of my supervisor's staff saw Ben's ad for a handyman on the Internet and decided to have it checked out as a possible hiding place for me while my leg finished healing.

"The men who came to look over Moon Lake spotted the Help Wanted sign in the coffee shop window and decided the ad over the net had to be legitimate. But it was the sign that gave me the excuse to ask Ben about a job.

"Henry and Brenda work for the department and provide references for me whenever I go undercover. If you hadn't hired me, I would've ended up working as a janitor for a dental clinic in Seattle until July, when my doctor figured I'd be ready to go back on active duty."

He looked at her. "That's the truth, Wendy. The whole truth."

CHAPTER FOURTEEN

WENDY HAD WANTED the truth, but this was more than she knew how to handle.

If it hadn't been for Ben's ad, Josh would be in Seattle right now. They would never have met. She would never have known him. That seemed inconceivable to her.

What were the chances of Josh's supervisor coming across that ad on the Internet?

"Has everything been a lie?" she whispered. "All the stories about your background, the farm..."

His eyes darkened. "No. What I've told you about my past is true. My grandparents raised me after my parents were killed. When my grandmother died, my grandfather needed me even more. He taught me how to farm. But he knew I didn't really like it, that I didn't feel about it the way he did. When I turned eighteen, he encouraged me to go to college and find out what I wanted to do with my life.

"After I received my degree, I attended Annapolis and went into the Navy as a commissioned officer. I trained as a fighter pilot. I thought I'd make a career in the military. That is, until my grandfather died.

"When I came home for his funeral, Henry, our neighbor—one of my grandfather's best friends—approached me. I had no idea he was a member of the FBI. He put me in contact with someone at the Bureau, who asked if I'd like to work for them. It meant more training, including helicopters.

"I found the offer so intriguing, I changed careers. I ended up doing classified aerial surveillance photography as part of the Bureau's forensics team."

"H-how did you get shot?"

"After monitoring the drug trafficking movement from the air for eighteen months, my partner and I became part of a massive sting operation. It involved making simultaneous arrests nationwide of corrupt police officers and motorcycle gangs working together in the drug trade."

"Motorcycle gangs? Like the one tonight?" she cried out

"Yes. Except that I was able to determine that the Scarlet Pimpernels are a riding club. There's a huge difference. On the particular morning in question, Barry and I, dressed as businessmen, flew a private plane to a small airport outside Topeka where we knew a large shipment of cocaine was expected to arrive from South America.

"But something went wrong. One of the rogue policemen, disguised as security, must have smelled a trap. As my buddy stepped off the plane, he was shot in the head. I was right behind him and took a bullet in the leg.

"We were taken immediately to a private hospital where Barry died without ever reaching consciousness. The bone in my leg was splintered so badly, I was told I might lose it." His voice grew hoarse. "Barry wasn't just my partner, he was my closest friend."

She couldn't stop the gasp that came out of her. As she stared at him, his handsome face seemed to darken.

For the first time since she'd known him, she thought he looked older than his thirty-five years.

"During the three months I was in the hospital, there were times I felt so responsible for his death, I wished I'd been finished off, too."

"But how could you possibly have been responsible?" she asked. "If you'd gotten off the plane first, it would have been your friend who was left to suffer. It must have upset Lisa to hear you talk like that."

"Wendy," he said quietly. "There is no Lisa."

She shook her head in confusion. "What do you mean? I met her."

"No. You met Agent Lisa Wood. She's happily married to another agent, Frank Wood."

That was too much to absorb. "I don't understand what you're saying."

"I'm saying I never had a fiancée. Lisa Delvie is the name my supervisor invented. The fiancée story was to give me a legitimate reason to walk away from here as soon as my leg got better. Whenever I'm on a job or in this case, on medical leave, it's routine to create a cover. That goes for any agent. Since our sting operation, the gang put out a contract on me."

"You mean they're trying to find you and kill you?" Her voice shook on the last words.

He drew in his breath. "In the beginning they were. But that was months ago, and some of the members have now been arrested. The good news is that one of them talked, and more arrests were made a little while ago. It's only a matter of time before they're all rounded up—including the leader—and put behind bars."

"But the danger's still there!"

"It's very slight. But to protect you and the children,

I'll remain under cover until my supervisor gets word to me that everyone's been caught.'' He moved closer. ''Wendy—the reason I told you Lisa broke our engagement was because I didn't want to lie to you any longer about my involvement with a fictional woman. I've longed to reveal the whole truth, but I was going to wait until the ba—''

''Mom? Josh?''

Their heads jerked around at Ben's panic-stricken voice calling from the back hall. In the next instant he burst through the door, then came to an abrupt halt when he could see he'd interrupted them.

''Are you guys all right?''

No. I don't think I'll ever be all right again. Would she ever be able to trust her own judgment again? Everything she'd believed about him had been a lie!

''Of course, sweetheart.'' His pale face alarmed her. She held out her arms, needing her son as never before. ''There was no problem. Those bikers belonged to a riding club,'' she explained, hugging him as tightly as the baby permitted.

Ben clung hard to her. She knew that after losing his father, he'd been frightened that something might have happened to her or Josh.

''How come you didn't stay at the Stobbes'?''

''Because I didn't want to. Kim's over there crying. Mr. Stobbe wouldn't let us leave, but I ran out anyway.''

Her son would never change; he'd always follow his protective instincts rather than act cautiously. In this instance, however, she was glad he'd come. Now that she knew the truth about Josh, being around him was just too difficult. ''We'll pick her up now, then go home to bed.''

"I'll drive Kim to the house in your car and leave it in front," Josh offered.

Wendy's first reaction was to say no. She could tell that Josh wanted to finish talking to her and would use the opportunity when he brought back her car. But she couldn't handle any more confessions tonight.

It was enough to know that he was an agent marking time before he returned to active duty. His insistence that he'd found his real life at Moon Lake had been pure fabrication; he'd said those things for her sake, to force her to keep the resort open so *she* wouldn't lose it.

In the beginning, he'd said he would find a new manager for her when the time came. Since he was a man who always kept his word, she had no doubt he wanted to finish their talk so he could reassure her of that.

Unfortunately, the exertion of her run through the woods had brought on more lower back pain. She told herself that if she could just lie down for a while, it would go away...but there was the niggling thought that early labor had felt a lot like this. With the pain growing worse, she decided she'd better take him up on his offer.

Avoiding his eyes, she said, "Thank you, Josh. I'd appreciate that. As long as you're going over there, would you mind returning the rifle to Mr. Stobbe, as well?"

"No," he murmured. "I'll hurry."

She whispered her thanks and rushed Ben out of the kitchen. Thankful for her son's support, she leaned on him most of the way. As soon as they reached the house, she headed for the shower. Maybe the warm water would soothe her.

"Ben, when Josh brings Kim back, tell him I'll talk to him tomorrow. I'm too tired now and I need to go to bed."

"Okay."

"I want you to get ready for bed, too."

"I will."

Ten minutes later, when she'd put on a fresh nightgown and slid under the covers, Kim came running into the bedroom to give her a hug. "I'm glad you and Josh are okay, Mom."

"So am I, sweetheart. Tomorrow I'll tell you all about it. But I'm exhausted and I want you and Ben to get to bed. Okay?"

Kim nodded. After another hug, she left the room and all grew quiet in their household.

To Wendy's alarm, the back pain persisted. She tried to get comfortable, but it was impossible. No position would relieve her distress. It seemed to be growing worse. Another fifteen minutes, and she started feeling twinges of stinging pain.

She'd only felt that kind of sensation when she went into labor. These pains had to be contractions. Turning on the lamp, she started to time them with her watch. Half an hour later, they were five minutes apart.

She phoned her doctor, who told her to meet him at the hospital.

Tears rolled down her cheeks. Josh had asked if he could drive her. She'd been looking forward to that, wanting his strength and support when the baby came. Before tonight she would have called him without hesitation.

But now that she knew the truth about him, she realized it was only a matter of days or weeks before he returned to his job. Under the circumstances, she felt this would be the best time to make a break from him, psychologically as well as physically.

He'll be gone soon. Don't get any more emotionally involved than you are already.

Long ago Carol and Steve had volunteered to drive her to the hospital. She'd take them up on their offer.

She quickly called the Irvines, and made one more phone call to her sister, who said she'd be there by early morning to take over from Carol. Wendy methodically packed an overnight bag, then checked on Ben and Kim. She left the house to wait for the Irvines on the porch, the children sound asleep inside. Her friends arrived moments later, driving two cars. An excited Eric was with them.

Carol assured her she'd stay with the children until Jane arrived. Steve took one look at her, hustled her into his car and they were off.

"Don't worry about the baby being two weeks early," he said, trying to comfort her when she told him her greatest fear. "Eric arrived a whole month before his due date, and he was able to go home from the hospital a few days later without any problem."

"I'm sure you're right. I ju—" She couldn't talk. Another pain, much stronger than the others, racked her body. This baby would be born within the hour.

Oh, Josh. What I'd give to have you here with me. But she didn't dare get in any deeper....

WHEN JOSH DELIVERED Kim to the house, he'd expected Wendy to be waiting for him so they could finish what they'd started in the kitchen. He felt a gut-wrenching pain when Ben answered the door and informed him Wendy had gone to bed and wouldn't be able to talk to him until morning.

It was going to be a hellish night.

He walked back to the Stobbes' for his motor home, then drove out to the barn to collect his things. Knowing he'd never get any sleep until he'd spoken to Wendy, he decided now was as good a time as any to make his motor home livable.

After parking it on the far side of the coffee shop, he got to work. But no matter how busy he kept physically, he couldn't turn off his tortured thoughts.

Had he truly misread Wendy's signals? If that was the case, it meant Lisa had been fooled by them, too. How could they both have been so wrong?

The night of the party, had the tears on Wendy's face been only on behalf of her children's pain?

Tonight, when she'd defended him with an unloaded rifle against thirty bikers, had she done it out of anger against them? Not because she cared for him?

Her actions defied logic.

How could she go to bed when she knew he'd just *started* telling her the truth about his situation? There was so much more to say....

Her refusal to talk to him tonight had shut him down, physically and emotionally.

He sat forward on the couch, his elbows on his knees, his face buried in his hands.

When the cell phone rang, his heart leaped. Praying it was Wendy, he grabbed it.

"Yes?"

"Josh?"

Much as he loved Ben, he almost sighed aloud in disappointment.

"Hi, sport. What's up?"

"You told me to call you if my mom was going to have the baby."

Josh reeled. Wendy had gone into labor! She was two weeks early. He'd been keeping track. "I'll be right there."

"She's already gone to the hospital with Eric's dad."

For a moment, Josh's world seemed to go black.

"Eric and his mom are staying with Kim and me until Aunt Jane gets here. I just thought you'd want to know."

Everyone had been told…except him.

"I'm still coming over," he said in a forceful voice. "Tell Carol to expect me in ten minutes."

"All right!"

Galvanized into action, he phoned Ross with the news about Wendy and asked if the younger man would be willing to come over to the resort and be on call until morning.

Ross acted more than eager. He needed the extra money and said he'd leave right away. Josh told him he could sleep in the trailer.

With that accomplished, he took a quick shower, changed into a clean shirt and khakis, then left for Wendy's house. When the children saw him from the front porch, they ran toward him.

"The baby's coming!" Kim cried joyfully.

"I heard." Josh swung her into his arms and carried her up the steps.

Carol met him at the door with a smile. "How are you, Josh?"

"I think I'm as excited as the kids," he said, putting Kim down.

"There's nothing like a new baby."

"You're right. Carol?" he murmured out of earshot of the children. "I'll explain later, but you'd be doing me a great favor if you'd let me tend Kim and Ben for the rest of the night. There's something important I need to talk to them about.''

She studied his face for a brief moment. ''Of course. I'll take Eric and go back home. Just so you know, Wendy's sister, Jane, will probably arrive before morning to take over.''

He nodded.

''Come on, Eric. We're going home.''

''How come? We just got here. I don't wanna leave!''

''Eric—''

''Okay,'' he muttered.

''Thanks,'' Josh whispered to Carol. ''I'll find a way to repay you.'' He gave her a hug.

She shook her head. ''I'll owe you forever for making sure I still have a grumpy little boy to love.''

Josh chuckled, then walked them out to the car. Once everyone had waved goodbye, he asked the children to come into the house. ''If you'll sit down for a minute, there's something I want to say to you.''

''What's wrong?'' The joy had gone out of Kim's face.

''Nothing, honey. I just wanted to get the two of you alone to ask you a very important question.''

''What is it?'' Ben asked with an equally sober expression.

''I guess you know I'm pretty crazy about the entire Sloan family. To be honest, I've grown to love you guys as if you were my own children.''

''We love you, too!'' Kim blurted.

''I've always wished you could be my dad,'' Ben said at the same time.

''At church, when our Sunday-school teacher told us

to pray for something good and never give up, I prayed you'd never go away,'' Kim told him solemnly.

Josh's throat swelled so he could barely swallow. ''I'm very thankful you feel that way because I'd like to stay with you forever, too. I could never take your dad's place, but I'd love to be your friend and do the things for you that your dad would have done.''

''You would?'' Ben sounded incredulous.

''Yes. You two are very special children. You've had very special parents to love you and raise you. When I think how hard you've all worked to try and keep this place going without your dad, it's made me love and admire you more than you know. But it frightens me, too.''

''How come?'' Kim asked softly.

''Because I've never been a father, and it would be impossible to fill your dad's shoes. But if we worked on it, I know we could have a wonderful life together.''

''We have one now!'' Ben's face was glowing.

''I agree. However there's a problem. Another member of the Sloan household would have to feel the same way about me as you do.''

Ben flashed him a shrewd look. ''If you mean Mom, she's been in love with you for a long time.''

Josh's heart raced out of control. ''Did she tell you that?''

''No. I just know she is. Besides, I heard her talking to Aunt Jane about you on the phone. I didn't mean to listen. It was the night of the rescue, and I couldn't sleep. So I got out of bed and went to Mom's room. She told my aunt she was afraid it was Moon Lake you loved instead of her. Then she cried.''

That was all Josh needed to hear.

''Naturally, I love Moon Lake,'' he murmured. ''It's

the greatest place on earth. But I'm in love with your mother, and I want to be her husband if she'll let me. Do I have your permission to ask her to marry me?''

Ben flung himself at Josh, almost knocking him down with a hug. ''Heck, yes!''

''After the wedding, can I call you Daddy?'' Kim had squeezed her way into his arms, as well.

''I'd like that more than anything, sweetheart.''

Cutty kept running around them, and Ben scooped her up to join their hug. Even as he laughed, Josh's eyes were smarting. He loved these kids so much, and he was so grateful for their love in return.

''When are you going to ask her?''

Before he could answer Ben's question, Wendy's phone rang. Ben dashed into the kitchen to get it. Josh put an arm around Kim's shoulders and they hurried after him, eager for any news.

''It's Mr. Irvine,'' he called out. ''Mom just had a boy!''

Josh had never felt such elation.

''He weighs seven pounds, ten ounces, and he's twenty and a half inches long.''

''Hey!'' Kim shouted. ''We've got a brother!''

Josh grinned. A boy. His premonition had been right, after all. ''Ask him how your mom and the baby are doing.''

Ben did, then repeated, ''They're both doing great!''

The news left Josh weak with relief. ''Let me talk to Steve, will you, sport?''

''Sure.''

As Ben handed him the phone, Josh said, ''You guys get dressed. We're going to the hospital to see this little guy. He's been hiding from us long enough.''

They both dashed off.

He put the receiver to his ear. "Steve, it's Josh. I sent your wife and son home a while ago. I'm going to take care of the kids until Jane arrives. Tell me the truth. How's Wendy?"

"She had an easy delivery, or so I'm told. But I'm a man. What do I really know?"

"I know a lot less than you," Josh muttered.

Steve laughed. "The OB said everything went like clockwork, and now they've given her something to help her sleep."

Josh cleared his throat. "Thank you for being there for her."

"Maybe now you know how I felt the night you found Eric and Ben."

"Yes, I think I do. Steve—I'm driving the kids to see Wendy now. I assume it's the same hospital where I dropped off the boys?"

"That's it."

"One more question. The baby's two weeks early. Is everything—"

"Don't worry," Steve interrupted. "I talked to the pediatrician. He assured me all the signs are good. Little Matt is breathing normally." *Matt.* Josh had always assumed she'd name the baby after his father. It was exactly as it should be. "Since his lungs seem to be fine, there's no reason he can't go home with Wendy in a couple of days."

"That's excellent news," Josh said. "Then we'll see you in a little while."

"I'll be in the waiting area on the fourth floor, east wing."

"Oh, Steve, I don't want Wendy to know I'm with the children. I'll tell them not to say anything, either. Let her believe you and Carol are taking complete charge. I don't want her concerned about anything but looking after her new baby."

After a brief silence, "I won't say a word."

"Thank you."

"Mrs. Sloan?" Wendy's day nurse breezed into the room with a wheelchair. "You're next. Who's coming for you?"

"My sister and brother-in-law. I'm expecting them any second."

Wendy couldn't wait to leave. She felt as if she'd been trapped inside this hospital room for months instead of three days.

Of course she adored her precious little son, who was perfect from his bald head to his square-toed feet. She'd spent every waking minute loving him. As for Ben and Kim, their delight in holding the baby so soon after his birth had been one of those transcendent moments for the Sloan family. Carol, Steve, Wendy's mother, Bob and Jane—everyone had been wonderful and couldn't do enough for her.

She should be grateful for so many blessings. She *was* grateful.

But there was a huge, hollow space in her heart, and only one man could fill it. She agonized over the fact that Josh hadn't come to the hospital—or even sent her a message via the children.

She had a roomful of flowers, but his weren't among them. In three days, his name hadn't been brought up once.

During her hospital stay she'd had a lot of time to think and had come to several conclusions. First, his silence over the past few days conveyed a clear message. He wanted to manage Moon Lake until he went back on active duty, but any feelings for her were simply those of friendship.

Her second conclusion: because she knew she couldn't live around him under those circumstances, she would ask Josh to find a manager to replace him as soon as possible. But she would wage that battle tomorrow.

Today, for the good of her family and her own sanity, she had to forget a man named Josh Walker existed.

An angry laugh escaped

Don't you remember? His name is Special Agent Joshua Quincy.

Josh Walker is pure fiction.

"Hi, honey." Her sister walked through the door and rushed over to kiss her. "My gosh—you're gorgeous! You're actually wearing a normal skirt and blouse. You don't look a day over twenty-five! No one would guess you'd just had a baby. It isn't fair! I still looked nine months pregnant two weeks after delivery."

Wendy knew her sister was exaggerating to help distract her and ease her heartache over Josh. But nothing was going to make that pain go away. The only thing Wendy could do was lavish all the love she had to give on her three children.

"When I stand up, you'll notice I didn't tuck in my blouse, and the waist is elastic."

"All the same, you do look pretty terrific," the nurse concurred as she placed the sleeping newborn in Wendy's arms. "Now we're ready to go."

"I'll tell you what," Jane murmured. "I'm going to run on ahead with all your stuff, then come back for the flowers. Bob's waiting at the east entrance. Is that okay with you?''

''Of course. Thank you,'' she called after her sister.

The nurse wheeled Wendy from her room to the elevators. ''There's nothing like family at a time like this.''

The comment didn't require an answer. Wendy knew how lucky she was and hugged her baby tighter.

Don't think about Josh today. She had to put him out of her mind. If she didn't, then she wasn't worthy of all the gifts life had bestowed on her.

The automatic doors opened to the outside of the hospital, and Wendy breathed deeply of the warm summer air. It was a beautiful June day with that brilliant blue sky Tahoe was famous for.

''Which car is your sister's?''

Wendy looked for their green van, but all she saw was a motor home parked at the entrance of the circular drive. Suddenly Ben and Kim climbed out the side door and ran toward her, calling her name. As they hugged and kissed her, a tall, dark-haired, powerfully built man strode up the ramp behind them.

Josh.

Her heart began to race. If she hadn't been in a wheelchair already, she would have needed one.

The children transferred their attention to the baby, but she wasn't aware of anything going on around her. Her gaze had fused with his. Josh's eyes blazed a more intense blue than the sky above. He wore the half smile she loved.

''I got cheated out of taking you to the hospital, so I'm driving you home,'' he announced.

He must have arranged this with Jane and Bob. ''All

right,'' she whispered. She was shivering with excitement.

The nurse wheeled her the rest of the way to the steps of the motor home. Josh walked alongside.

''I've installed an infant car seat. Hand me the little guy, will you?''

''Y-yes.'' The shock of seeing Josh had robbed her of any coherence. She could hardly talk, let alone think, before she gave up her precious bundle.

Josh took the baby in his arms. He held him so naturally, you'd have thought he'd done this before. She watched him study her son.

''He's beautiful, Wendy. Perfect,'' he said in a hoarse voice she didn't recognize.

''I think so, too,'' she whispered.

''Wait here. I'll be right back.'' He sounded like his usual confident self again. ''Come on, guys. I'm pretty sure I know how the car seat works, but I might need some help getting this little tiger settled.''

The children clambered after him, eager to play with their new brother.

Little tiger.

Wendy got out of the wheelchair on shaky legs and stood there until Josh returned.

How amazing that before he'd arrived, she'd felt strong enough to walk out of the hospital. The few stitches after such a short labor and easy delivery hardly hurt at all. Now her whole body seemed to throb with feelings that were part pain, part pleasure.

When he put a hard-muscled arm around her waist, she thanked the nurse, then clung to Josh as he lifted her over the two steps to the floor of the camper.

''All right?'' he murmured near her ear. It sent the most delicious tingles through her nervous system.

"Yes."

"Good. Come and lie down on the couch next to the baby, and I'll strap you in."

"Thank you, but after lying in a hospital bed for three days, I think I'd rather sit up."

She walked to the couch and sat down near her baby. The children had crowded around, cooing and giggling, obviously entranced with their infant brother. Josh leaned over to find the seat belt for her. Their eyes met again as he fastened it. She felt the warmth of his hands against her hip.

"Are you ready to go home?" His lips were only a few inches from hers.

Her breathing grew shallow. "I can't wait."

"Neither can I."

Those words gave her heart a serious jolt, but there was no opportunity to explore his meaning. He stood up and headed for the front of the motor home. Within seconds it pulled out of the drive and joined the main stream of traffic.

"Mom? Do you want a drink? You're nursing the baby, so Josh stocked the refrigerator with all kinds of juice. He said you'll need lots of liquids."

"I'd love an apple juice, Ben," she murmured in a daze, afraid that something might wake her from this heavenly dream. Josh was acting like...like...

"Give me peach," Kim called out while she examined the baby's tiny hands. "Take Josh a grape. That's what he likes."

It was clear that her children had spent a lot of time with him while she was in the hospital. Wendy felt envious that they seemed to know so much about him.

"Here you go, Mom." Ben handed her and Kim

their drinks. "I'm going to ride up front with Josh."
He held two bottles of grape juice.

"When's the baby going to wake up?"

"Not for a while, I don't think. I just fed him."

"He's so cute." Kim couldn't stop kissing his
cheeks. Every time she gave him one, the baby made
a funny face in his sleep. Wendy chuckled along with
her daughter.

I'm too happy. I have to be dreaming.

But if it *was* a dream, it showed no sign of ending.
By the time they pulled to a stop in front of the house,
she was still enveloped by an indescribable sense of
euphoria.

"I'll be back for you shortly." Josh had reappeared
to take the baby inside. The mere sight of him quick-
ened her pulse. From the motor home window, she
watched the children scurry after him. After a few
minutes, she saw him leave the house and stride toward
the motor home. His limp had disappeared completely.

When she realized he might have lost his leg in that
shooting...

"It's your turn."

Once again he supported her waist while he walked
her to the house and half lifted her up the stairs. She
hoped he attributed her trembling to weakness from the
birth. If he had any idea how desperately she loved
him...

"Surprise!"

Wendy collapsed against Josh when she saw what
greeted her. There had to be at least a dozen bouquets
of long-stemmed red roses placed in vases around the
living and dining rooms. Blue-and-white streamers had
been fastened to the ceiling. Amid a pile of presents,

a big white cake with a baby tiger motif stood in the center of the dining-room table.

"Josh—" She managed to say his name past the lump in her throat. "Children—this is so wonderful…I don't know what to say."

"You don't need to say anything," Josh murmured. "We've put the baby next to your chair. Even if he's asleep, we want him to be part of the festivities. If you're up to sitting a little longer, we'd like you to open your gifts."

It didn't take her long to unwrap her packages, while Josh and Ben took videos with a camera she'd never seen before. This was better than Christmas. Since the children had no money, Josh had made it possible for them to give her a new robe, nightgown, perfume, a sleeper outfit for the baby. His generosity, his goodness, his kindness to the family overwhelmed her.

When she looked up at him, his features had become a blur. "How do I thank you for all this?" she asked in a tremulous whisper.

"Do you really want to know?" Now it was his voice that shook.

"Yes."

"Then let me put this on and promise me you'll never take it off." In the next breath he slid a dazzling solitaire diamond onto the ring finger of her left hand. The white-gold band was a perfect fit.

"I already have the children's permission to marry you. The rest is up to you."

Forgetting she'd just been released from the hospital, Wendy jumped up from the table so fast, she knocked the chair to the floor in her urgency to reach him.

"Oh, Josh…" She threw her arms around his neck.

"I was afraid you'd never ask. I'll marry you today if you want."

Half sobbing with happiness, she begged, "Come into the bedroom with me where we can be alone. Please…"

CHAPTER FIFTEEN

JOSH STOOD THERE with his pulse racing. She'd just given him his heart's desire. Now he felt as though he was in a trance as she led the way to her bedroom, tugging on his hand.

Once the door closed behind them, she walked over to the bed and lay down on top of the quilt. "I think I've been waiting for this moment since the night you showed up at the resort asking for a job," she told him softly. "Don't make me wait any longer."

She reached for the hand nearest hers and clung to it.

"Wendy…" He couldn't move, couldn't breathe. "I'm so in love with you, I'm almost afraid to touch you for fear I won't be able to stop."

"Please…kiss me. I love you, Josh."

He let out a low groan before he lay down beside her, stretched on his side. He was still trying to believe this was really happening when her mouth lifted to his with primitive urgency.

Then he was kissing her.

Deep, long, hungry kisses.

Nothing hidden, nothing held back.

Over and over they took each other's mouths, enraptured by sensations of pleasure only they could give each other.

The passion between them was so electrifying, he knew he needed to slow things down, but he had no idea how. Not when her breathtaking response held him prisoner.

It was ecstasy to finally be able to hold her the way he wanted. How many times had he longed to bury his face in her gleaming hair?

Her legs tangled with his, bringing new sensations to life. He'd never experienced anything as erotic as the pressure of her body nestled firmly against his.

He couldn't stop kissing her, caressing her. When he heard her moan, he tore his lips from hers. "Did I hurt you, darling?"

"No," she whispered, smoothing the hair from his brow. "I'm...overwhelmed. Too much feeling. That's all."

Josh could believe it. The luster in her eyes showed the measure of her entrancement. He knew his eyes reflected the same passion. So many times he'd dreamed this dream. The reality was almost impossible to comprehend.

"I know how you feel. I've wanted this longer than you could possibly know. Before you were even aware of me..."

"Do you want to bet?" Her voice caught.

He swallowed hard. The unselfishness of her love, her honesty, humbled him.

"Steve told me I should wait until your six-week checkup before I make love to you."

"You've already talked to Steve?" Her smile melted his bones.

"Weeks ago he and Carol figured out how things were between us. Last night I needed the advice of a man who's been a father."

"Well, my love, technically speaking he's right. But

I think if you asked Carol, she'd tell you her husband didn't wait that long after Eric was born."

"I need to marry you right away, Wendy. I love you and the children. Two nights ago, I resigned from the Bureau. I'm a free man, ready to make you my wife. I have a special wedding present for you. While you were in the hospital, the gang leader was apprehended. There is no more contract. I don't have to be under cover anymore. We can tell everyone the truth."

"Thank heaven," she whispered.

"The thing is, I know how much you loved Matt, how much you'll always love him. I could never replace him as a husband or father."

"Josh... There will always be a place in my heart reserved for him. And in the children's hearts. That's only natural. But it doesn't mean there isn't room for someone else. The children adore you. I want you for my husband. There's no time to waste," she whispered against his lips. "Our baby needs his mother and father."

Tears pricked the back of his eyelids. "God forgive me, but I feel like you all belong to me. Even the baby."

She rained kisses on his face. "Matt left me a very precious gift, so I named the baby Matt, in honor of him. But he died before I even realized I was pregnant. Please make no mistake. This baby is yours, my darling."

Too consumed by emotion, he buried his face in her neck.

"Maybe in a year or two, we'll have another baby. A little Josh, Jr.," she added softly.

He lifted his head to stare down at her. "You would do that for me? You'd go through all this again?"

She traced the outline of his mouth with her finger.

"As long as it's possible, I would like you to know the thrill of finding out you made a baby, that you're responsible for creating a life that—"

"Mom?" Kim called through the door. "The baby woke up and he's really hungry. And guess what? Grandma's here with Aunt Jane and the family. So are the Irvines. When are you and Josh coming out so we can cut the cake?"

Wendy lifted her head. "In a minute!"

"A mother's work is never done," he whispered against her ear.

She kissed him with deepening passion. "Neither is a father's, as you're going to find out. You thought the FBI gave you thrills and chills? My darling Josh, just you wait until we're married."

He kissed her back, never wanting this to stop. "What date shall we choose so we can go out there and make an official announcement?"

"Three weeks?" Her eyes implored him.

"That's ages from now. Three weeks, huh?"

"By then we'll certainly be able to enjoy a real honeymoon." Her voice trembled as she spoke. "I want that more than you can imagine."

"No," he said in a gruff tone, "not more than I can imagine. But what about the baby? Can you leave him?"

"He'll survive on a bottle for three or four days."

"But, darling—"

"Josh, I intend to make you as happy as you make me. That means a honeymoon where we can concentrate totally on each other. We need it. Every marriage needs it. In fact, we're going to go on lots of little honeymoons for the rest of our lives.

"I've learned so much from my first marriage. Never

take your love for granted. I adored Matt, but I wish we'd taken more private time to renew our love. I refuse to repeat that mistake with you.''

Her eyes filled with tears. ''You've lived this long without a wife. Now you're taking on a family, too. I don't ever want you to regret our marriage.''

He swallowed with difficulty. ''Remember the night you sent me packing to the hotel, saying you'd call me if you were interested?''

''How could I forget?''

''That was the night love happened for me. I lay awake all night wondering what I'd do if you didn't phone. You put me through hell, woman.''

Her seductive smile provoked another breathtaking kiss. There was so much he needed to share with her.

''Unlike you,'' he went on, ''I never met the right person to settle down with and have a family. I had hoped to find love in college, but it never happened there or in the Navy. Later, the nature of my work with the Bureau made it difficult to sustain a relationship.

''I'm not saying there haven't been other women, but none to whom I wanted to make a commitment. Your husband was a lucky man. Even though his life was cut short, he had the unqualified love of a beautiful, adoring wife, two wonderful children he could be proud of, and the most glorious place on earth to live.

''The other night, when you thought I was in trouble and came to my rescue at the risk of your own life and the baby's, I got a taste of what it would be like to be loved like that. I prayed you weren't simply defending the castle the two of you had built with dreams and hard work. I hoped you were fighting for me, too. But for a moment, I knew a terrible envy—a need to have all that love for myself.''

She clung to him. "When Ben woke me up and told me about that motorcycle gang, all I could think was *I'm not going to lose Josh.* I grabbed Mr. Stobbes's rifle off his mantel and took off through the woods."

"You went into early labor because of me," he whispered into her silky hair.

"Not necessarily. The baby was only two weeks early and he's a healthy weight. We'll never know what triggered labor, and it doesn't matter." She paused, smiling. "I don't think you have a clue how much I love you, Joshua Quincy."

"I'm beginning to find out." He wrapped her more tightly in his arms. "If you can wait three more weeks, then I'll prove exactly how I feel about *you.*"

"Promise?" she teased, but her eyes radiated green fire. Josh was living for the moment when she became his wife in every sense of the word.

"Mom?" This time it was Ben's anxious voice calling out. "Aunt Jane gave the baby some water, but he's still hungry!"

Wendy's body had already let her know it was time for his feeding. She cupped Josh's neck and pressed a swift kiss to his lips. "Darling? Will you bring little Matt in to me, and then play host until I can put him down again?"

"Your wish is my command."

"I'll remind you of that a month from now when our son starts crying at three in the morning, and you're too tired to hand him to me."

"You think that'll happen?"

Her saucy smile captivated him. "I can guarantee it, but I forgive you in advance."

"Wendy, I'm so happy, it scares me."

"It scares me, too. But I trust it, Josh. It's real."

"Mom!" both children cried at once. But this time their voices were drowned out by the baby's siren-like cry. He had extraordinary lung power.

"He must be in pain!"

She broke into a sunny smile. "That, my love, is the sound of anger. Men get like that when they're hungry."

Josh laughed out loud as he headed for the door. "Is that a fact?"

"You know it's true."

"You know something?" he said before he opened it. "The children were right. They said you were so smart it was scary."

"The smartest thing I ever did was listen to Ben when he begged me to give the stranger in the coffee shop a job."

"Hmm. We can be thankful Ben inherited your smarts. That ad of his changed my life."

"Mine, too."

"Wendy?"

"Uh-oh. That's your mother. I don't dare get on her bad side before we've even said our vows."

"INASMUCH AS Wendy Carlisle Sloan and Joshua Lyman Quincy have pledged their love before God and this congregation of family and friends, I now pronounce them husband and wife. May they live together in the bonds of joyous and holy matrimony, loving and supporting each other until the day they die."

The minister lifted his hands. "You may now kiss your bride, Mr. Quincy."

Before Wendy could take a breath, Josh swept her in his arms and kissed her with fierce possession. Finally their wedding day had come. Until now, they'd both had to hold back. But no longer.

"Whoa, Mom!"

"Ben!" his grandmother shushed him.

It didn't take a lot to make Wendy blush. Her son was old enough to understand that she and Josh had been having a hard time keeping their desire for each other under some semblance of control.

The last three weeks had been a time of pure joy as everyone helped plan the wedding. But it had also been a time of frustration because their physical needs had to be held at bay while her body healed from the delivery.

"I'm sorry," Josh finally whispered against her hot cheek. "I got carried away."

"No more than I did," she responded in a trembling voice before they turned to greet family and a few close friends, among them Josh's supervisor Harve, Agent Wood and her husband, and Josh's longtime friend, Henry.

Because of Josh's former association with the FBI, they'd kept their wedding private.

"That lavender silk dress looks heavenly on you," her mother murmured, hugging her. "You'd never know you're a brand-new mother, not with that figure. Today you're every bit the beautiful bride you were when you married Matt—only more so."

"You're just prejudiced."

"That too, but I'm so proud of my daughter. Proud of the way you've handled your life, the good and the bad. I'm so thankful you met Josh. I can see you fulfill each other. Be happy, my darling girl!"

"I am, Mom." She sniffed. "Happier than I ever thought possible."

As her mother turned away, Henry Kendal, a distinguished-looking man in his seventies shook Wendy's hand.

"What did I tell you? The minute that highfalutin fiancée of Josh's took off, he went and found himself a real Nevada showgirl."

Wendy burst into laughter and threw her arms around him in a hug. "One day soon we'd like to come to Ohio to visit you."

"I'm counting on it."

"Well, well." Josh's attractive, sixty-year-old supervisor broke in, giving her a quick once-over. "I wondered what force had been unleashed to lure Josh away from the department. I finally have my answer—and I can't say I blame him."

"Thank you, Harve."

He winked at her. "It was Josh's lucky day when I sent him out here. Little did I know we were going to lose one of the best men who ever worked for the Bureau."

"I love him, Harve."

"You've made him happy."

"You have," Lisa Wood interjected as she stood in the circle with her husband.

Harve nodded. "I heard it in his voice over the phone the first time he called me to check in. I've learned never to underestimate the power of love...when it's the right woman." He drew her to him for a gentle hug.

"I'm going to try to be the right woman. When you go on vacation, please plan to stay here. We'll reserve a cabin for you and your wife."

"We'll come without fail," he vowed, then moved on to hug her husband.

"Well, you did it, sister dear. You pulled it off. If I didn't love Bob as much as I do, I'd be jealous."

"Jane." Wendy embraced her sister, unable to express her overflowing emotions with words.

"Don't worry about the kids or the baby. I have everything under control."

"I know. I'll leave you the hotel number at Laguna Beach. If you run into any problems, Josh and I can be in Sacramento within a couple of hours."

"Wendy?" Bob gave her a hug. "We know your itinerary, but no one's going to need anyone. You and Josh go have a great time, okay?"

"Okay. Thanks for everything, Bob. I love you both."

As he moved on, Carol grabbed her and whispered, "This is such an exciting day. Besides your wedding, I just found out this morning that I'm pregnant!"

"That's wonderful news! Our children will be able to play together."

Carol rolled her eyes. "Steve couldn't believe it. He made me do the test three times to be sure."

"Don't worry—he'll get used to the idea."

"No, I won't," Steve chimed in, putting his arm around Carol. "I'm not quite as young as Josh."

"Did I hear my name taken in vain?"

Josh pulled Wendy back in his arms.

She kissed his smooth-shaven jaw. "Steve is going to be a daddy again in about eight months. He's worried about being too old to get up for those three o'clock feedings."

Josh chuckled deep in his throat before clapping their friend on the shoulder.

Steve flashed Josh a meaningful glance. "We'll see who's laughing in a couple of weeks."

"Don't scare the poor man!" Carol chided her husband with a smile. "Have a wonderful time, you two."

"We will," Josh answered for them. "Come on,

Mrs. Quincy,'' he whispered against her neck. ''Let's say goodbye to the children.''

Wendy felt a pang as she embraced Ben and Kim. As for little Matt, she'd spent the entire morning with him. She'd given him one last feeding right before the ceremony. Now he was sound asleep next to his aunt Jane.

''Missing him already?''

She lifted her head to her husband. When his eyes devoured her like that, her bones turned to liquid. ''No. I wish we were at the beach right now, away from everything and everyone. But we still need to greet the staff before we go.''

''Then let's hurry, darling.''

She heard the urgency in his tone, felt it in the way his body trembled when he so much as brushed against her.

Their tension was becoming intolerable. They needed to be alone....

WENDY LOVED DAWN when the tide came in. Enormous waves crashed against the sand. A heavy gray mist stole through the open doors of their beachfront cottage.

The rhythmic pounding of the surf dictated the pounding of her heart, as she lay on her side to watch her husband. He'd turned on his back with one arm above his head, the other hooked possessively around her hips.

Last night she'd told him he was a beautiful man. He'd only laughed before loving her into oblivion. But it was true. From the first moment she'd met him, she'd found him perfect, inside and out.

After three days and nights together, she'd memorized every exciting masculine feature that set him apart from other men. Anticipating another morning of lovemaking thrilled her so much she couldn't sleep.

Later in the day they'd have to fly home. Much as she missed the children, she couldn't bear to leave this room, this bed where she'd known rapture in her husband's arms.

She couldn't resist pressing her lips to his shoulder, where she could still smell the soap from his shower. She ran her palm over his chest, and before she knew it, she'd practically covered him with her body so she could kiss the corner of his mouth.

"What took you so long?" he whispered against her lips. But he didn't give her a chance to answer because he'd started kissing her as if he were starving for her.

"You've been awake all this time and didn't let me know?" she gasped the words when he allowed her to draw breath.

The look of raw desire deepened the blue of his eyes. "That's right," he said. "I can't believe my wife of four days still doesn't know that she doesn't need my permission to wake me up whenever she damn well pleases!"

She framed his cheeks with her hands. "I was just afraid you might think you'd married a...a wanton. We haven't left this room in three days!"

"If I had my way, we'd never leave." He stared into her eyes. "Would you?"

She moved her head from side to side. "I love you too much. It hurts."

"That's good," he whispered before bringing his mouth to hers again. "I want it to hurt—to remind us how lucky we are to have found each other."

"We are," she breathed. "When we get home, I'm going to be useless. I won't want to let you out of my arms in the morning."

His eyes held a lascivious gleam. "You're going to

be even more useless when I find excuses every hour to come back to the house for something I need.''

A wave of heat washed over her, and she responded with a seductive smile.

Josh laughed deep in his throat. ''In case I didn't inform you yet, Mrs. Quincy, bedtime is going to be strictly observed at our house. Lights out at eight o'clock every night without exception for every member of the family, starting with mom and dad.''

She buried her face in his shoulder. ''It sounds like heaven.''

His chest rose and fell. ''Heaven is being married to you. Do you have any idea how beautiful you are? How wonderful? Six months ago I felt like my life was over. This morning I have you in my arms and all is perfect with my world.

''Come closer to me, my love. Much closer. Hold on to me, Wendy. Promise you'll never leave me,'' he begged.

His vulnerability was a revelation.

Josh had been robbed of parents and siblings. He needed a family of his very own to give him that sense of connection and belonging every human craved.

She sealed her promise with her body. Heaven willing, one day soon she'd be able to tell him she was pregnant.

You think your life is perfect now?

Just you wait, Joshua Quincy. Just you wait.

HARLEQUIN®
SUPERROMANCE®

By the Year 2000: **BABY!**

What have *you* resolved to do by the year 2000?
These three women are having babies!

Susan Kennedy's plan is to have a baby by the time she's forty—in
the year 2000. But the only man she can imagine as the father of her
child is her ex-husband, Michael!
MY BABIES AND ME by **Tara Taylor Quinn**
Available in October 1999

Nora Holloway is determined to adopt the baby who suddenly
appears in her life! And then the baby's uncle shows up....
DREAM BABY by **Ann Evans**
Available in November 1999

By the year 2000, the Irving Trust will end, unless Miranda has a
baby. She doesn't think there's much likelihood of that—until she
meets Joseph Wallace.
THE BABY TRUST by **Bobby Hutchinson**
Available in December 1999

Available at your favorite retail outlet.

HARLEQUIN®
Makes any time special ™

Visit us at www.romance.net

HSR2000B

Looking For More Romance?

Visit Romance.net

Check in daily for these and other exciting features:

Hot off the press

View all current titles, and purchase them on-line.

What do the stars have in store for you?

Horoscope

Hot deals

Exclusive offers available only at Romance.net

Plus, don't miss our interactive quizzes, contests and bonus gifts.

PWEB

HARLEQUIN®
SUPERROMANCE®

Three childhood friends dreamed of becoming firefighters. Now they're members of the same team and every day they put their lives on the line.

They are

AMERICA'S BRAVEST

An exciting new trilogy by

Kathryn Shay

#871 FEEL THE HEAT
(November 1999)
#877 THE MAN WHO LOVED CHRISTMAS
(December 1999)
#882 CODE OF HONOR
(January 2000)

Available wherever Harlequin books are sold.

HARLEQUIN®
Makes any time special ™

Come escape with Harlequin's new

Series Sampler

Four great full-length Harlequin novels bound together in one fabulous volume and at an unbelievable price.

Be transported back in time with a Harlequin Historical® novel, get caught up in a mystery with Intrigue®, be tempted by a hot, sizzling romance with Harlequin Temptation®, or just enjoy a down-home all-American read with American Romance®.

You won't be able to put this collection down!

On sale February 2000 at your favorite retail outlet.